PROVIDENCE

Richard Sezov

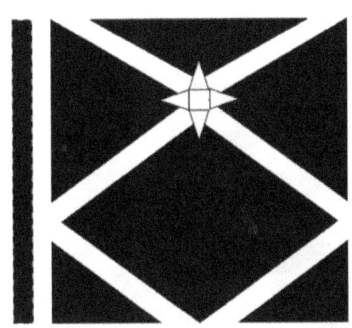

© 2021 by Richard Sezov

All rights reserved. No part of this publication may be reproduced, stored in a retrieval system, or transmitted in any form or by any means electronic, mechanical, photocopying, or otherwise, without prior written permission of the publisher.

ISBN 978-1-7367657-1-5

Library of Congress Control Number: 2021904813

This book is a work of fiction. Names, characters, places, and incidents are the product of the author's imagination or are used fictitiously. Any resemblance to actual events, locales, or persons, living or dead, is coincidental.

Cover image by Louis Ciavolella, www.ciavo.com

For my wife, Deborah, and my children, Julia and Alex.

Also for Nate Cavanaugh, my first and perhaps most enthusiastic beta reader. I'm sorry I didn't finish it in time, man. See you in glory.

1

∞∞∞∞

7:45 AM

*L**ate* did not adequately describe Gerald Foster this morning. He was something past late, beyond even that, and this could not happen; not today. He had an important presentation to do for upper management precisely at 8:00 AM. This morning's meeting meant the difference between preserving a key software platform—a distinct advantage for his company—and replacing it in the name of "standardization," with some outsourced, untested, unproven, cloud-based thing.

It really meant the preservation of his job.

Gerald had been up till three in the morning polishing his presentation, and it shined. He now felt fully prepared to knock the board's socks off. The past six months of his life culminated in this morning's meeting, and he could not be late. His smartwatch, however, had had different ideas. He'd been working so hard the past few days that he hadn't given a second thought to charging it, and now this simple, *stupid* thing—a failed battery leading to a failed alarm—might cost him his career. He had fifteen minutes to make it to Center City Philadelphia, and he lived 20 minutes away without traffic. During rush hour, it could be a 45 minute trip.

His car roared down the entrance ramp to Route 55. Panic exploded in his core and moved out to his limbs as he mashed the accelerator to the floor. Traffic or no traffic, he *would* make it, no matter what. The weather was his only ally: a crisp, brightly lit January morning. The previous week's snow had all melted.

Ba-da-dink! A text. He grabbed his phone from the passenger seat. Harvey, his co-presenter.

Where are you?

He did his best to poke out *on my way*, hit *send* before verifying his phone's attempts at auto-correction, and threw the phone back on the passenger seat. In those few seconds, his foot had raised itself unbidden from the accelerator as he'd attempted to concentrate on too many things at once. The speedometer said 86. Annoyed, he cursed under his breath and jammed the pedal back down again. This part of the journey was where to make up time, so he needed to take advantage of it: anything below 90 was too slow. He checked his car clock again—his useless smartwatch left at home—and it didn't look good. Anything *above* 90 might also be too slow.

He rounded the curve to the left just before the approach to the Deptford exit, swerved into the cruising lane to go around a dirty minivan with *School Bus* stenciled on its back, and jerked back into the passing lane to avoid a slow-moving tractor trailer. Finally, he reached the curve where he'd get his first inkling of how bad this morning's traffic jam was.

With relief, he didn't see any stopped cars before the right-hand curve past the Deptford exit. He began to be hopeful. He jumped back into the cruising lane to pass a (relatively) slow-moving Camry and decided to stay there. He knew by experience that if traffic slowed ahead, the right lane moved faster.

Ripping past the Deptford exit, he hoped with everything in him that it wasn't jammed beyond that curve. Why today? Of all days, why did he forget to charge his smartwatch last night, on a career-boosting or a career-ending day? He gripped the steering wheel, grimacing in frustration as he began to round that last curve, the curve that jammed every morning because the lanes thinned down to one as Route 55 merged into Route 42: the gateway to Philadelphia, Camden, or Cherry Hill.

An uncomfortably close Honda Civic loomed before him: it *was* jammed in the worst possible place, in the middle of that curve, where he couldn't see the jam coming. At more than 90 miles an hour he couldn't stop, so he veered off to the right onto the shoulder, the rumble strip making his tires emit a loud "haaaaaaahh" and vibrating his clenched teeth. He flew past the cars at a good clip, grateful that he still had room to keep moving forward, to make progress. He hated people who drove up the shoulder during a traffic jam, but he had no choice now. He had to make that meeting. The dashboard clock now said 7:50. He approached the ramp, beside the traffic, more than one car honking at him.

Ba-da-dink! Had to be Harvey again. Did the guy not understand that distracted drivers cause accidents? He decided to look but not respond this time. Gerald had, after all, promised his wife that he would be careful driving. He leaned over to his right and fumbled for the elusive phone, which had bounced somewhere toward the far edge of the seat when he'd tossed it. Keeping his eyes on the road, he felt for it with his fingers. He felt forward, backward—it wasn't there. He leaned over further, stretching. His fingers touched it in the crack between the seat and the door, among a sticky wrapper and a rock-hard french fry. Grimacing and stretching further, he finally retrieved it.

His car climbed the ramp on the shoulder, next to traffic that had already merged by now, a little too close to the concrete barrier. One hand on the steering wheel, one hand holding his phone, he adjusted his trajectory. He had to concentrate here on the shoulder; it was tight next to the jammed traffic, and he would have to merge soon. The coast looked clear. Maybe he could steal a glance at that text.

Meeting postponed. Take your time, but get here.

A wave of relief washed over him as a jagged piece of metal left over from a previous accident shredded his right front tire. Euphoria tingled down his spine at the thought that everything would be all right. As he took his foot off the accelerator to slow down and merge back into traffic, he felt his car, still going 90 miles an hour, jerk violently and skid sideways. The car slammed into the concrete barrier at the start of the left-hand curve at the top of the ramp and flipped upward and over, spinning and turning end over end in what seemed like slow motion.

Flying coffee and jangling coins ricocheting off the windshield made him realize that he shouldn't be feeling relieved any more, but he didn't have time to fully understand his predicament before his car landed on Route 42 below and everything went black.

7

2

∞∞∞∞∞

7:55 AM

Gloria Williams commuted from her home in Sicklerville to West Deptford High School every day to teach math. This required her to travel up Route 42 and get off at 130 South. She was running a little late this morning because her dog, James (her ex-husband, a Star Trek fan, had named him), had thrown up on the living room floor, and it had taken some time to clean it. The older that dog got, the more trouble he gave her, it seemed.

Traffic lagged, as usual. She would probably be a few minutes late, but her teacher's aide, Christine, would cover for her. She wasn't worried. She stuck to the middle lane so she wouldn't have to think too much about passing anybody. Her mind began to drift as she guided her white VW Jetta through slow but steadily moving traffic.

For three years, she'd been alone in the house with the dog. She hadn't even wanted him—her ex-husband had—but she loved him, and the feeling was mutual. The dog was like every project Willie had ever done: a great start, with hopeful promise, but no follow-through. When things got tough or responsibility reared its ugly head, Willie found something else to pique his interest. He loved having the dog, but didn't want to scoop poop or even feed the thing. He loved having a house, but wouldn't maintain it. He loved having a salary, but working was not how he wanted to spend his time. As with everything else, so went their marriage. *No fault* is what they'd called it, as though it had just fallen apart by itself with no other intervention. Gloria missed Willie, missed the excitement and adventure that he'd brought to her life. Willie sure made things interesting. It turned out, however, that long-term commitment didn't agree with him. His passion burned out too quickly, and as he'd lost interest in everything else, he'd also lost interest in Gloria. That didn't make it *no fault*; it had been his fault. *No fault* was just another euphemism told to make it easier for people to get out of their responsibilities.

She didn't like dwelling on these things, but they came to mind whenever something happened that she could've used a little help with. For example, it would've been nice if there'd been somebody else around to clean the dog puke this morning. Someone to trade lateness with. Someone who—

Oh no! She couldn't be sure if she'd said it or thought it. The sun glinted off the windshield of a spinning blue car turning end-over-end in a twisted Olympic dive in the air above her. It seemed aimed at her car. She closed her eyes and slammed on the brakes, her tires joining the chorus of skidding, squealing, and crashing cars around her. A deafening impact and sickening screech of grinding metal coupled with breaking glass interrupted the other sounds as the plunging car landed close—very close—behind her.

Gloria opened her eyes and realized she'd been holding her breath. Still maintaining her death grip on the wheel, she breathed great gulps of air, thankful she hadn't been hurt. Incredibly, both she and her car were unscathed. Traffic had frozen in both directions. She opened her door and got out, her mind distractedly registering that she stood in the middle of Route 42, and that this wasn't normally a safe place for pedestrians. The cold winter air made everything except her puffs of breath seem sharper—too sharp; the jumbled cars and smell of exhaust caused immediate sensory overload.

Despite the cold, sweat trickled down the small of her back as Gloria fought to control a body that seemed to want to do its own thing. Her heart attempted to leap out of her chest, and she shook violently. Leaning against the car to prevent her knocking knees from tipping her over, she placed her trembling hands against the driver's side door and forced herself to take deep, calming breaths. *In through the nose, out through the mouth. In through the nose, out through the mouth.*

She smelled gasoline. In front of her, the empty freeway stretched into the distance, the absent cars having escaped calamity. Behind her, a jumble of cars in ragged fender bender formations lay scattered like a child's toys. The stunned hush gave way to dozens of car doors opening and the sound of people dialing 911. Others—*idiots*—tried to sneak around the accident, still attempting to make it on time to wherever they were going. She found it incredible how selfish, how stuck to their own routines and patterns people could be.

The damage looked horrific. The blue car, *Impala* stamped on its back, had come to rest upside down across the hood of the green Land Rover directly behind her car. The gas, she could see, dripped from the rear of the Chevy, creating a slow rivulet that started on the road outside the Land Rover's driver-side door and ran back behind the accident. Gray smoke rose from underneath the Impala, possibly from the Land Rover's crushed hood. She couldn't see the Impala's driver because the car's underside faced her. Slowly and with careful steps, she made her way over to the driver's side door of the Land Rover, her knees still shaking. She stepped carefully to avoid the stream of gasoline trickling past on the road.

The air bag had deployed, and particles of propellent still hung in the air, creating a fog-like haze. It looked like a man: unconscious, slumped over. The sun's glare put him in shadows, but she could see medium-length hair hanging down from his forehead. There was blood on his face and a line of blood or saliva hanging down, headed toward his lap. She could discern no movement. Glass covered him, the windshield having exploded inward. It looked like the Impala's driver's side had crashed down on the Land Rover's hood, and its rotation had flipped it all the way around on its other side, crushing the windshield. When its forward momentum had stopped, gravity had rotated the Impala back down on its top, precariously balanced on the hood of the Land Rover. She didn't want to think about the state of the lower half of the man's body. He needed help, quickly. Since it seemed everybody else around was calling 911, Gloria didn't feel any pressure to do so; instead, she tried to pull open the door.

It wouldn't budge. The misshapen hinges refused to move. She yanked on it a few times just to be sure, and then she backed away from the SUV and looked around.

Multiple men from other cars arrived, trying as fruitlessly as she had to get the Land Rover's door open. Some of them went around front to try to get a look at the other driver. Behind the accident there had been fender benders in both lanes. Traffic on Route 42 was completely stopped, except for those trying to get around on either shoulder. Distant sirens became audible.

Where had the blue car come from? She looked up.

Of course. The ramp from Route 55 was in front of and above her. It curved from left to right, crossing Route 42 and lining up with it so traffic could merge. The morning sun was behind her, which made it easy to see the people up on the ramp looking in the opposite direction, shading their eyes, squinting down in her direction through the sunlight and pointing. Whatever had happened up on the ramp to knock this car down must also have created at least one accident up above, and traffic was stopped up there too. The Impala must've been going incredibly fast to jump the barrier and still have enough momentum to cross both lanes of 42 to land where it did.

She wasn't sure if she wanted to try to see how badly the other driver was hurt. The car precariously balanced on the Land Rover's smashed hood, and the small crowd of people that had now gathered around it were so far unsuccessful in freeing either driver. Thankfully, flashing lights in the distance now joined the growing siren sound as the police approached, heading south in the empty northbound lanes. The enormity of what had just happened, and how close she had come to injury or death, washed over her, and she began to cry. She cried not just for herself, but for the man—and his loved ones—in the Land Rover, as well as for whomever was in the blue car.

She'd better call Christine. She wasn't going to make it in time for home room.

3

∞∞∞∞

8:15 AM

Sal Fuchetti whistled a recent tune with the radio as he traveled up Route 55 for his job. He needed to get to Pennsauken to run some pipe in a recently renovated row home—scratch that—*town*home, he corrected himself. Now that he'd relocated to South Jersey from South Philly, he needed to use the right word. The local 322 had accepted him as a contractor from the local 690, his business was taking off, and things seemed finally to be going his way. His transition from the city to suburbia might actually work.

He hit a small bump, and pipes rattled in the rack in the bed of his truck. Traffic seemed to be thickening. He didn't really care. He'd get there when he got there; that was one of the great things about owning your own business. As he rounded the curve before the Deptford exit, he noticed the traffic jam. He stopped whistling, whispered a curse, and turned the radio up. It shouldn't take long to hear a traffic report.

Okay, he thought, *I guess I do care if it means I'm gonna be really late.* It looked like traffic was backing up quickly; something bad must've happened ahead. Making a quick decision, he joined the cars stacking up on the shoulder, heading for the Deptford exit. He'd take the back roads. He could hang a left off the exit and go up Almonesson into Westville, then go up 47 and take 130 up to Pennsauken. It was slower than his normal route, but his normal route wasn't moving. This way he'd go around whatever horrible thing had happened up ahead.

The traffic report confirmed his suspicion of a horrendous accident up ahead. Pleased he'd made the right decision, he waited through the exit ramp traffic, made his left turn, and headed toward Westville.

Clearly, he wasn't the only person who'd thought of this. Getting through the lights around the mall took a lot longer than it should have, but then things freed up a bit. He passed through open country, the empty space between towns. It would have been beautiful through here if it weren't the middle of winter. Now, however, the trees, the grass, and the shrubs were a mixture of browns and grays. Recently they'd been covered decently by a blanket of snow, but now were revealed as a result of the temperature fluctuations common to Southern New Jersey in the winter.

As Sal got closer to town, traffic froze again. This road emptied out onto Delsea Drive, the main street going through Westville. He crawled, knowing from past traffic jams that up ahead drivers alternated one car at a time: one car from Almonesson, one from Delsea, as the two roads merged. He couldn't do anything but wait through it.

Finally, he approached the intersection. The car ahead of him turned right onto Delsea, and Sal moved up. He intended to let the car already on Delsea go ahead of him and then get in line behind it, following the pattern every other car had followed. When he looked to his left, however, the other car didn't move. It was a woman in an old blue Oldsmobile. He waved her forward. She waved him forward. He looked to his right; the line of cars had moved ahead, and a large space had opened between the intersection and the end of the line. He figured maybe the woman was just being nice. His clearly marked plumber's truck indicated he was on his way to a job. Plenty of people had given him the right of way before. He stepped on the gas and made his turn, anxious to catch up with traffic.

As soon as he completed the turn, he sped up a bit to close the gap, failing to notice the pothole that proceeded to eat up his left front tire. *Bam!* The truck lurched to the left, climbed out of the pothole, and bounced to the right. The plastic ties holding his pipes in their racks snapped, and PVC pipes tumbled out all over the road, bouncing and ponging and rolling. He had time only for one expletive before he heard a screech of tires and a loud bang somewhere behind him. He pulled over and got out, dreading that somebody might've gotten hurt, fearing a serious delay to his work schedule.

Behind him, his pipes rolled randomly in the street. Some had made it to the curb; some spun randomly in passing traffic as cars swerved to get around them. Some had been flattened under the crushing weight of a vehicle and lay in the street like roadkill. With rising dread, he realized the pipes had been run over by a car that moments ago must have passed him going the other way but now sat on his side of the street kissing a telephone pole. He didn't see any live wires sparking or anything like that; in fact, the pole looked fine. Traffic had slowed, of course, and people were gawking. Holding out hope the driver was unhurt, he decided he'd better go find out. Sal jogged over to the car, a worn Ford Fiesta, smoke rising from its hood. As he approached the driver's side window, he saw tangled, long brown hair. The woman looked up at him, large round glasses askew.

"Are you all right?" he shouted through her closed window.

She seemed to have trouble focusing on him. She had a small cut on her forehead that was just now beginning to bleed. She said something he couldn't hear.

"Roll down your window; I can't hear you," he shouted.

Through her clouded expression, understanding dawned on her face. She tried to fix her glasses, but the bent left temple didn't cooperate, and they didn't fit right. This distracted her for a moment; then she seemed to remember what she'd originally set out to do and rolled the window down, her arm rotating slowly on the manual lever.

"Are you all right?" Sal asked again.

"Oh, uh, yeah. I think so," she said. "I'm actually not sure. My head hurts."

"I'm really sorry," he said. "It's all my fault."

"It is?" she asked. "What did you do?"

His mouth clicked shut in surprise. "Well," he stammered, "I think I hit a pothole back there, and my pipes came off—"

Honk! Sal turned around. A still-rolling pipe had now blocked traffic, and an angry driver, now that he'd gotten Sal's attention, indicated in unfriendly terms that Sal should do something about it. Embarrassment leaped in his chest.

"I'll be right back!" he said and dashed off, intending to kick the pipes remaining in the street to the curb. Halfway there, he realized he'd been too abrupt with the woman, and he yelled back, "I-I'll call for help!"

"What?" she asked.

"I'LL CALL FOR HELP!" he shouted. "JUST GIVE ME A MINUTE!"

She nodded, and another horn honked, uncomfortably close because he was standing in the middle of the street. "Sorry, sorry," he yelped and retreated out of the way, ran back to where a few of his pipes still spun and rolled in the street, dodged traffic to gather them, and dropped them near his truck. Some were definitely not salvageable, but at least they were out of the way. Traffic began moving again, and now nobody had a reason to yell at him. Grabbing his phone from the holster on his belt, he dialed 911, explained what had happened, and the dispatcher said she'd send help, which made him feel much better. He told her he needed to get his insurance information together, and that there was no need to stay on the line.

After hanging up, he sat sideways in the driver's side seat of his truck, legs dangling, head in his left hand, and sighed. This was disastrous. He glanced back at the woman's car. She still hadn't gotten out. He decided to see if he could try once more to make sure she was all right, to smooth things over. He slid out of his seat, shut the door, and approached her car again. Though it was cold this morning, she hadn't raised her driver's side window. She'd lain her head back on the headrest, eyes closed. The wound on her forehead had stopped bleeding. It looked like she'd dabbed it with something. She'd also worked a bit more on her bent glasses, but they still sat crooked on her face.

"Hey," he said gently.

She opened her eyes. They were green.

"Hey."

"I just wanted to let you know that I called 911, and they're sending help."

"Oh. Good. That's good. Who are they sending?"

Sal went blank at the unexpected question. "Uh, almost surely, the police. Possibly an ambulance. Hey, are you sure you're all right? You don't seem like you're all here, if you get my meaning."

"I get that a lot."

Sal suddenly wished he could take back his last sentence, but before he could backtrack, she spoke again.

"When you said it was all your fault, what did you mean?"

To Sal, it was obvious. He'd hit the pothole. His pipes had come off his truck. Was she asking this to get some admission out of him? To make sure his insurance paid instead of hers? Was she recording him now? He glanced over at her passenger seat, but he could only see a purse. She could have something in there, recording him. He glanced over, but didn't see a dash cam. Maybe he'd have to choose his words carefully. But again, before he had a chance to speak, she spoke.

"Because I don't see how it could be your fault. I hit this pole all on my own. I'm not a very good driver, really. I get distracted because I think too much. I assume those pipes fell off your truck, and you've been nice so far, though you haven't introduced yourself, which is kind of rude. But you're probably an honest man. You wouldn't have come right out and said it was your fault if you weren't. So you probably weren't rude on purpose." She paused. "It's clear that this is a different sort of day for both of us."

She'd hit him with so many things that his brain overloaded, and didn't know what to say. He decided simply to introduce himself.

"I'm Sal Fuchetti." He stuck his hand out. She ignored it.

"Just Sal?" she asked.

"No, uh, Salvatore."

"Salvatoré. Salvatoré," she said, pronouncing the *e* (which Sal never did) and enunciating slowly, as though each syllable were a relished mouthful of delicacies dancing delightfully across her tongue. She seemed lost in thought, as if remembering something. She finally took his hand.

"Pleased to meet you, Salvatoré Fuchetti. I'm Mary Simmons. I must say, you have a much more interesting name than I have."

"Uh, thanks," he said, letting go of her hand.

"Were you named for a famous Salvatoré, like Salvatoré Ferragamo, the Italian shoe designer?" She paused. "Or better yet, Salvatoré Quasimodo, the Nobel prize winning poet?"

"Uh, no. It was my grandfather's name. On my mother's side."

"Oh." She looked disappointed at first, then seemed to reconsider. "Italian on both sides?"

"Oh, yeah. I'm pure-bred," he said proudly.

She smiled. "Was your grandfather a plumber too?"

"Naw. Roofer."

Suddenly she looked troubled. She turned away, eyes down in her lap.

"I'm sorry," she said. "I didn't mean to ask personal questions."

"Hey, no problem. If it bothered me, I woulda just not answered."

"I can get carried away with facts," she explained.

"That's okay, really." he said, then added: "Hey, how did you know about them other Salvatores? I never heard of any of them guys."

Now she seemed reluctant to answer. She didn't look up.

"Oh, I work at the library—the Deptford one," she said. "I'm on my way to work right now, or at least I was. It's a small library. Not a lot of traffic anymore; kids these days just use Wikipedia. Lots of time to myself. I can look up anything I want. I learn a lot of random facts that way."

Sal searched for something to say to put her at ease. He couldn't guess at why she seemed to lose her confidence. Finally, he said, "Well, the facts don't seem too random today," and then immediately regretted it. What was that supposed to mean?

She looked up at him and smiled. He liked her smile. The faint sound of sirens approaching hit his ears.

"No," she said. "No, they don't."

"Hey, listen," he said. "I just came over here to see if you were all right."

"I'm fine, really. I hit my head pretty hard, and I'm a bit dizzy, but other than that, I think I'm okay."

"I'm pretty sure they're gonna want to take you to the hospital to see if you have a concussion. My brother hit his head pretty hard playing touch football when we was kids. They don't mess around with head injuries."

"That probably means I'll miss work."

"Well," he explained, "if you do have a concussion, you also probably shouldn't drive. Do you have somebody to come pick you up and take you home? Somebody you can call?"

She sighed inwardly. There were no relatives nearby. She didn't have close friends, but she had co-workers she could call. She didn't like revealing details of her life because she lived alone, had cats, and was a single librarian. When people heard that, they acted as though they could sort her into some category that made them feel they knew her rather than take the time to actually get to know her.

"Yeah," she said. "I can call one of the girls from work, or somebody like that."

The sirens were louder.

"Okay," he said. "Look, we're gonna have to exchange insurance info when the cops get here anyway, so let me just give you my card now."

He offered her his business card, and she took it.

"My day's shot now anyway," he said. "I gotta see how much of that PVC back there I can use; how much I gotta take a loss on, and then get it replaced. By the time I do that, it'll be late in the day. Though I'm gonna try, I may not get back to the job till tomorrow. It's no problem for me to come pick you up and take you home if you can't find nobody."

She looked up at him doubtfully.

"Yeah, I know what you're thinking. Look at that card. I'm a licensed plumber, member of the local union. I have a reputation to uphold, and there are about 500 ways to track me down if I don't. You can trust me. I just want to make sure you're all right. I feel responsible for this, okay?"

The police and ambulance arrived. EMTs bounded out of their vehicle, and Sal waved them over.

"Okay," she said.

4

∞∞∞∞

8:30 AM

Greta Stratton-Foster, Ph.D, Sociology, always checked her inbox first thing upon entering the department every day precisely at 8:30 AM. She grabbed the thin stack of mail and proceeded to her office while flipping through it. Decades ago, the paper inbox was the primary means of communication, but now it existed as a vestige of a bygone era that somehow lingered in the modern age. It sufficed to check it once in the morning, as there were still forms of communication based solely on paper. It had, of course, mostly been replaced by her email account.

The Sociology department was not a big department at Rowan University, but it had endured a long time. Nestled in a corner of Robinson Hall in the center of the campus, the department saw most undergraduates pass through, because the department's intro course was a popular General Education requirement for many of the majors. Greta had been there for about 16 years, so she'd taught her fair share of students. That wasn't what excited her, though. For her, it was the research.

She was well into gathering data on her latest project: *The Role of Religion in Intergenerational Transmission of Mores and Values in a Cross-Cultural Society*. In fact, she'd almost completed her data gathering, and the preliminary results were exciting. Her partner in this project, David Greshom, also in the department, was excited too—about the data and about Greta. They'd had a friendship prior to the research, but the project had caused it to blossom. There'd been dinners in Philadelphia after a hard day's work gathering data; there'd been late nights crunching numbers; they'd shared inside jokes, inside stories, inside feelings. She liked working with David. He was funny, energetic, and very, very smart. He could make data analysis programs like SAS and Mathematica sing. And truth be told, his advances were flattering; he showed more interest in her than her husband did of late. Each day they grew closer, closer than Greta cared to admit, because she sensed an approaching line—a line she feared crossing. She'd informed David in no uncertain terms that she was a happily married woman and intended to stay that way. But she found herself thinking about David and looking forward to spending time with him.

Part of it was that she and Gerald didn't have a lot in common anymore. Now that Jenny had left the house and gone to school across the country, they found they had little to bring them together without her. Gone were the days of their youthful romance, with all the passion and heat and excitement that went with it. Now, she couldn't remember life like that, let alone try to recapture it. Jenny had come out of that and had been the catalyst for their marriage ever since. Now that she was gone, Greta and Gerald found their marriage had been on autopilot. After the initial adjustment to the quiet and lack of activity, they'd settled into a pattern where they both did their separate things. They had everything they needed, so it was easy for life to run itself. That had sort of worked for the prior semester, and now Jenny had gone back after the winter break. But it didn't make for much adventure and excitement or camaraderie and partnership, much less love.

She reached her office and opened the door. David sat at her desk, waiting for her.

"Hi!" he greeted her enthusiastically.

Greta didn't like him letting himself into her office. This was about the third or fourth time. She really needed to remember to lock it.

"Didn't I tell you not to come in my office when I'm not here?" Greta threw the forgotten contents of her inbox on the desk.

"Hey, what kind of 'good morning' is that?" he asked.

"It's not one," she said.

David got up from her chair, came around her desk, and grasped both her hands in his.

"I'm sorry," he said, leaned in, and kissed her on the cheek.

She looked up at him. "Don't do it again," she said.

"I won't. I promise," he lied. "Boy, you smell great! I'd like to go in again." He leaned down as if to kiss her again, but she smacked him across the chest.

"Trespassers do not merit kisses," she said.

"So if I want more kisses, I have to be nice. Noted. I can be *very* nice." He smiled devilishly.

That wasn't what she'd meant, of course, but he had a way of wringing additional meaning out of the things she said.

"Stop," she said, annoyed, realizing she frequently told him to stop. She considered adding something to further dissuade him, but checked herself. She did enjoy the attention.

"Okay, I'll stop. For now. But you need to know you drive me crazy, woman."

"I'm not driving you anywhere; it's all in your head."

She successfully moved around him, took her coat off, hung it up, and sat down at her desk. He sat in the chair opposite, where a student would sit if she'd been having office hours.

"So what brings you in here this early in the morning?" she asked.

"Nothing really. I just wanted to be the first to see you," he said.

"Oh."

"Well," he added, "I was analyzing the numbers last night after inputting our data from over the weekend. The trend seems to be going in our direction."

"Wow!" She looked down at her blotter, slapped both hands on the desk, and again exclaimed, "Wow!"

"Yeah, I know. Seems we're on to something here. But of course, we predicted that, didn't we?" He winked at her.

"We sure did. This is fantastic, David!"

"It is. I'm really excited. I think all we need is a few more weekends to get our sample size up a bit, and as long as the trend continues, we'll be able to publish soon."

"Wonderful! Oh, I'm so happy about this."

"Well, *I* think it calls for a celebration. Dinner tonight?"

"Let's just stick to lunch. Gerald had a big presentation this morning, and he may want to celebrate tonight." This was true, but she knew he'd be far more likely to celebrate at a bar with his co-workers than with her. He'd be home late, and she'd eat alone.

"Oh, Gerald. What's he been up to?" David sounded disappointed.

"I don't know. I don't really understand what he does anyway. Something to do with implementing a new website to track something-or-other."

David sighed. "Gerald my nemesis. He has no appreciation for what he has." He stood up, moved around the desk, and then knelt down by her chair so they were face-to-face. "You deserve better."

"You're calling yourself better? You've been trying to break up a marriage."

"Because I know it isn't working. And I know what I want, and it's you. I know you're unhappy. We could be so happy together, Greta. We have so much in common, and I'm not just talking about work—"

"I know," she said.

"When you love somebody," he said, "you do what's best for them. I love you. It's best for you to get out of your marriage, Greta." He reached out, caressed her cheek. "You're not happy. You know as well as I do that there's no way he's celebrating with you tonight. Why spend another night alone, when you could be with somebody who truly cares about you?"

She looked at the floor. "Oh David, I don't know," she said quietly.

"Yes you do," he said. "You know it's right. You're just afraid to start. Don't be afraid. I'll be with you every step of the way."

The trouble was, he would, and she knew it. She couldn't count the number of small, thoughtful ways he'd cared for her over the past few months. What did Gerald do when her car had died on 8th Street in Philadelphia? Told her to call the roadside service, and then hung up—he needed to get back to work. She'd called the service, and then called David. He immediately came, waited with her until the tow truck arrived, and then drove her home.

"Okay," she said. "I'll have dinner with you tonight."

"Excellent," he said. "You won't be disappointed, I promise you that."

He leaned over and kissed her on the cheek. She surprised herself by kissing him back—on the cheek. They stared for a moment into each other's eyes; he leaned in again and this time, kissed her lightly on the mouth. She didn't resist. Instead, she put her hand behind his neck, pulled him in, and they began to kiss passionately. She felt desire burn within her, and she realized he'd finally worn her down, though at the moment, she didn't care.

Elation exploded within David. He hadn't thought this would happen, maybe, until tonight, after some dinner, some wine—

The phone rang. They ignored it. One, two, three, four rings, then to voice mail. Finally, they pulled back. They smiled at each other.

"What was that?" David asked.

"I miss being loved," she said, the warning in her heart having almost completely waned.

"Well, I love you, and I want to love you."

"You've made that abundantly clear." The voice mail light on her phone went on.

"So tonight? 6:00. I'll pick you up here; no need to go home."

"Okay."

"Okay," he said. He stood up. "I, uh, better get to my office. Have some stuff to do before my 9:30 class."

"Okay, David. See you later."

He turned to leave, but stopped when Greta's cell phone rang from within her purse. She frowned, wondering if the same person had called her office phone. Could it be Gerald? Only he and a few close friends had both numbers. She fumbled through her purse and found the phone. She didn't recognize the number, but answered it anyway.

"Hello?"

"Hello, this is Sergeant Pete McCaffrey of the New Jersey State Police, Bellmawr station. May I speak to a, uh, Mrs. Gerald Foster?"

She didn't know what this was about, but they could at least get her name right. "Speaking. This is *Dr. Greta Stratton-Foster*."

"I'm sorry, ma'am, I just need to make sure I'm speaking to the right person. Are you the wife of a Mr. Gerald Foster, and do you reside on Wildwood Avenue in Pitman, NJ—"

"Yes. Yes, I do."

"I regret to inform you, ma'am, that your husband was involved in a car accident at approximately 7:50 AM—"

"Gerald!"

"Yes, ma'am. He was air lifted to Cooper Medical Center in Camden, and is in critical condition."

"My God!"

"Yes, ma'am. I'm sorry to be the one to bring this news to you."

David put a hand on her arm and gave her a questioning look. She shook her head, which began to pound along with her heart.

"Is he all right? How badly was he injured?"

"I know they needed the jaws of life to remove him from the car, ma'am. I do not know the extent of his injuries; I would suggest, however, that you visit the hospital as soon as possible."

"He's at Cooper?"

"Yes, ma'am. In critical condition. Usually, that means he'll be in surgery right away. I'm sorry, ma'am, that I don't have any further information."

"No, that's okay. Thank you for calling."

"You're welcome, ma'am. Good luck."

He hung up. She glanced down at the red voice mail light that now looked surreal, knowing that the message it represented was the same as this, that they'd called work first, then her cell phone. And what had she been doing when that call came in? When they were trying to tell her what had happened only moments ago to her husband? The red light, now representing tragedy, blurred as tears filled her eyes.

"What happened?" David asked.

"Gerald. Car accident. I have to go to the hospital," she said.

"Oh, no. I'm so sorry, Greta." There went tonight's plans.

She didn't say anything. Tears began to trickle down her cheeks as she put on her coat. He tried to help, but her movements were sharp, manic, angry. She shrugged him off, dropped her phone on the floor instead of in her purse, and bent to pick it up.

"Can you—I have two classes today. Can you—?" she couldn't get the words out.

"Of course. I'll take care of everything. You just go."

"Thank you. Thank you, David."

She stormed out of the room, the scent of perfume in her wake.

5
∞∞∞∞

8:45 AM/5:45 AM Pacific

The pitch-dark room made sleep blissful until the musical chimes of her phone—on its charger and lying on her desk next to her head—intruded into Jenny Foster's peace. At first she tried to ignore it, and then she remembered her roommate in the bed across the room. She sat up and grabbed the phone.

Mom? Why was Mom calling now? Didn't she know how early it was out here in California? Maybe she just forgot. She answered the phone.

"Hello?" she whispered, the sleep definitely not out of her voice. She stood and headed into the bathroom she and Emma shared with the occupants of the other room—the totality of which the University called a suite.

"Hi, honey; I'm sorry to wake you." Her mother's voice sounded shaky, quivering. Something was wrong.

"Hey Mom; that's okay. What is it?" She could hear the slowing of Mom's characteristically fast footsteps clicking and clacking on pavement, then the unlocking and opening of a car door.

"Well, I don't know all the details yet, but apparently your father's been in a car accident."

"What?" She momentarily wondered why she referred to him as *your father* instead of simply, *Dad*. "What happened?"

"I don't know yet." The car door slammed; she heard a jangle of keys, and then the engine started. "I just found out myself. The police called. They said he'd been airlifted, so I think it's pretty serious." She heard a click as her mother's phone switched to the car's audio system.

"Oh no. Airlifted where? Philadelphia?"

"Cooper. The accident must've happened on the Jersey side; the call was from the State police." Her mother sniffed; she'd obviously been crying. "Hold on a sec, I have to find a tissue."

There was a maddening pause while Jenny's mind raced. Snow had been on the ground when last she'd seen New Jersey for winter break; maybe Dad had hit an ice patch? She found it hard to picture now that she was back here in Berkeley where the wintertime temps vacillated between the 60s and 40s, but at home it could get pretty nasty this time of year. As far as she knew, Dad had never been in an accident: he was a careful, if somewhat impatient driver. How could this happen? The thought of Dad lying on a gurney, an oxygen mask attached to his face, IV in his arm, eyes closed, unspecified injuries covered by emergency blankets, was almost too much to take. Her eyes welled up with tears.

"I'm back," her mother said.

"Mom," Jenny said through her tears, "is there snow on the ground? Were the roads dangerous?"

"No," she said. "Everything melted late last week. It's a bright, sunny day. I have no idea how this could've happened; it must've been somebody else's fault." Greta doubted this, but thought it would reassure Jenny.

"Okay," Jenny said. She sniffed, had trouble focusing, sniffed again, and finally wiped her nose with the back of her hand.

"Look, honey, I've told you everything I know at this point. I just left Rowan for the hospital. I should be there in about a half hour. When I find out more, I'll call you back. Do you have classes today?"

"Yeah. I have a couple classes down in Wheeler Hall later today." She lived in Stern Hall, on the edge of campus. Wheeler was in the center of campus.

"Okay; it's still early out there. I'll try to give you an update as soon as I can, before your classes."

"Mom, I don't think I can go to class like this!"

"Well, what would you do with your time otherwise?"

"I don't know.... Sit around. Think about Dad. I certainly couldn't concentrate in class."

"You can sit around and think about Dad just as easily in class as in your room, and who knows? You might pick up something in class. I don't expect you to be at your full potential, but—"

"Do you want me to sit and cry in class?"

"Well, no, honey, but—"

"I'm not going to class, Mom."

"Okay. Okay, I'm sorry. I'm not exactly at my full potential right now, either. Look, you try and get some rest, okay? I know I got you up early. I'll give you a call in an hour or so when I find out what's going on."

"Okay, Mom. Thanks for letting me know right away."

"Sure thing, honey. I love you."

"I love you too."

"Okay, bye-bye."

"Bye."

Jenny put the phone down on the bathroom counter and stared at it, thinking about Dad. Her awareness retreated backward from her field of vision, overcome with so many memories. Never in her wildest dreams did she ever think Dad could be taken away from her so suddenly, so *randomly*. But she could still hope, she reminded herself. He'd been airlifted. That meant that he was alive, and they were trying to save him. She could hold on to that.

Mom was another thing entirely. She could be so detached, so insensitive. Dad was always the one who understood her, who could put her at ease. Any time she had a problem, she could always go to Dad. He would understand, would identify with the issue, and he always seemed to have the right thing to say. Mom approached things so coldly, so logically. For a sociologist, she certainly didn't understand people very well.

Despite what her mother wanted, Jenny wasn't going to class. And she wasn't getting any rest either. Maybe she could find something online about the accident.

6
∞∞∞∞∞

9:00 AM

It felt surreal to be getting back in her car and carrying on with her day, but Gloria didn't see any reason not to. She'd given her statements, her thoughts, her opinions, her drivers' license number, her insurance, her address, her phone number, her email address, and most of all, her support to anyone who needed it. It was the least she could do, she felt, after having come so close to the accident and escaping it. Now, after all her testimony had been given, the cars had been cleared, and traffic flowed again, she was free to go.

It had been two men: the one in the Land Rover was the younger of the two. Mid-thirties, light brown hair, an empty car seat in the back. His legs had been crushed, and they'd had to cut him out of his vehicle. He'd regained consciousness soon after the accident, howling in pain. Gloria couldn't bear to listen, and she'd been glad when the paramedics arrived and they'd given him something for the pain. His words had haunted her, though:

"Terri! I'm coming to get you, Terri! I won't leave you there, I promise! Oh, Terri, I'm so sorry!"

This would give way to screams and cries of pain, but he would always come back to Terri. Gloria brushed away a tear. Perhaps Terri usually occupied the car seat, but of course she couldn't be sure.

The other man, the one in the blue Chevy, had been in worse condition.

He'd sustained a head, neck, or back injury of some kind and had never regained consciousness. They'd landed a medical helicopter and flown him directly to Cooper. She wasn't sure if he'd make it. She wondered how he'd created this horrible accident, where he'd been going this morning, and if someone who loved him was now in pain. She hoped he'd be all right.

She looked out at all the cars going by. Each one of them held people with their own dramas, their own stories, and each of those stories was unique and vitally important to those who were in them. Hundreds, thousands of cars went by this spot every day, just a small and normally inconsequential part of all of those stories. But today, this place had become a nexus of sorts, diverting thousands of stories in different directions, ways in which they would not otherwise have gone. For some, the result was minor inconvenience and delay, and most of them would complain about their own circumstances, never knowing about the serious, life-changing things that had happened here to other people, in this spot, today. Would they care if they did know? Some would; some wouldn't, Gloria thought.

All other injuries came from minor fender benders separate from the main accident. Most of those people were gone now, cars towed away or driven, loved ones having come and picked them up. A few police officers managed the rest, but Gloria had nothing more to say or do. It was time for Gloria to move on herself. She started her car, checked her face in the mirror, and wiped away a stray tear. Shifting into gear, she merged in with the traffic and continued on her way to the school. She drove very slowly.

Thankfully, the rest of her drive was uneventful, and she arrived at West Deptford High School at 9:32 AM, according to her car's clock. She pulled in and began to circle the lot, looking for a space. Since she was very late, of course, the front lot was full, and so was the side. That meant she'd have to use the back lot and walk past the fields to the school building. Normally she'd sigh inwardly and complain about this, but after what she'd witnessed this morning, she knew in the scheme of things, it didn't matter.

She went around the building from the side lot and turned onto the access road that went past the fields. The lot was toward the end of this road on the left, before the water tower. She pulled in. This lot was almost full too, but she found a space near the end on the left, facing the woods.

Grabbing her bag and her purse, she got out and locked her car.

Unexpectedly, she could hear voices. She paused a moment, waiting for a car to pass on Red Bank Avenue, to determine where the voices were coming from. The woods. Classes were in session now; nobody should be out here. She decided to go investigate. Arriving at school had transformed her; the crash victim had disappeared. She was Ms. Williams now, with authority over these kids. If any of them were out here, there would be detentions and suspensions with no exemptions.

Of course, navigating in the woods was no easy task in her high heeled shoes, and she had to leave her bag and purse behind. The wet and spongy ground gave way under her feet, her heels sinking into the mud, and more than once she thought she'd lost a shoe. As she approached, the voices sounded like they were arguing. She couldn't make out what they were saying yet, but their words became more audible with each step.

"...told you...be coming back...." A male voice.

"I know...didn't think..." Another male.

"Look, man, I fronted you that stuff...said you'd have it."

"I will! I get paid on Friday, Freddie!"

"I need it now, Jameel!"

"Whoa, what's that for?"

"Persuasion. How much do you have right now?"

"Stop it, Freddie!" A female voice. How many of them were there?

"Shut up!" shouted Freddie. "How much do you have?"

"I don't have nothin', man," stated Jameel. As Gloria got closer, she could see figures through the trees. Freddie was probably Frederick Dietrich: a troubled kid. He'd had so many infractions he was barely in school. If he was up to no good, this might be the thing that got him kicked out. Gloria quickened her pace to try to get there before anything serious happened.

Jameel had to be Jameel Jones. Gloria could not guess why he was hanging out here with Freddie Dietrich. Jameel was an Honor Society kid, a basketball player, a shoo-in for any university he wanted. He'd probably be Valedictorian this year. He had the respect of many teachers in the school, not just because of his grades, but also because he came from a poor, single-parent home. In other words, he worked for everything he had. He'd earned everything he'd accomplished through effort and determination. What was he doing out here with Freddie

Dietrich?

Freddie spoke again: "I don't believe you."

"It's true, man. Don't do nothin' stupid, Freddie."

"Are you threatening me?" Freddie asked.

"Freddie, don't!" said the female voice again. It was probably Sheila Masterson, Freddie's girlfriend.

"Stay out of this, Lana." Not Sheila. Somebody new? "I said, are you threatening me?"

"No, Freddie. Just explaining."

"Empty your pockets, right now!"

"Why?"

"'Cause I *told* you to. I'm not gonna say it again. I want any money you got on you, right now. Empty your pockets."

There was a pause. Gloria was almost there now; she could nearly see them.

"The wallet. Give it to me."

"How 'bout I just empty it for you?"

"No, I want it."

"There's no money in it!"

"I'd like to see that for myself. Plus, I could keep your driver's license as collateral."

"I'm not giving it to you."

"Then I'm gonna take it."

Gloria could hear the sound of rustling leaves and a struggle. She burst into the clearing in time to see Jameel and Freddie fighting. Freddie had charged Jameel, whose hands gripped Freddie's wrists, holding them back. Freddie had a knife clamped in both hands, shoving them forward, forcing the knife at Jameel. Before Gloria could say anything, Freddie pushed hard with his legs and backed Jameel up against a tree; as Jameel's back slammed into the tree, he lost his grip on Freddie's wrists, and the knife plunged into Jameel's stomach.

"Freddie, stop!" Gloria shouted, too late.

The girl screamed. Jameel grunted and dropped to the ground in a sitting position. Freddie stood up straight in surprise and let go of the knife, which fell to the ground. He looked down at Jameel, then back at Gloria, turned, and fled. The girl turned to see who Freddie had seen, saw Gloria, and sprinted after Freddie. Jameel slumped to the side, a stain spreading on his shirt. Gloria ran over to him as fast as her shoes would allow. Jameel looked up at her, breathing hard, clearly in pain.

"Ms. Williams! What are you doing here?" he asked.

"I might ask the same of you," she said, "but now is not the time."

She grabbed his hands, pressed them together, left palm on the back of the right, and pushed them into his wound.

"Ugh. That hurts!" he said.

"You have to apply pressure to slow the bleeding. I'm gonna call 911; you apply pressure."

"Okay."

She reached for her purse, but it wasn't there. Her purse. Where was her purse? Oh no; she'd left it by her car.

"I left my phone in my purse; I have to go get it."

"I'd give you mine if I had one," he said.

"That's okay; I'll be right back."

She stood up and left the clearing as quickly as she could. Picking her way among the roots, leaves, and mushy ground, she again cursed her shoes. She'd taken a different path this time seeking a more direct route, and when she emerged from the wooded area, she was further down the line from her car. Instead, she faced a black, aged Nissan. It was running. She looked up to see the driver, and Freddie stared back at her, panic in his eyes. His girlfriend jumped in and slammed the passenger door in one motion. Without waiting for her to belt herself in, Freddie peeled out of the space backward, turned, and raced out of the parking lot, leaving the smell of burnt rubber in his wake. Gloria fumed. Whatever charges could be pressed, whatever penalties could be levied, whatever sentences could be carried out, she would see to it that he paid for this.

Gloria turned left and sprinted for her car. When she was almost there, she turned her right ankle, stumbled and fell, sliding into the back of her car and banging her head in the process. Her surging adrenaline meant that she hardly noticed the pain, but she did curse her shoes again. She pulled them off and threw them both down. The purse was right where she'd left it. She got up, and then felt the pain when she tried to walk on her ankle. It didn't seem too bad; she could manage for now.

Digging through her purse, she found the phone and dialed 911 as quickly as she could. She explained what happened and asked them to dispatch an ambulance. The operator, a man, asked her to describe the car.

"It was a black Nissan. Old, beat up."

"Four or two-door?"

"I'm not sure. I know it was a Nissan because it reminded me of the 280ZX my boyfriend had when I was in high school. But it must be something newer; whatever they replaced that one with."

"And you didn't get the license plate, but you know the driver?"

"Yes."

"We'll get the police out there right away."

"And an ambulance."

"Yes, ma'am."

"Thank you! I need to get back to Jameel. I'll be here when they get here." Without waiting for a reply, she hung up.

She became increasingly aware of the pounding pain in her ankle. It might be worse than she thought. But she couldn't leave Jameel by himself. She stood up. Yeah, it was definitely getting worse. She'd better return to the clearing before she couldn't walk at all. Digging through her purse for her keys, she unlocked her car, threw her bag and her purse in, pocketed her phone, and shut and locked the car again. She set off into the woods, limping this time.

She'd arrived at school hoping the rest of her day would be normal. Clearly, there was nothing normal about today.

7

9:30 AM

The ambulance left, and Sal headed back to his truck. After doing some weird stuff with lights to see whether Mary's pupils were dilating properly, they had decided she had a concussion and took her in for some x-rays. The hollow feeling in his chest from having caused all of this got a little bigger every time he thought about it. For the umpteenth time, he looked at where the plastic ties that were supposed to have held his pipes securely should be: snapped off somewhere and missing. It made no sense; everything had been fine when he'd attached those pipes—in exactly the same way he'd been doing it for 10 years now. An absolutely freak accident.

He had a lot more of them in one of the truck's compartments, so he retrieved them and set about re-fastening both the salvageable and the unsalvageable pipes to the top of his truck. This was quickly done, and then he was on his way—not without vigorously shaking the re-mounted pipes to make absolutely sure they weren't going anywhere.

As he headed to the plumbing supply store, his thoughts turned once again to Mary. He'd stayed with her while they examined her, and he was thankful that her injuries didn't go beyond the bad bump on her head. Mary seemed to have appreciated his being there, and just before they wheeled her away to the ambulance, she'd grabbed and squeezed his hand. That was more attention than any woman had paid him in a long time, and he couldn't say it was unwelcome.

Sal had the curse of always being the *nice* guy, the guy you could rely on, who'd never let you down, and was always ready to do you a favor. His friends had been saying that since high school, but the niceness didn't seem ever to provide him any benefit. Did nice guys really always finish last? Maybe. He wasn't bad looking; he could probably stand to lose some weight, but he didn't think looks were the issue. No, the problem sat squarely on Sal's shoulders. He was perfectly comfortable relating to women in "safe" ways: family members, wives of friends, and other acquaintances loved him. When, however, he made the mental mistake of considering a woman a potential partner, he froze up and became awkward.

His friends tended to make it worse, because they frequently prodded him to approach women in bars. He'd embarrassed himself enough times to know several things about that scenario: 1) He was not good at what sales people called the "cold call;" 2) Women in bars that *wanted* to be approached—at least the ones that he'd tried—usually made it obvious after a couple weeks that they weren't interested in a long-term relationship like Sal was; and 3) The same people seemed to frequent the same bars, in a futile circuit orbiting the next "experience." Sal wanted more than an experience; he wanted a partner. Bars did not seem like the right place to find his life-partner.

Rather than keep doing the same thing and expecting a different result, Sal had learned not to pursue the type who frequented bars looking for the next good time, the next party, the next high. Those relationships only lasted long enough to create the opportunity for the next high. After piling up a decade of party-highs and looking back on his accomplishments, Sal had started asking questions like *What does it all mean? What is this life I'm living accomplishing? Is this all there is? What will be my legacy when I'm gone? Will anyone remember me or care that I was here? Does that even matter?*

Asking those kinds of questions, alone in your *just-having-transitioned-from-apartment-to-mostly-empty-townhouse*, in the early morning hours because you couldn't sleep, did not contribute to a positive outlook on life. He tried talking to his brother Tony about it, but Tony's interest lay in his political career and his new town council seat, and he didn't seem to have time for Sal and his problems. Sal had considered putting it in terms Tony would understand:

WHEREAS a certain Salvatore Fuchetti is unfulfilled in his daily life; and

WHEREAS it is the intent of the aforesaid Salvatore Fuchetti to live a full, rich life, complete with all the experiences and relationships pursuant thereunto; and

WHEREAS it is the desire of the previously aforementioned Salvatore Fuchetti to leave the world in a better state than that in which he'd entered it; and

WHEREAS this individual has the legal, moral, and actual authority to adopt such measures as are necessary, proper, and relevant to achieving these goals;

NOW, THEREFORE, BE IT RESOLVED that this individual hereby:

What? What should he do? How could he break out? He'd already started backing off. When the guys wanted to go out for drinks on Friday nights, he'd started making excuses. Since that life, that endless pattern, that orbit leading to nowhere, was not what he wanted, it didn't help him to hang out with people—male or female—for whom that kind of life was fulfilling. He'd begun avoiding those situations. Now, however, he had nothing to replace it with, and he found himself to be really lonely. He didn't want that either. And Tony was no help. He had something fulfilling his life at the moment, and he couldn't spare time to think about Sal's life.

Maybe this new thing, this connection he'd unintentionally made with Mary—a woman he'd almost inadvertently killed—signalled the start of a change in his life. Admittedly, guilt currently drove his nascent relationship with her—a desire to make right a mistake that could have had much worse consequences. But maybe that was the ice breaker he needed. Time would tell. He had not set out today to begin any relationships. Now that he'd had these thoughts about her, he'd see if he could even talk to her again when she called, or if he'd freeze up as usual.

You're getting ahead of yourself, he told himself. *You don't even know if she's going to call. She could have any number of other people willing to come pick her up from the hospital.*

But now he hoped she would.

Mary thought all this was ridiculous. A simple bump on the head, that's all—this unnecessary fuss would wreak havoc with her health insurance. The word "concussion" had been mentioned, however, and that turned a minor bump on the head into a big to-do over nothing. This thought repeated over and over each time some new embarrassing thing happened: the rush to the hospital, siren blaring, EMTs expertly jumping out of the ambulance, the pop of the wheels on her gurney as they unfolded with a snap upon exiting the rear compartment, rushing to enter the emergency room, the streamlined sign-in, the concerned faces appearing, fluorescent light fixtures passing by as they wheeled her down the hall and then transferred her to a somewhat private compartment in the emergency room.

The doctor—he could hardly be called a doctor really; he looked so young—had said, after shining a light in her eyes and making her follow the tip of his pen over and over, that they'd be taking her down to get a CT scan of her head. They needed to make sure she wasn't bleeding on the brain or some such thing. She had to ask what a CT scan was, and they'd informed her it was a CAT scan. She wondered when they'd changed it from a CAT scan to a CT scan. Certainly not because it was easier to say: they'd added another syllable, for Pete's sake. It made no sense, but not much did these days. Everything changed so fast. As usual, the world had passed her by somehow, and she'd forgotten to get on the ride.

So here she lay alone with her thoughts, waiting for some unspecified amount of time to get an x-ray. How could she have known this day would wind up so, so...dramatic? It all started the same as any other day: up, shower, eat, feed the cats. Noodle around on the Internet, poke at that last paragraph of the novel she knew she'd probably never finish. Then off to work, at precisely the same time every day. There'd been practically no change in her routine for 10 years, and then suddenly today that all changed. She'd imagined all sorts of interesting breaks in her patterns: a sweepstakes win, a call from the President, being swept off her feet by a tall, dark, and handsome Library patron with a love of Henry David Thoreau. Today, however, was not what she'd had in mind.

The only intriguing thing about today so far was that plumber she'd met. He'd given every indication of being what her mother called a Nice Man:

Why don't you go out and meet a Nice Man? Think how different it would be to have a Nice Man around.

I met a Nice Man at the bus stop the other day; he helped me with my umbrella, and he didn't have a wedding ring on!

Sometimes *Nice* and *Man* sandwiched *Young*:

I had lunch with Sally, and she said there's a Nice Young Man who just started working in her office.

It's been a long time since you brought a Nice Young Man home. Surely, there's a Nice Young Man at work? In your neighborhood? At the park?

Mom meant well; she really did. She didn't seem to be aware, though, that pointing out the obvious—that Mary led a solitary existence—hurt just a little each time she did it. The cumulative effect on Mary of all those small wounds would horrify Mom if she knew about it. Mary had filled enough tissues after phone calls with Mom to paper her walls. Truth be told, that was the big reason why she hadn't gone home to Ohio for so long: she couldn't bear the direction in which the conversation would inevitably turn, and at Mom and Dad's, she couldn't hide anywhere once the tears began to flow. Mom didn't understand how different things were now than they were when she and Dad were young. She'd met Dad at a town fair, for Pete's sake. He'd been the only one who could hit that lever with the sledge hammer hard enough to make the ball go all the way up and ring the bell. Mom had batted her eyes at him, and the rest was history. She'd heard the story so many times, and Mom thought Mary should just do something like what she did. Mom didn't understand that things weren't that *simple* anymore.

That plumber, though—*Salvatoré*, she corrected herself—might fit Mom's description of a Nice Man. Of course, guilt over his supposed culpability in the accident could explain why he'd been nice. But Mary wasn't sure; she didn't think he'd been driven solely by guilt. Or maybe that bump on her head had given her delusions. She didn't know; she didn't know! How were you supposed to think straight when you didn't have all the information?

She still had his business card in her purse, which they'd kindly placed on the chair next to the bed. She could, of course, use that card and call him. But that was putting herself out there, making herself vulnerable, and maybe she wasn't ready for that. Then again, maybe she'd be wiser *not* to play it safe this time. What did she have to lose? A little embarrassment? In the scheme of things, she'd get over that quickly. If she didn't call him, would she forever wonder what might have happened, kicking herself for not taking the risk? Probably. If anything, at the very least she'd likely have a more interesting conversation on the way home than if she called Nancy or Vivian from work. But wait; she didn't even know him. What would she say, if she were to call him?

Gaaah! Why was this so hard?

8
∞∞∞∞∞

10:00 AM

Fatigue lurked at the edges of Officer Bob Blake's perception as he drove home. He'd just gotten off the night shift and had almost reached the station when the call had come in: traffic duty on Delsea Drive at Snyder Avenue until the next shift could take over. Apparently there'd been an accident, and they needed someone to direct traffic around it. Since he was coming off shift, Bob was elected. Oh well. It didn't take that long for someone to relieve him, and he got some overtime out of it.

Traffic duty went uneventfully. At least he hadn't been asked to process the accident itself, though that also seemed to go pretty smoothly. Some kind of paperwork delay had kept him from being relieved until 9:30, but soon he would be home. He looked forward to getting rest.

Bob had just gotten off Route 130 and made the left onto Red Bank when the call came in. His mind automatically translated the code: a stabbing. The location, however, caught his ear—West Deptford High School, just up the road on his left, not even a minute away. Though this was not his jurisdiction, under the circumstances he had a duty to respond. A stab wound could be a life or death matter.

Radioing in his response, he flipped on his lights and picked up speed. The school's back parking lot entrance appeared. Bob turned onto the access road and made a right into the parking lot.

He didn't see anyone, but he knew from the call that the incident had occurred in the woods, the suspect was a white male with black hair wearing a denim jacket and a concert T-shirt, the victim was a black male, and a teacher had witnessed the whole thing. He briefly hit his siren so the teacher and the boy would know he was here. Before getting out of the car, he noted now his fatigue had been pushed to the edge of his consciousness as adrenaline took over.

He got out and immediately noticed the rubbery smell of someone who'd beaten it out of here in a hurry. He must've just missed him; if Bob had been two minutes earlier, the guy might have made his escape right in front of him. This sort of thing happened all the time: Bob called it Criminal Luck. Sometimes these guys wound up in the right place at the right time to evade detection and pull off their nefarious deeds. He plunged into the woods.

"Hello? This is Officer Bob Blake, Westville Police," he called.

"Over here!" he heard faintly. A female voice. He trudged through the underbrush toward it. After a while, he wasn't sure he was going in the right direction, so he called out again, "Am I getting closer?"

"We're right here!" He was indeed much closer. He made a minor course correction, and soon he entered a small clearing. He could see a woman kneeling by someone, taking off her tan overcoat. He quickened his pace and jogged over. Though tall, the prone figure was a kid, a young man really. The woman pressed a wad of tissues into his stomach and then covered him with her coat. He looked over at Bob, but he didn't say anything. He looked ashen and shook violently as he desperately gulped air.

"The ambulance is on its way," Bob said, squatting down. "Good, you're keeping pressure on it."

The woman turned to him. She looked to be in her early thirties, of African descent. "Wow, that was really fast," she said.

"I happened to be in the area," he said. He noticed her disheveled hair, and she had a welt rising on her right cheek.

"Hey, are you all right?" he asked. "Were you involved in the, uh, altercation?"

She smiled. "No. I did all this to myself, by wearing the wrong shoes today."

Despite himself, Bob laughed. He looked down at her muddy, stockinged feet.

"I'm guessing your shoes did not survive your wrath."

"No," she said. "No, they didn't. I left them by my car."

He turned to the boy. "How 'bout you, son? Are you doing okay?"

"Hurts."

"Yeah, I'll bet it does. You wanna know something, though?"

"What's that?"

Bob leaned down so he could whisper in his ear: "Chicks dig scars. And you're gonna have a doozy."

He leaned back and gave him a wink. The boy managed a wan smile.

"Well," he said to the woman, "it looks like you've got everything under control here." He reached out and patted the boy's hand. "I'm Officer Bob Blake. Most people call me Officer Bob, but since you've been stabbed, you can just call me Bob." The boy smiled again.

He offered his hand to the woman, and she took it. "Gloria Williams," she said.

"Pleased to meet you. Now that I know where you are, I'm gonna go watch for the ambulance and guide the EMTs up here. You stay put and keep that pressure on." He stood up.

"We will," she said. "Oh, one other thing." She pointed to the ground, next to Jameel's left leg. "The weapon. It probably has prints on it. We didn't touch it."

"He actually dropped it here, after the stabbing?"

Gloria nodded. Bob sighed and looked up into the sky. "A gift," he said. "Maybe this isn't a case of Criminal Luck after all."

"Criminal luck?" she asked.

He smiled. "I'll explain later. I wanna make sure those guys—" He pointed in the direction of the parking lot, and Gloria realized she could hear a faint siren in the distance. "—find you as fast as possible."

He left. "Not long now," Gloria said to Jameel. He didn't say anything. Her ankle pounded; she wondered if she'd be able to walk on it.

Officer Bob and the EMTs arrived soon with a stretcher. Bob had fetched an evidence bag from his car and with latex-gloved hands, picked up the knife and carefully dropped it into the bag. While the EMTs worked on Jameel, Bob gathered from Gloria the information he would need for his report. Though they were as gentle as they could be, Jameel yelped when the EMTs lifted him onto the stretcher. Gloria had agreed—even insisted—on accompanying Jameel to the hospital. His mother didn't have a phone either, and she would be at work until 6:00 PM. Bob assured Gloria they'd get in touch with Jameel's mother, but she wanted to stay with him anyway.

Expertly, the EMTs picked up the stretcher and began carrying it off. Gloria rose to follow, stumbled, and Bob caught her by the arm before she could fall. She hissed a breath through her teeth.

"Ow."

"Sounds like you hurt yourself."

"Yeah, I knew I'd twisted it, but it wasn't this bad before."

"Can you walk on it?"

"I think so." She tested putting some weight on it. It felt like somebody jammed a spike through her heel up into her shin.

"Ah!"

"I'm guessing that's a no," he said.

"You're a very perceptive man."

He grinned. "That's me. I'm so perceptive that once I almost noticed I was wearing two different colored socks. To the beach. Here, let me help you. The EMTs seem to have left prematurely."

He put her arm around his shoulders and his arm around her waist and waved another EMT over. "She needs to go too," he said. The EMT, a six-feet-something, two-hundred-something pound behemoth, took her other side.

"Go slowly, please," Gloria said, wincing.

"Okay. You lead; we'll keep your pace."

They picked their way through the woods and were soon back to the parking lot, because the two men nearly carried her the whole way to the ambulance. She took a seat next to Jameel.

"Rest here for a minute," Bob said. "I need to go talk to these guys."

Two other police cars pulled into the parking lot. They looked different from Bob's, which caused Gloria to look more closely at Bob's car. Westville. He was a Westville cop? This wasn't even his jurisdiction. What was he doing here?

Bob went over and spoke to the two officers who emerged from their cars. Clearly, he was explaining what had happened, pointing past the parking lot to the woods and handing over the evidence bag with the knife. He seemed to be agreeing to something, and one time he gestured over toward her. The conversation seemed amicable enough; he shook hands with both officers, turned, and came back.

"You're not even from this town," Gloria said.

"On the contrary. I *live* here. I *work* in Westville, which really isn't very far away. I was actually on my way home when the call came through—"

"—which is how you got here so quickly," Gloria finished.

"Exactly." The EMTs seemed ready to leave. "I happened to be in the right place at the right time, lucky for you and for that kid." The ambulance's motor started, and Bob slammed the back door, leaving Gloria to her own thoughts.

9

10:00 AM

Pastor Sean Peterson usually tried to enjoy a relaxing morning on hospital days. Two years since taking this small pastorate in West Deptford, his session—the leadership board of his church—had decided he should do some more "outreach," or ministry to those outside the church. He'd begun volunteering at Cooper hospital once a week, going from room to room and offering—well, whatever he could do to help. Mostly, patients considered him just someone to talk to, a friendly voice, a companion. Sometimes he had the opportunity to do a little more: pray, read the Bible, or impromptu counseling. Though he'd originally been skeptical about the need for him to be involved in this ministry, now he found it was often the highlight of his week. After six months, it hadn't resulted in any new church members, but he felt he'd definitely made a difference in some people's lives, people he would not likely otherwise have ever met.

He shared his responsibility with other clergy who were part of the chaplain program. Since he was the new guy, of course they'd given him Mondays: the day most Christian ministers had off. He didn't usually arrive until after lunch, and he stayed as long as necessary. This usually translated to two to four hours; normally he got home in plenty of time for dinner, and his activities of the day provided much fodder for dinner conversation and prayer with his wife—and even the occasional sermon illustration.

All things considered, the ministry had enriched his prayer life and gotten him out of his comfort zone, so he was grateful for the opportunity.

He realized he'd been thinking all of this while he'd also been reading, and he had no idea what he'd read for the last few paragraphs. Clearly his mind had wandered, and it was time to put the book down. He did so, then stood up and stretched. At that moment, the phone rang. As he headed for it, he could hear his wife's quick footsteps doing the same thing. Wendy had been cleaning up in the kitchen where the phone was, humming to herself as she worked, and he knew if he didn't head her off, she'd beat him to the phone.

"I'll get it hon," he said.

"Okay," she replied.

He had a sneaking suspicion for some reason that this was an important call. Grabbing the phone, he looked at the caller ID. Arthur Hasbrook. Arthur coordinated the ministry at the hospital. He hit the *answer* button.

"Hello?" he said.

"Hello, Sean!" Arthur had a loud, hearty voice, and he wasn't afraid to use it. "I'm glad I caught you."

"Just getting a little R&R this morning before I head off to the hospital," Sean said.

"Wonderful! Always good to recharge," said Arthur. "Well, I'll get right to the point. I had a cancellation today, and I need someone to fill in this morning. I know you normally do afternoons, but I wondered if perhaps you could spare some time over at Cooper this morning as well as this afternoon, sort of a double-shift? I hate to ask you, but there isn't anybody else I *can* ask."

"I don't know, Arthur; this is usually time I carve out to spend with my wife." Wendy looked at him sharply. *Don't bring me into this*, that look said. Sean was immediately chagrined.

"I understand how important that kind of time can be," Arthur said. "There may be a great opportunity to do some good today, though. Have you heard the local news this morning?"

"No, I haven't."

"There was a terrible accident. Lots of people involved, and some were airlifted to Cooper; it made a real mess of people's morning commute. I'm sure there are families at the hospital who could use good counsel today."

He knew right where to hit him. Sean had privately confided to Arthur once that he hadn't been gunning for the ministry when he'd gone to seminary. No, his goal had been an MAR: Master of Arts in Religion, with a specialization in counseling. Though the MAR had sparked his interest in theology—which itself motivated his switch to the Master of Divinity program—he still felt like his first love was counseling people. Lost people. Directionless people. Successful people. All of them, with hopes, dreams, aspirations, some fulfilled, some dashed, some never attempted. Working with people was his main motivation for ministry. To connect people with their "chief end," as the catechism put it, to see them made anew, healed, filled with new purpose. That was what he lived for; that was why he was a pastor. Arthur knew this, and Sean couldn't suppress the suspicion that he used this knowledge to manipulate him. Of course, that was a terrible thing to think, but that didn't make it untrue. Regardless of whether it was true or false, though, Sean needed to make sure that he believed the best about his friend and colleague. That was love, right?

Sean sighed. "Hold on a sec, Arthur."

He put his thumb over the receiver and turned to his wife.

"Wendy, Arthur wants to know if I can fill in for someone this morning, and then do my regular shift this afternoon. He said that there'd been a few bad accidents today and that it'd be a good opportunity to help those families."

"Go," Wendy said. "I'll be fine. In fact, it'll give me an opportunity to get some classwork done." Wendy helped out at the home school co-op that met in their church. "It sounds like you're needed. I'll be praying for you."

Sean smiled. "Thank you, Wendy. I'll make it up to you later."

"I knew what I was getting into when you said you wanted to go into the ministry."

Sean took his thumb off the receiver and brought the phone back up to his ear. "I'll do it," he said to Arthur.

"Excellent! Thank you so much, Sean. I'll be praying for your work today."

"Thank you, Arthur."

"Okay, you better get on the road then. I'll see you later."

"Okay, bye-bye."

Sean hung up the phone. His relaxing morning had just turned into a busy day. He stood, went into the kitchen, and began to massage his wife's shoulders.

"I love you, Wendy Peterson," Sean said.

"I love you too," she replied.

He kissed his wife and headed into the bedroom to get himself ready to go.

10
∞∞∞∞

10:00 AM

Greta pulled into the parking garage at Cooper Hospital and began the long spiral ascent, looking for the first available parking space. Traffic had still been slow on the way over; this must've been a whopper of an accident. Her eyes felt puffy and swollen; her nose, stuffed and runny. She did not present the poised and professional appeal she believed she usually did. Part of the problem was how wrong everything had gone this morning: the rush to get out of the house, the encounter with David, the accident, Jenny's recalcitrance, the traffic jam, and even this stupid, endless spiral up the parking garage. The other part was frustration at herself. She prided herself on always being in control, and this morning—even before the news about Gerry—she'd been out of control. Way out of control. She'd let David get to her this time. What had she been thinking?

And as she struggled to get herself back into control, she unwittingly thwarted herself at every turn. When she thought of David, she gripped the steering wheel, her fingernails biting into her palms. When she thought of Gerry, more anger welled up, and she wanted to scream. When she thought of Jenny, up too early and not going to class, she clenched all her muscles and accidentally accelerated up the parking garage ramp for a few seconds. When she thought of her work, it became ghostly; a wisp of fog that evaded her grasp and receded out of reach.

She had to find a parking space soon, or her nose would run right down to her chin. The garage seemed endless; she'd been going so long, she had no idea what floor she was on. Not a single car had passed her going the other way, and still up, up, up she went. She wondered if she'd already passed Gerald, if she'd already driven up higher than where they were working on him.

How could he have been so stupid as to get into a car accident?

No, she shouldn't think that way. That thought had pushed itself into her head more than once, and every time she pushed it back. There were accidents every day: all you had to do was tune into any Philly radio station and you'd hear about all the delays in all the problem places: I-95 South between the Betsy Ross Bridge and the Ben Franklin Bridge, I-95 North between the Delaware state line and the airport, the Schuylkill Expressway (I-76) all over the place—but always the "Conshohocken Curve"—the Blue Route (I-476), and of course, Routes 42, 55, and I-295 in New Jersey. Gerry had a better commute than most. He only had to navigate the Jersey stuff, get over the Ben Franklin Bridge, and get downtown.

Finally! A parking space. She pulled in, squeezing herself between a black Ford F-150 and a green Toyota Highlander. She'd never be able to see fully to back out, and she'd probably have dings on both the driver's and passenger's side doors by the end of the day, but she'd made it. She cut the engine, dropped her keys into her lap, and reached for another tissue. She blew her nose thoroughly and then inspected herself in her sun visor's mirror. Her eyes *were* puffy and bloodshot. Not much she could do about that. At least her makeup hadn't run; a quick mopping of the tears, and she looked somewhat satisfactory. Grabbing her keys and her purse, she opened her door only to have it slam into the Ford truck, partially open. At least one of the dings would obviously be her fault. Cursing, she squeezed herself into the space between the door and the car, exiting the car through much effort and disheveled clothing. She closed the door as best she could, locked the car, threw the keys into her purse, straightened her blazer and blouse, and headed for the elevator.

It had taken nine floors to find a parking space, and now she had to go all the way back down to get to the lobby. When the elevator finally arrived, she stabbed the button for the lobby and then waited as it stopped twice on the way down to admit people from other floors. She had no idea how *these* people found parking spaces lower down; there certainly hadn't been any when she'd gone through. The mixed dread and anticipation of not knowing what had happened to her husband tore at her composure, and she nearly yelled, "Oh, come on!" when the elevator stopped for a third time. Finally the doors opened on the lobby floor, and she made sure she was one of the first ones out.

She couldn't rush ahead without being conspicuous, so she was third in line when she reached the front desk. When her turn came, she gave them Gerald's name and her name and learned that he was in surgery.

"Surgery? What kind of surgery?" she asked.

"Trauma," replied the woman behind the desk. She looked to be, oh, about 86 years old, viewing the computer screen with her head pointed up and her eyes pointed down so she could read it with her bifocals. "That's all I can access on this system, ma'am. There's a waiting area outside the surgical unit; if you register yourself there, the doctor'll come out and explain everything to you when he's done."

She gave Greta the floor and directions, and Greta was off to the elevators again.

11

∞∞∞∞∞

10:00 AM

Freddie Dietrich checked one final time to be sure no cops had followed him and turned down Green Street. He parked in front of a nondescript duplex, cut the engine, and slumped over the steering wheel, his arms above his head.

"Why are we here?" Lana asked. "Can't you just take me home now?"

The girl was so stupid. Why were they all so stupid? He would've loved to have dumped her on the side of the road somewhere, and then she wouldn't be so much extra baggage—except of course that she'd find some way to get caught up with somebody he knew, his name would be mentioned, and suddenly the cops would be on top of him. No, he had to keep his eye on her for now.

What did it matter now anyway? He was screwed. Ms. Williams had seen him. They had his name, his description, his license plate number, his car, his home address—shoot, they'd probably be calling his phone any minute. They had an eyewitness, and even worse, they had his knife with his fingerprints all over it.

He may as well have gift-wrapped himself.

"No, I can't take you home now," he said impatiently.

"Why not? I don't want to be a part of this, Freddie."

"That's not my problem, is it? You were there. You're part of it. Now you're stuck with me."

"I don't like this, Freddie! Just take me home, please!"

"Shut up! Just shut up and let me think!"

The house he'd parked in front of belonged for the moment to Brick Johnson. Brick wasn't his real name, of course; he'd acquired the nickname (Brick thought) for his body: he worked out regularly, and he was ripped. In reality, Brick was the youngest drug dealer to come out of West Deptford High in recent years, and the nickname came from the stockpile of various drugs packaged in a brick shape everyone assumed he had, somewhere. Freddie had never seen Brick's brick collection, and he wasn't sure he'd still be alive if he had.

Brick had been industrious since high school: he began selling drugs his senior year and now, a mere three years later, he could afford not only to rent the right side of this duplex, but also to buy that beautiful red Corvette parked around the corner—as well as other things like the Kawasaki he had in the back yard. Freddie had always admired him; in fact, Brick had introduced him to pot when he was in eighth grade and Brick was a junior. Weed had carried him along for a while, and he still liked it every now and then, but he knew right away that it wasn't Brick's style. You won't wear tight jeans for long if you're smoking dope all the time.

Pretty soon they'd started dropping acid: a totally different experience. Acid had led to crack, and crack had led to meth—both of which were way better than weed, because they made you sharper and better instead of dull and stupid. The kids that hung around Brick—Ted, Mick, Len, and his skanky girlfriend Penny—never really liked Freddie very much, and Freddie wasn't the only younger kid Brick had let into his circle from time to time. But Brick was always nice to him, always friendly, and most importantly, always backed him up. He'd nearly put that wrestler kid—Mike Murphy—in the hospital as a reminder to everybody that you don't mess with a kid under Brick Johnson's protection. When Brick had approached Freddie to see if he wanted to help out with his distribution business, Freddie was eager and willing. He could not only make some extra cash, but also dip in a bit himself.

The problem was, this month he'd dipped in a bit too much to impress Lana, as the prestige of seeing an older woman had a great effect on his status at school. Couple that with the extra stuff he'd fronted to Jameel to ensure he was hooked (a standard practice, and one he still didn't recognize had been performed upon himself), and he found himself way short. The money was due today, and he knew Brick would hold him responsible for it. Freddie's take went to Brick, Brick's take went to somebody else up the chain, and he always made his numbers. *That's what separates the winners from the losers, Freddie,* Brick had told him. *The winners make their numbers; the losers get addicted and come up short. I always bet on the winners, Freddie. Always. You remember that, because I'm betting on you.*

Freddie'd been doing just fine since school started. He'd even gotten a nice Christmas bonus from Brick, represented now in this car. He was a winner. Winners find a way; they always find a way. He just needed more time, so he planned to ask Brick for help. He knew he was in it deep, but maybe Brick would know what to do. Freddie surely didn't. He reached across Lana and grabbed an envelope out of the glove compartment.

"C'mon, let's go," he said, and without waiting for a reply, got out of the car.

"Where—" she said, but Freddie ignored her; he headed up the front walk, stuffing the envelope in his back pocket. He heard the passenger door slam and Lana's heels clicking their way behind him, trying to catch up (oh, the complaints about the mud from the woods he'd had to hear on the way here). She made it to his side by the time he reached the front door and waited silently while he banged on it. He heard a muttered curse from within, and soon came the sound of approaching footsteps. The door opened.

"Freddie, my *man!*" Brick exclaimed in a puff of cigarette smoke. The lack of a screen door over the front door made it easy for him to encase Freddie immediately in a bear hug. "Come on in; I was just playing some video games." He ignored Lana; she was an accoutrement, and they never really had anything interesting to say. This actually made Freddie grateful; Brick had those all-American good looks made famous time and again by too many boy bands. He wore only a white t-shirt and faded jeans, but he looked like he'd just stepped out of a catalog. One sideways glance made it clear that this fact hadn't escaped Lana either.

Brick indicated a brand new couch on which a game controller lay. "C'mon, sit down. You want anything?"

"No, man, I'm good." Freddie replied. Brick looked over at Lana.

"Can I have a soda?" she asked.

"Coke okay?"

"Sure."

"Be right back."

Brick went down the hall to the kitchen and soon returned with a fizzing glass and ice. He handed it to Lana and sat down on the couch. Freddie just stood there, not sure how to begin.

"Hey, you want to play some?" Brick asked, offering a game controller.

"Naw, man, I'm good," Freddie said.

"You cut school to come here today?" Brick asked, grabbing a burning cigarette from the ash tray on the coffee table and taking a long drag.

He supposed technically, that was one thing he'd done. "Yeah," he said.

"So what's on your mind? Just business? You got the money?"

"Yeah, here." He pulled the envelope out of his back pocket and handed it to him.

"Seems thin."

"Yeah, it's thin, Brick." Freddie looked at the floor. Brick's countenance changed from friendly to serious.

"What's going on, Freddie? You've never been short before."

"Look, man, I need your help."

"You need *my* help?" Brick flipped through the bills in the envelope. "Looks to me like I need about a thousand more dollars."

"Dude, I woulda had it this morning, I swear!" he lied. Even if he'd gotten what Jameel owed, he'd still have been short.

"Yeah, right," Lana said.

"Shut up, Lana!"

"What does she mean?" Brick asked.

"There's this kid at school. Smart kid. He came up to me one day, wanted to know if I had somethin' to, you know, keep him goin'. I said, 'Yeah, I got somethin'." Another lie. He was on a roll.

"And?"

"So I did what you showed me. What I've done a hundred times. I fronted him some, told him to let me know if it worked, and there was more where that came from."

"Sounds good so far."

"Until today," Lana said.

"Shut up, Lana!"

"What's she got to do with this, Freddie?" Brick asked, concern in his eyes.

"Nothin', man. She don't know nothin'."

"Okay, go on."

"He came back a week later, said it worked and he needed more. I told him what it would cost; he said he almost had enough, and he'd have the rest by Friday when he got paid. So I fronted him some more on condition that he pay me on Friday."

"Bad idea, man. Get the money up front; establish a good pattern from the beginning."

"I know. But he's a *good* kid, Brick! I knew he'd come through, and he did."

"All right."

"So that's how we've been workin it. He needs the meth to get through whatever he does all week, and he pays me on Friday. He's always been good for it. Except last week."

"What happened last week?"

"I went to meet him, you know—" He trailed off. Brick didn't need or want to know the inner workings of how Freddie ran his part of the business. Plausible deniability. "He didn't show. I tried gettin' him all weekend, but he wasn't home, and he doesn't have a phone. So I decided to catch up with him at school today. He's a good kid. He's not gonna miss school."

"Okay, sounds good so far."

"Until you killed him," Lana said.

"What?"

Freddie looked incredulously at Lana, his mouth open. He turned back to Brick, the color of whose face now began to redden.

"I didn't kill him, Brick! I swear!"

"Stabbed him!" Lana said almost gleefully. "In front of a teacher!"

Brick stood up, a blue vein pulsating in his forehead. Freddie had never seen him like this; wouldn't have believed he possibly could make a face like this. Any semblance of friendliness, brotherhood, or camaraderie had disappeared. What replaced it stabbed Freddie with fear: pure, unadulterated, unmitigated hate. It should not be possible that a human being could make a face like that; it seemed unhuman, perhaps subhuman, demonic. Instinctively, Freddie recoiled, taking a step backward. Expecting him to shout, Brick surprised him again when he asked very softly:

"And you came here?"

And then despite himself, it all came out in a torrent: "It was an accident I didn't know what to do I needed help you always helped me before, man, always been there, I don't wanna get arrested what am I supposed to do how do I get out of this I need your help oh man oh man—"

Brick slapped him across the face.

"What're you doin, man—"

"Get out." Brick said.

"Wha? I need your *help*, Brick!"

"You stab a guy, in front of a witness who *knows* you! Knows your car, where you live, your— Give me your phone."

"My phone? What do you want with my phone?"

"GIVE IT TO ME!" Brick shouted.

"All right; here it is." Freddie dug his phone out of his pocket. Brick dropped it on the floor, picked up the end of the coffee table, and slammed it down on the phone, over and over again.

"What are you doing? That phone cost me over five hundred—"

"SHUT UP!" Brick continued slamming the table down on the phone until its circuit board became visible through its screen, now ground into powder. He threw the table down one last time, went to the end table beside the couch, and pulled something out of its top drawer.

"Get out, man. Get out now."

"I drove around a while before I came here; nobody followed me. It's cool."

"*I HAVE SEVENTY-FIVE THOUSAND DOLLARS AND DRUGS IN THIS HOUSE! You will NOT lead the cops here!*"

"I didn't, I swear!"

Brick revealed the object he'd taken out of the drawer: a 9mm semi-automatic handgun. He pointed it at Freddie.

"Get out now, or I swear to God I'll shoot you."

This had gone far beyond anything Freddie was prepared for. He burst suddenly and without any warning into tears.

"Okay, okay man j-just don't—"

An electronic tone went off as Brick's security system registered someone attempting to use the alley to get behind the house. Brick grabbed a remote control from the coffee table and switched his screen from the video game to a feed of several cameras showing the approach to his house in all directions. Cops filled every one of them except the backyard, but as the alarm had indicated and as the cameras showed, they'd be surrounded in seconds.

"You *idiot!*" Brick said. Without looking behind him, he switched the

9mm to his left hand, opened the second drawer on the same end table next to the couch, and pulled out a .38 special. He pointed it at Lana, and she screamed.

"Thank you," he said, and fired at the large living room window. The glass shattered, and almost immediately, gunfire erupted from outside. As a bullet whizzed by his head, he threw the .38 to Freddie.

"Defend yourself," he said.

Freddie had no idea what to do with the gun, but he'd watched enough movies to get the idea. Relieved that Brick seemed to know what to do and still considered him an ally, he looked around for a place to shoot. In panic, he took a few steps over to the door and began shooting through it. Lana continued screaming and ducked down low. Brick glided like a ghost behind him somewhere, likely to back him up. An explosion shook the house, nearly knocking him off his feet. Even as he splintered the front door with shot after shot, he felt calm: gratefulness washed over him. Brick hadn't shot him; he was still on his side. Pride swelled his heart to know Brick fought the cops beside him. They'd get out of this together. Glass shattered behind him and he began to smell smoke.

After an impossibly small number of shots, Freddie could hear only the distinctive *click! click! click!* of an empty gun.

"I'm out!" he said, turning to Brick, "Where—"

Brick had disappeared.

The door burst open. Freddie heard an explosion of gunfire, and somehow he lay on his back looking at the ceiling. As he heard multiple footsteps approach, he tried to shout for Brick, his friend, and ask him for more bullets. For some reason, however, he could only make a gurgling sound, and Lana's Coke must have spilled; he could feel a pool of something wetting his chest and back. He needed help to hold them off, but he knew despite this setback, Brick would come through. Brick always knew what to do. Brick had given him the gun. They didn't have a —

Freddie had no further thoughts in this world.

12
∞∞∞∞∞

11:00 AM

Sean arrived at Cooper Hospital three hours ahead of his regular shift. Arthur had been grateful for his help. Sean would be filling in for a priest from the diocese of Camden, who was sick. Arthur knew Sean wasn't Catholic, but that didn't seem to phase him. He said it was more important to minister to the spiritual needs of the patients than it was to worry about whether they shared your faith or not.

This seemed rather odd to Sean. If he were a patient, he'd certainly want counsel only from someone of similar beliefs. Otherwise, how could he trust the counsel? On the other hand, trials that required a hospital stay might be the only contact some people had with anything spiritual. He'd do what he'd been called to do and leave the things he couldn't control to God.

He began making his rounds. He thought first he'd visit the trauma centers. Families of those who'd been seriously injured would be in the various surgical waiting rooms, and he might be able to talk to some of them there.

The first waiting room he visited contained a woman, maybe in her mid-60s, visibly upset and being consoled by two men: one older and the other younger. The older man wore clothes similar to those Sean had on: blue button-up shirt, tie, slacks. The younger man had on khaki pants, a green shirt, and no tie. He held the woman's hand in his. As he entered, they all looked up at him.

"Hi, I'm Pastor Sean Peterson; I'm part of the hospital's clergy on staff. Is there anything I can do to help?"

The men stood up and walked toward him, a protective gesture. The shorter, younger, pudgy man stayed behind the older, thin man. The older man spoke first.

"Hello, Pastor," he smiled, "I'm Pastor Dan Livingston, of Turnersville Baptist Church. This is Colin Donnell, a Deacon in my church." They shook his hand, one by one.

"Pleased to meet both of you," said Sean.

"Do you just work for the hospital, or do you have a flock of your own?" asked Dan.

While Sean's views on church government made him object to the idea of "having a flock of his own," to be polite, he answered the question.

"I volunteer here on a part-time basis. Full time, I'm the Pastor of Living Waters Independent Reformed Church in West Deptford."

Dan visibly brightened. "A brother! Very pleased to meet you." He shook his hand again. "Yes, maybe a fresh perspective might help our sister here."

They turned to the woman, whose head was down. Pastor Dan spoke while Colin looked on.

"Margaret?" The woman looked up. She'd been making an effort—and failing—to control her tears. "Margaret Fitzpatrick, I'd like you to meet Pastor Sean—I'm sorry; what was your last name?"

"Peterson."

"Sean Peterson. He works here in the hospital. He's come to bring some words of comfort."

"Hello, Pastor."

"Hello, Margaret." The two men sat on either side of her, and Sean pulled up a chair so he could sit directly across from her. "What's happened?"

"It's my son," she said, her voice wavering. "He was in a car accident this morning on his way to work."

She paused and swallowed hard. Sean intended to wait until she was ready to continue, but Dan broke the silence.

"Margaret's a member of my church," he explained. "So is her son, Nathaniel. Grew up in the church, he did; I remember when he was just this high." He held his hand out to indicate the size, perhaps, of a five-year-old boy.

"And how old is he now?" Sean asked, looking at Margaret.

"He's thirty-two." She let out a sigh, her face resolute.

The Deacon, Colin, put his hand on her hand as he had had it when Sean first arrived. "Maybe you should just rest, Margaret," he said. "We could all just pray together."

"No, it's all right. Talking about it actually helps." Another sigh came as she brought herself under further control. "This isn't all about the accident. I'm told he'll be all right, though they didn't know the extent of the damage when I got here. His—his legs were crushed under the weight of another car."

"Oh Margaret, I'm so sorry," said Sean.

"If that were all, it would be bad, but I think I could handle it."

"Well, that's bad enough, Margaret." Sean pulled out a small notebook from his jacket pocket. "This is my prayer notebook. If it's all right with you, I'll just write down your name and your son's name, and my church and I will pray for you."

"Certainly, Pastor. We could use all the prayers we can get."

Sean wrote their names and a brief description of their situation in his notebook, then closed it and put it and the pen back into his pocket. He glanced over at Dan, who nodded. He then turned to Colin, who looked worried. He decided to press on and treat her as though she were a member of his church.

"If you are able, can you tell me, Margaret, how you are processing all of this? What are you thinking about your relationship with Jesus?"

Margaret, who had been leaning forward, sat back and began wringing her hands. "Oh, I don't know. It's hard."

"You said there was more to it than just the accident."

"Yes."

"Is Nathaniel in some kind of trouble?"

She began to cry again. "Yes, but it's not his fault." She buried her face in her hands. Dan had a tissue ready, and eventually she took it. She spent time wiping her eyes and blowing her nose, while the men uncomfortably attempted not to watch.

Sean decided to try a different approach; he'd talk for a while instead of trying to draw her out. "Would it help if I read a short passage of Scripture?"

She nodded. From his other jacket pocket, he produced a small Bible. He could have used his phone, but he'd found that in the hospital and particularly with older people, the Bible app on his phone was more of a distraction than a help. He turned quickly to Psalm 91.

"He who dwells in the secret place of the Most High shall abide under the shadow of the Almighty. I will say of the Lord, "He is my refuge and my fortress; My God, in Him I will trust.""

"You've heard that before, haven't you?"

"Yes, Pastor." She was regaining her composure now. "I've read it many times."

"Okay, I'm going to read another short passage."

"Okay."

Sean turned to Psalm 13.

"'How long, O Lord? Will You forget me forever? How long will You hide Your face from me? How long shall I take counsel in my soul, Having sorrow in my heart daily? How long will my enemy be exalted over me?'"

"Which passage do you identify with more fully, right now?" he asked.

"The second one."

"Thank you for being honest with me, Margaret. I want you to know it's perfectly normal to have these feelings."

Dan and Colin glanced at each other briefly, but Margaret raised her eyes and looked directly at Sean.

"It is?" She produced a somewhat wan smile and her eyes flitted briefly over toward Dan. "Yes, I suppose it is, if it's expressed in the Psalms. I'm so used to having to hold things together for everyone else, I think I started believing I wasn't allowed to have those feelings. I honestly don't think I can handle what God is throwing at me anymore."

"That happens in life, to most, if not all of us," said Sean. "Our suffering is real, and the Bible doesn't shrink from that. It also doesn't tell us to ignore it, because that's not healthy. But for some reason when we're suffering, we only remember the passages about being joyful and not hiding our lights under a basket, and the incongruity between that and our suffering makes us feel worse. Do you know what I've discovered about that?"

"No."

"It means that since things were going well before our suffering, we fell into the practice of finding our sufficiency in ourselves and our own abilities instead of in the Lord. You've been a Christian for a long time, haven't you Margaret?"

"Yes I have."

"Then you know that really, a Christian's whole life is lived the same as when you first became a Christian. Every day, you have to put your faith and trust, solely and completely, in Jesus. As we first trusted in Him for the forgiveness of our sins when we become Christians, we also have to learn to keep doing that, to trust Him in everything, every day. And really, He's the only one who can be trusted to get us through the horrible kinds of things that can happen to us in this fallen, sinful world. We can't handle it ourselves."

"No, we can't. I can't," she said.

"So the proper response to our suffering and problems on the one hand is not to be super-competent and think that through training and discipline, we can handle anything. Then we just set ourselves up for failure when we learn there are things we can't handle. On the other hand we're also not to ignore our suffering and problems, trying to pretend we're doing okay. That makes us try to deal with our problems in unhealthy ways, like denial or hardening ourselves so we don't feel anything. Both of these wrong ways draw us away from God. Instead, we have to acknowledge them and run immediately to Him, saying things like 'How long, O Lord?' Did you know that Charles Spurgeon, because of the repeated 'how longs,' called Psalm 13 the Howling Psalm?"

"No, I didn't know that."

"Isn't that what we do when we're in pain? If you stub your toe, you howl. How much more should we howl when we're in anguish, when we're going through the kinds of things you're going through? It's okay to do that. You *should* do that. Just make sure you don't start attributing bad motives to God—he never has those. Remember Matthew 6. God loves you, knows all about your needs, and tells you not to worry, but to trust Him. He's not abandoning you, and you don't have to face this alone, on your own strength. Run to Him. He will bear you up, and He'll use His people, like those in your church, to help you."

Margaret took a deep breath and let it out slowly. She lowered her gaze, and Dan and Colin looked at her expectantly. Finally, she looked back up at Sean.

"Thank you, Pastor. That's extremely helpful. I honestly think I was starting to despair."

"I don't think you can be blamed for that. You've obviously been through a lot, and we still have to wait to find out how your son is doing. We should go to God in prayer about that."

"Absolutely, but you don't know the half of it, Pastor. I've been through a lot, but only as an observer. I've been helpless to do anything except lend my support. Nathaniel is the one who has really been suffering."

"I'm sorry to hear that," said Sean. "If there's a family matter, I'm sure Pastor Dan has been providing you with good counsel—"

"Yes, our church has been heavily involved in ministering to Nathaniel and his family," said Dan.

Sean really didn't want to get into the depths of a family matter, especially if her church was already involved. He wanted to help Margaret and to give her comfort during the acute pain of dealing with her son's injury. But he'd rather leave a family matter to her church and to her church's leaders. He considered it outside the scope of his hospital ministry, but of course it would be very much in scope if she and her family were members of his church. He didn't want to step outside his bounds with Dan there, and he also didn't want to delve into something that could take up the rest of his time at the hospital.

"All the same, Pastor, it will help me if I get this off my chest," Margaret said.

Sean glanced at Dan, who looked resigned. Colin gazed at him expectantly. He didn't see a way of getting out of it.

"Very well, Margaret. I'm here to help in any way I can."

Margaret had a look of resolve that she didn't have before. Her eyes, though bloodshot, had now lost their dullness, and she held his gaze steadily. She took a deep breath.

"About five years ago, Nathaniel met a girl named Tammy," she said, letting out the rest of the deep breath. "She just showed up at church one day. My son was single and in his late twenties, and was beginning to feel at the time like he'd missed the boat. He'd always wanted to get married, but he hadn't had any serious relationships in college, and there wasn't anyone in the church he was interested in pursuing a relationship with.

"So here comes Tammy. She's young and attractive, and newly converted to Christianity through a rock band or something like that."

"It was some musician she listened to who'd converted to Christianity," put in Dan. "I don't remember his name, but it's in my notes."

"Pastor Dan counseled her," said Colin.

"Right," said Dan. "I looked this musician up; the guy wasn't thinking clearly himself. He said he had a personal relationship with Christ, but didn't believe in organized religion."

"I see," said Sean. *Depending on the type of organized religion,* Sean thought, *I might not believe in it either.*

"Anyway," Margaret continued a bit impatiently, "she'd come to the church because she lived nearby, and as a result of this musician's influence, had been reading the Bible. She said she'd become a Christian and wanted to find other Christians. Nathaniel took to her immediately. Their friendship developed very fast. She seemed wonderful; everything seemed wonderful. Though I was worried at first, I grew to like her.

"About a year went by. Tammy was in membership classes and was receiving counseling from the Pastor." Strangely, Margaret emphasized the word *counseling* and briefly caught Dan's eye. Sean wasn't sure, but she might even have glared at him. Sean kept his eyes focused on Margaret to reassure her that she had his full attention, which meant that he missed whatever reaction (if any) that Dan had.

"I thought I knew her pretty well by then," Margaret continued. "About this time, Tammy and Nathaniel got engaged. They wanted a quick wedding; three months was all they wanted to wait. The church really rallied for them."

"It was actually great for the church—the wedding was to be in the church and the reception in the fellowship hall, and the whole church really pulled together to make it happen," said Dan.

"The wedding was wonderful. Just wonderful. I got to dance with my son at the reception, and they went off on their honeymoon to celebrate with each other. After the whirlwind wedding, I was a bit lonely for those two weeks. Nathaniel is an only child, and his father died many years ago in the Gulf War. He'd had a whole career in the Army, and was planning to get out after the war. Nathaniel and I have always been close, but even more so after his father died."

"I'm so sorry, Margaret," said Sean.

"Thank you, Pastor. And I'm sure you can tell where all of this is going."

"No, actually; I have no idea. Please continue."

Margaret cleared her throat. "The problems started shortly after they returned from their honeymoon. Fights. Arguing. Unhealthy ways of dealing with both. And of course, there was the pregnancy."

"Pregnancy?"

"The reason they wanted the whirlwind wedding was that Tammy was already pregnant. Nathaniel told me shortly after they returned. He wanted to know how I thought the church would react."

"And how did they react?"

"The congregation was divided," said Dan. "Of course, we had to discipline them. They were both members."

"What did you do?"

"I met with them and the board of Deacons. Colin here was a part of that." Colin nodded, and Dan went on. "They said they were embarrassed, that it shouldn't have happened, that passion overtook them. The usual stuff, really. They'd wanted to get married anyway in order to 'make it right,' as they put it. They knew the deception was wrong, and they repented of it.

"We kept them from the Lord's Supper for three months and asked them to come before the church in a special congregational meeting after worship one Sunday to confess and to seek the congregation's forgiveness. Tammy didn't want to do it. Nat agreed—"

"Nathaniel," corrected Margaret.

Dan smiled. "Everybody but his mother calls him Nat. Nathaniel agreed to do it over Tammy's objections. He did all of the talking when it came to it; she stood before the congregation quietly. The congregation readily forgave and restored them. They rejoiced in her pregnancy. The ladies scheduled a baby shower and everything."

"I think that experience, though, soured Tammy on the church," said Margaret. "She never seemed the same after that."

"Pre-marital sex didn't seem like anything serious to her," explained Dan. "She'd lived most of her life with the view that it was a good thing to just go with your feelings, and that what they'd done had all the seriousness maybe of cursing or littering. In hindsight, I don't think she ever viewed her and Nat's—Nathaniel's—action as something wrong that she needed to repent of, because they'd always intended to get married."

"I see," said Sean.

"Anyway, the baby was born six months later. My granddaughter. Theresa Margaret Fitzpatrick." Margaret beamed. It was the first real, unadulterated smile Sean had seen on her. "She was beautiful; still is. Seeing her for the first time was one of the happiest days of my life."

"I'm sure it was."

"I'd hoped that the baby would help Nathaniel and Tammy in their marriage. You really have to work as a team to raise a child."

"I can only imagine," smiled Sean.

Margaret's eyebrows raised in surprise. "Well, having the baby only seemed to make things worse. I don't think they were ready for the responsibility. Tammy especially. Nathaniel came home from work one day to find Tammy watching TV at an incredibly loud volume, alone. When he came in and turned the TV off, he heard Theresa screaming in the back bedroom. He found her soaked to the skin and slick in her own poop. It took him forever to clean her up, he said. When he confronted Tammy, he found that she was drunk."

"Drunk?"

"Apparently, she'd had a drinking problem before she met Nathaniel. Only three people in the church knew about it: Tammy, Nathaniel, and Pastor Dan."

"It was a confidential matter that came up in her counseling," explained Dan. "She'd done AA and had been clean for a year prior to my meeting her. There was never any reason to broadcast it, and she wanted to keep it confidential."

Margaret glared at Pastor Dan for a moment. "You should have told me."

"I couldn't, Margaret. It was a confidential matter."

"Look, let's not get into this again now," said Colin. "What would or would not have happened doesn't help us deal with what *did* happen."

"You're right, of course," frowned Margaret. "I'm sorry, where was I?"

"Tammy was drunk," Sean said.

"Drunk and violent. During the course of their argument, she threw a bunch of things at Nathaniel. She told him she was trapped with this screaming baby she couldn't comfort, trapped in the house, trapped away from normal, adult interaction, alone and miserable. She slept there, on the couch that night, and Nathaniel slept in the bedroom with Theresa. Theresa hadn't been fed properly; Nathaniel was up with her half the night while Tammy slept off her drinking binge. He stayed home from work the next day and helped out, and things got better. He told me he felt like it had been a one-time thing and that he felt safe going back to work the next day."

"Nathaniel doesn't have much experience with addicted people, does he?" Sean asked.

Margaret shook her head. "No, he didn't, not at the time." She sighed. "But he went back to work, and everything was okay for a few weeks. Then it happened again."

"She was drunk?"

"She was gone. He came home from work to find Theresa in the back bedroom again, screaming. Tammy wasn't in the house. Nathaniel called everybody. He called me, he called the Pastor, he called a couple of her friends. Nobody had seen her. Finally he called the police. No sooner had he done that than she came staggering through the front door. She'd been at a bar. She looked all disheveled. Said she'd driven there and back, but Nathaniel didn't know how that was possible in her state. Nathaniel asked her about the baby, and she said that she didn't leave her for that long, and she thought she'd be fine. Nathaniel was livid. He called me, and he called the Pastor. We both came over, along with Dan's wife. I helped clean Tammy up and put her to bed: she was in no condition that night to talk about anything. Pastor Dan, his wife Christine, Nathaniel, and I all had a, uh, conversation. That's how I found out that Dan knew about her problem and never told me."

"It was a confidential counseling matter," Dan emphasized.

"Uh huh. Yeah. Sure."

"She'd been clean and sober for 19 months, and she still went to AA meetings. There was no indication she'd backslide."

Margaret ignored him and spoke to Sean. "I was very angry, as I'm sure you could imagine. If I'd known, I could have been a sounding board for her. I could have counseled my son on what to look for." She glared at Dan again. "I wasn't afforded the opportunity for any of those things."

"I'm sorry, Margaret," said Sean.

"Well, it gets worse."

Colin looked at his watch. "It's 12:00. Anybody else hungry?"

"Not so fast, Colin. I'm going to finish."

"Okay, Margaret. Go ahead and finish."

"It was late that night; everybody went home. We agreed to have a sort of intervention for Tammy the next day. It was a Saturday, so Nathaniel didn't have to go to work."

Dan said, "We took Terri for the night—"

"Theresa," said Margaret.

Colin explained, "Everybody calls her Terri; Margaret is the only one who calls her Theresa."

Sean smiled. There was a pattern emerging here.

"As I was saying," said Dan, "my wife and I took *Theresa* for the night, so that Nathaniel could get some rest, and because Margaret wanted to run interference for him with Tammy in the morning. Tammy, of course, was out cold. We just put Terri in between us in our bed, and she slept very soundly."

"I slept on Nathaniel's couch," said Margaret. "Tammy, as you can imagine, was quite hung over the next morning. She got up about nine or ten o'clock, came into the kitchen, and drank almost a carton of orange juice, like an old pro."

Margaret gazed down at her hands for a moment and then continued. "She was sullen and defensive. She certainly didn't appreciate my presence there. Made me wish I'd taken Theresa for the night instead and left Pastor Dan there to deal with Tammy in the morning. She got worse when Pastor Dan and Christine arrived."

"I can imagine. How was Nathaniel?"

"Quiet. Exhausted. I could tell that he was ready for somebody else to take the reins. He'd obviously been dealing with this himself in various forms for a while. There had been other, uh, events—less spectacular ones—than the two I've mentioned here. I probably don't even know half of what went on in that house."

Sean nodded; Margaret continued. "We confronted her with her behavior. Not all Baptist churches are teetotalers, Pastor, but we are. I've gone over that day many times since then, and I'm afraid that we were pretty hard on her and pretty judgmental. We have lots of Scriptural support for our position, but we should have realized we weren't dealing with someone who was actively considering Scripture an authority in her life."

"We told her the truth," said Dan.

"Do you see what I'm dealing with?" pleaded Margaret to Sean.

"What?" asked Dan.

"If I may," said Sean to Dan, "I think Margaret is saying that using the 'alcohol is evil, thus drunkards will not inherit the kingdom of God' tactic was not the best idea. All Christians agree that drunkenness is a sin, but the use of alcohol itself is an issue on which good, professing Christians have a difference of opinion, and that's not what's at issue here anyway."

"But—"

"Let me finish. I'm sure you're strongly convicted of your position. I think what Margaret is getting at is that the use of alcohol is only the surface issue. It might have been better to identify with Tammy, help her recognize that running to alcohol isn't a solution to the problem she was facing, and give her support in her struggle. You're certainly not without struggles, are you Dan?"

"Well, no, but—"

"People do all kinds of things to avoid facing their problems. Alcohol, drugs, binge watching shows, porn. It's called 'escape.' Escape leads to addiction, addiction leads to unbalance, and unbalance eventually causes you to fall down on your face. How do you think it feels when you've fallen down on your face, and instead of pulling you up, someone yells at you for being so stupid as to fall down? Will that help you feel better? Will that help take away your embarrassment at falling, or will it turn it into something else, like anger and resentment?"

Dan looked at the floor. "She professed faith. I—we—were trying to make her see the seriousness of what she'd done, and how that displeased the Lord."

"I understand that," said Sean, "and under certain circumstances, you need to do that. I think Margaret is saying that perhaps, this was not one of those circumstances."

Dan looked up and nervously twiddled his thumbs. "Maybe not."

Margaret looked over at Dan sympathetically and put her hand on his.

"Well, the discussion turned into a shouting match, up to a point. Then there was a sudden turnaround. Tammy agreed that abandoning her child to go get drunk was irresponsible and criminally negligent. She agreed that her behavior was not becoming of a Christian, regardless of the reasons she had for it. And she had reasons. I don't think Nathaniel was as supportive as he could have been. It's hard to be the mother of a small child. You miss adult interaction. You feel very lonely. Nathaniel had his job, and he'd often go out at night as well for meetings and such. Tammy really had no outlet like that. It was just her and the baby most of the time. Eventually it got to her, she snapped, and went back to old habits. That's what she told us, anyway."

"But she wasn't being honest with us," added Dan.

"No, she wasn't. Duplicity is something I'll never understand, but she was apparently telling us one thing while making other plans," said Margaret. Dan put his head in his hands.

"Plans?" asked Sean.

"Yes. What happened after that is what's got me so upset. They were divorced. There were just too many other incidents. The problem was beyond Nathaniel's ability to help; Tammy wouldn't get help; and she finally left him. All that Christian talk really meant nothing. She served him with divorce papers, offering joint custody. I urged him not to sign, to sue for divorce with cause so he could get full custody of Theresa. But he was so tired. He wanted it to end. So he signed."

"And now he has joint custody."

"Yes. They split weeks and weekends. Theresa's four now, and in fact, he just dropped her off at Tammy's apartment this morning, before the accident."

"I'm guessing that this is a source of stress for him?"

"That would be an understatement. When he drops her off, she doesn't ever let him into the house. He has no idea what kind of environment she provides. When he goes to pick her up, she's often dirty and wearing ill-fitting clothes. Theresa actually never wants to go there; she cries when the time comes to drop her off at Mommy's house. Nathaniel's doing the best he can under the circumstances. But now, with this accident—he's going to have a long and difficult recovery."

"I see. And because of that, Theresa will now have to spend more time than usual at Mommy's apartment rather than at Daddy's," Sean concluded.

"Exactly. So now you have the whole thing. This is what's tearing me apart. Don't get me wrong: I love my son, and I'm equally upset about his injuries and his prognosis. But he's a big boy; no matter how difficult it is, he'll mend. I know he will. I have no idea what's going to happen to Theresa—what's happening to her right now, in that awful apartment. I'm scared. I'm scared she won't be loved or cared for. I'm scared to death that Tammy will abandon her again, with no one around this time to find her."

The tears began to well up in Margaret's eyes again. Dan looked up, and Colin put his arm around her.

"Thank you for telling me the whole story, Margaret," said Sean. Margaret, her hand covering her mouth, nodded, unable to speak for the moment. "I think it's high time now that we went to the Lord in prayer about all this."

"Amen," said Dan.

"How about I lead off, and you close?" Sean asked Dan.

"Sounds good to me."

"All right, then. Let's pray."

13
∞∞∞∞

12:00 PM

Gloria found herself in the emergency room, waiting. Jameel had been whisked away to who knew where. Sitting here, or rather, lying here on the hospital bed with nothing to do (they'd promised she was next to go down and get x-rayed) gave her time to think about what had just happened.

She'd registered with a minimum of fuss. Of course, the school's health insurance plan helped. Most people's insurance couldn't come close. She hoped, however, that she could get done whatever they were going to do for her ankle quickly so she could go see Jameel. She'd already called the school and explained what had happened, and she didn't envy the person who had to Jameel's mother.

Her thoughts wandered further back, to the beginning of her day. The narrow escape from the accident loomed in her mind. She'd been really, *really* lucky. One second earlier and she'd have been the one airlifted to Cooper, or dead. Had she been spared by blind chance? Or was there some meaning or purpose to it?

The accident had delayed her arrival at school. If she hadn't been in the accident, she would have been either right on time or barely late. At that time of the morning, she almost certainly would have found a parking space in the front lot, and she would've been there much earlier than she had been. Arriving earlier meant she would've missed Jameel's and Freddie's argument completely. And if that had happened, what would've happened to Jameel? Would Freddie have stolen his wallet and left him to bleed to death in the woods? She bet he would have. Up to now, Freddie had been a small-time juvenile delinquent, but today he'd brought things to a whole new level. He hadn't looked exactly comfortable with his actions either, and he sure had left in a hurry. She didn't think his panic had been solely her fault; he had already committed to irrational behavior before she'd surprised him. If she hadn't been there, that same panic and anger might have caused him to leave Jameel there to bleed to death or—she shuddered—something worse.

The accident, however, had changed everything. She'd been delayed and had intervened, which had saved Jameel's life. She didn't believe she deserved any special credit; she did only what any decent person would do. It had been the accident that had directed her to the proper place and the proper time. The same accident that seriously injured or killed several people had, then, also been the catalyst to save Jameel's life.

There was more, of course. What was Officer Bob doing there, again, just in the right place and at the right time? He'd been just in time to help her and Jameel, and had barely missed Freddie. If he'd been one minute earlier, Freddie would've pulled out of the parking lot right in front of him, and he might have chosen to chase down and arrest Freddie rather than help them. But that didn't happen; instead, he'd been too late to see Freddie peel out of there, but right on time to find them in the woods and direct the EMTs to them. Why had he been there? Had he also been delayed in some way by the accident? She didn't remember him saying anything about it. But what if he had?

That would mean that this one event, this catastrophic accident this morning, had orchestrated all these other complex events that had resulted in saving Jameel's life, Bob helping them, her sprained ankle, and her presence in the hospital right now. She hadn't taken much philosophy in college, and what she had taken she didn't remember very well. But she couldn't escape the feeling of being caught up in something bigger than she was, that she was living out some sort of plan.

And what about Jameel? What was he doing there having an altercation with Freddie about money of all things? Why were they meeting at all during school hours? Both of them should have been in class. She could understand Freddie; he didn't have an exemplary attendance record, and she highly doubted he cared about how many suspensions he had. She bet he flirted with the maximum number of sick days allowed every year. But Jameel was not that kind of kid. When he could talk, she would have to ask him about it. For now, she'd leave him alone.

A cheerful orderly parted her privacy curtain. "Hi there; I'm here to take you down to Imaging." He had a wheelchair with him, ready to receive her.

"I'm ready whenever you are."

As she descended down into the wheelchair, she asked herself again: *What was Jameel doing there?*

14

∞∞∞∞

12:30 PM EST/9:30 AM PST

When you really wanted to know what was going on, news reports could be extremely frustrating. Jenny Foster could find online only the same information she already knew: that the male driver of the Impala had been airlifted to Cooper Hospital, and he was in critical condition. They didn't show the accident; instead, helicopter images of miles-long backed-up traffic filled the screen as the female voice-over lamented the accident's effect on everyone's commute. The callousness of the news struck her; it didn't seem like the writer of the report considered how it sounded, focusing more on the inconvenience to commuters than on the serious injuries of those involved and the worry of families who loved them.

Sleep had been out of the question, so she'd instead showered, dressed, eaten, and now she was back in her room seated at her desk, feeling more drained than she thought she should. Her roommate, Emma Liu, had pointed out that she'd both been up early and had gotten some really bad news, so she had every reason to be out of sorts. But Jenny knew the source of the problem: the lack of news. Why hadn't Mom called yet? Certainly she should have some news by now, right? But so far, nothing.

Emma had gone off to class; they both usually had the same class down in Wheeler Hall (Environmental Economics), and then they would split up. Jenny had an English class from 10:00 to 12:30, and Emma went off to

Barrows for another environmental class. Instead, Emma had gone off alone and here Jenny sat, alone with her thoughts, with most of the building empty.

Dad. He'd spent most of his spare time, as far as she knew, with her. He was a technical guy who spent most of his working hours in air-conditioned server rooms, making sure all the systems stayed up, stable, and were patched regularly. As such, he didn't have a lot of experience with outdoorsy stuff, but that didn't stop him. She'd heard him say it many times over the course of her life: he wanted her to be "well-rounded." That meant having as many different kinds of experiences as possible—even if those experiences were also new to him.

She remembered a time when she was about 13 or 14, they went down to Wildwood, rented a boat, crab traps, and all the gear they needed, and attempted to go crabbing. Mom couldn't go for some reason; it might have been a conference. With the boat rented and a full tank of gas, Dad suddenly informed her that he wanted to go "off the beaten path," as he put it, because there'd be more crabs where fewer people had gone. So he attempted, with admittedly poor-to-nonexistent navigation skills, to go "where no one had crabbed before."

Jenny didn't know the various creeks, sounds, channels, lakes, and islands surrounding Wildwood very well, so she couldn't remember exactly where they'd gone. She knew Sunset Lake in Wildwood Crest had been part of it, and she only remembered that because it was the last known area on their route. After that, Dad made some turn, and then some other turn, and then got himself turned around. Admitting he was lost, he started making random guesses as to where to go, keeping his original goal in mind. He certainly achieved getting off the beaten path, and they did catch a whole bunch of crabs. The problem, however, was getting the boat back to where they'd rented it, or even getting back to civilization at all. They'd been in a land of small creeks surrounded by marsh in every direction. They could hear various sounds of marsh wildlife: chirps and croaks, the cries of water fowl, and unnerving splashes always out of sight, ripples giving away the presence of some creature they'd missed seeing that now lurked under the water's surface.

After trying for about an hour to return to an area they recognized, Jenny began to see the concern on Dad's face as he noticed the fast approach of low tide. Back in these small creeks and channels, even a small boat like theirs could run aground at low tide. If that happened, they'd be stranded for hours. They wouldn't get back (if they got back at all) until after dark, and they'd also be starving, sunburned (they were well on their way already), and dead tired, not to mention fined for returning the boat late. Dad seemed keenly aware of this, and Jenny, not perhaps for the first time, began to doubt his ability to get them home. She said nothing, however. After so many years of their inseparability, Dad was still Dad: fun, adventurous, and even sometimes heroic.

Dad had slowed the engine (an outboard 45 hp Johnson—she knew nothing about boat engines, but she'd unwittingly etched its image in her mind, as the logo had been a point of fixation for her eyes as internally she worried and wondered how they'd get out of this). The boat crawled along a narrow channel surrounded on both sides by tall marsh grass and cat-tails. They created only small ripples in the water as they went, and even these ripples disturbed wildlife on either side of their path. Each species created ripples of its own or caused the grass to part as it fled the boat's approach. As they came near to an area of shorter marsh grass on their left, the sun hit Jenny's face and she raised her hand to shield her eyes. Suddenly she realized something.

"Hey Dad, what time did we get here?"

"Oh, about 11:30 I guess. Why?"

"Well, since we ate first before we got the boat, it's got to be late in the afternoon now, right?"

Dad looked at his watch. "Yeah, it's almost 4:00."

"If it's in the afternoon, the sun should be more toward the west than the east, right? So since it's on our left, we are currently pointed north, if I'm right."

"Right!" he said with dawning realization.

"Should we be pointed north?"

"No," he said. "Wildwood's a barrier island, and we're in the space between the island and the mainland. To get back, we actually have to go south and east to get back to Sunset Lake, and then turn north. I think. I'm going to turn the boat around."

With that, he rotated the wheel to his right, the boat began to turn, and then promptly stopped moving.

"Oh, no," he said. He revved the engine a little, and the water churned behind them, kicking up bits of black nastiness. They moved a little, but in the wrong direction: they were now stuck worse than before.

"Shoot!" he said, and Jenny smiled. She bet that if she'd not been there, he'd have used a different word. "I should have put it in reverse!"

He now did so, revving the engine more than before. The boat shuddered and more of the black stuff kicked up, but this time it spewed over the sides of the boat. A piece of it hit Jenny's cheek, and she yelped. Dad gave up. The front of the boat (the *bow*, she reminded herself) now rested uncomfortably close to the tall marsh grass, some strands of which now leaned over, reaching toward the pilot's area. Dad cut the engine.

Dad made the understatement of the year. "Well, now we're stuck." He sat down, dejected. Jenny couldn't help feeling a stab of fear. Dad had been in over his head before (remember that pheasant shoot last year?), but never this far over. What were they going to do?

Before she could voice her concern, Dad seemed visibly to force himself onto another train of thought. He looked over at her and smiled. "Well," he said, "if I have to be stuck in the marsh for a few hours, there's no one I'd rather be stuck with than you."

Jenny smiled, got up, walked over to him (the boat felt much more steady now that it sat on solid ground), and gave him a hug. "Me too, Dad, except for one thing."

"What's that?" he asked.

"I have to go to the bathroom."

He laughed. "So do I. Let me see how bad it is. Maybe I can push us out." He stood up and began to lean over the right side (*starboard*, she reminded herself) of the boat. As the boat began to tilt dangerously, he realized the error in his plan, but not before he fell out with a loud splash. The water hit Jenny's face, and droplets of it hit the pilot's chair and ran down in rivulets. In alarm, Jenny peered over the side of the boat (it also tilted for her, but not enough to lose her balance) to see Dad sitting in water that reached only to his stomach. His feet were under, but his bent knees rose above the surface of the water. He rubbed water from his eyes.

"I'm all right, I'm all right!" he said, and then there was a pause. "Ahhhh."

"What?" she asked.

"Well, I don't have to go to the bathroom anymore," he said.

"Dad, that's gross!"

"Sorry, sweetie. Just trying to lighten the mood a little." Whether he really had relieved himself or not, she never found out. He stood up.

"Wow," he said.

"What?"

"You really sink down in this muck. It's not sand; I'm not sure what it is." He reached down and dug some of it out with his hand. It was black like soil, but it stuck together in clumps. He closed his fingers on it and massaged it. "Feels slimy."

"Nasty," she said.

He let the stuff fall back into the water, and she noticed it had stained his hand. He bent and washed his hands off in the water. "It doesn't seem natural, does it?" he asked.

"No," she said, staring down into the water. She noticed rainbow-colored oily patches floating on the surface here and there. "I think it's polluted."

"You think?" Dad said sarcastically. "I'm going to try to get us out of here."

With that, he attempted with much effort to walk around to the front of the boat, where presumably he would try to push them out. Each step was laborious. When his foot entered the water, it sank surprisingly deeply, and the black slime gripped it with an unexpectedly strong force. When his foot left the water, it was accompanied by a slurping sound as he freed it from the muck.

"If I'm not careful, I'm going to lose a shoe," he said.

"That would be no big loss," she replied. He'd worn his old, worn-out pair of sneakers, the ones he used whenever he went out to till his small garden, and they had definitely seen better days. She wore only flip-flops.

He finally reached the bow of the boat. "Okay, I'm going to push now! Hold on!"

Jenny gripped the sides of her seat. "Okay, Dad!"

He grunted with effort, and the bow of the boat lifted up a little bit, but didn't budge from its spot. The grunting stopped, and the boat settled back into place.

"Wow, we're really stuck," he said, sighing.

"Do you want me to get out?" she asked. She didn't relish stepping into that muck, especially in bare feet.

"No, honey, that's okay. I'm going to try something else." He slurped his way around to the stern and examined the motor. "I bet the motor's stuck down deeper in this stuff than the bottom of the boat is."

"Sounds reasonable."

"Do you think the motor rotates up out of the water?"

"Yeah; I've seen people with boats on trailers, and the motor was definitely up." Boy was Dad clueless, yet he had tried doing this with her anyway, and she loved him all the more for it. She examined the motor from inside the boat, and soon found a latch release. "I think I've found how it works."

"Okay, you pull the latch, and I'll try to lift the motor from here."

She pulled the latch up, and he reached down. "Wow, it's really buried," he said, and sighed without much hope. "I'll try." He bent his knees, reached down to grab the motor, and said, "There's no good grip." He scrabbled around under there, his face close to the water but turned sideways to avoid accidentally breathing it in, and then suddenly pulled with all his strength. The motor didn't move, but he seemed to shrink as his legs sank down deeper into the muck. He sighed again, breathing heavily from the effort. "It's no use. We're going to have to get help."

Extracting himself from the black slime took him several minutes, but he carefully worked at it until he freed himself, shoes and all. Jenny gave him a hand as he pulled himself into the boat. He sank into the chair across from her and sighed. Glops of the black stuff oozed down his legs. His face frowned with the effort of figuring out how he was going to get help. Suddenly he perked up.

"Do you hear that?"

She realized it was much quieter with the motor off and without him trying to muscle something around. She could hear the faint white noise of traffic passing somewhere nearby.

"Yeah," she said.

"I bet that's Route 47!" he exclaimed. "I know where we are!" He suddenly stood up, attempting to see over the tall marsh grass, but it blocked his view. He then put one foot on the back of one of the seats and stepped up, placing his other foot on the back of the seat across from it. From this added height, he saw something that gave him hope.

"I can see the marina on Route 47!" They hadn't rented the boat from there, but it represented civilization, which clearly enhanced his elation. But he was also torn, and Jenny could see why. Should he set off for the marina and leave her here? If he did that, would she be safe? Should they go together? There didn't seem to be a good solution. Finally, though, he made up his mind.

"I'm going to try schlepping my way over to the marina, Jenny. I think you'll be safe here; certainly safe from other people. If you just stay in the boat, you should be fine."

"But Dad, I don't want to be here by myself!"

"I don't think I have any other choice." He pulled his phone out of his pocket. "Yeah, I just fried my phone when I fell into the water. I'd love to take you with me, but you don't have any shoes, and that stuff is nasty. There's more than just slime too; I hit something hard and sharp once, and I could've cut myself. I think it's much safer if you stay here."

"I don't like this at all."

"I don't either, honey. I just don't see any other way."

Jenny considered the options for a while. Dad did not always think clearly under stress, and she thought he was missing something. She wished she'd paid more attention when the guy from the rental place had gone over the boat's systems. She had, however, blissfully left all of that to Dad, and had spent the time listening to her music.

"Okay, Dad. Please hurry back."

"I will," he said, and kissed her on the forehead. "I promise."

With that, he jumped out of the boat and headed in the general direction of the marina. She hoped his sense of direction was at least keen enough to get him close to the marina even though he couldn't see it. He soon disappeared into the marsh grass with a wave.

She stared at the floor of the boat, wondering how long he would be. Since they hadn't rented the boat from this marina, he'd need to get somebody to call the rental place they'd used. Then he'd need to get a ride or something to the rental place, where presumably they'd send another boat to tug them out. She guessed two hours, at least. Suddenly she heard his voice shouting back to her.

"Lost a shoe!" he yelled cheerfully.

She smiled and shouted back. "Sorry Dad!" She loved that he was trying to put the best face on this disaster that he could. After a while, she heard his voice again, fainter.

"Lost the other one!"

She didn't try shouting back; she knew he'd probably never hear her. She resigned herself to some alone time for a while.

Jenny looked up at her apartment ceiling and smiled. She had for years tried to imagine what it had been like for the people in the marina to see this wet and bedraggled, sweaty, sunburned, and black slime-stained man enter their spotless establishment and ask for help. According to Dad, the wait had been interminable. "I would've had you out of there in half an hour," he used to say. He'd had to explain his story "about twenty times," and it took convincing, cajoling, and eventually money to get somebody to agree to help him out.

Meanwhile, Jenny had taken an interest in the small console by the steering wheel. Attached underneath it was a marine radio, along with a small drawer that contained complete, laminated instructions for what to do if you got into trouble. She'd turned to the right channel, made the proper call, and it turned out that she'd gotten the ball rolling on the rescue, probably while Dad was still arguing with the guys at the marina—if that hadn't been an embellishment in his story, of course. According to him, when Dad finally got one of the marina guys to call the rental place, they were already aware of the situation and were preparing to send somebody out. Dad took a taxi to meet the boat before it left, and, well, the rest was history. Beyond her love for Dad and the mileage he'd gotten out of the story over the years, there had been one main benefit.

They'd never tasted better crabs than the ones they caught that day.

Jenny sighed. And now Dad fought for his life—and might even be gone. Not knowing made everything worse. For all his faults, Dad was a warm, wise man who loved her dearly and believed in her, and she drew strength from that. He'd been the one who'd supported her decision to come out here to Berkeley, who'd done the bulk of the work packing her bags so thoroughly and densely that they'd had to pay extra to get them on the plane. He'd flown out here with her and gotten her set up, had met her roommate and given her a thumbs up, and had left with a tear in his eye and a smile.

Oh Dad, I hope you're all right, she thought as a tear trickled down her cheek. *Please be all right. I don't know what I'd do without you.*

She crossed her arms on the desk and buried her head in them.

Mom, why haven't you called?

15
∞∞∞∞∞

1:00 PM EST/10:00 AM PST

The faint *pop!* sound coming from the open window barely registered with Jenny's roommate Emma Liu; in fact, she'd probably have ignored it completely if it hadn't been for the fainter screams that accompanied it. She turned her head to the left, away from her professor at the front of the room. The open classroom window on the sixth floor of Barrows Hall normally admitted a nice, cool breeze. As she stood, it now gave her a commanding view in the direction of the sound. She heard two more rapid *pops!* and more screams followed. Dr. Li stopped in mid-sentence, her mouth hanging open in a perfect O.

Trees partially blocked her line of sight, but Emma could see people streaming out of Wheeler Hall, clearly panicked. As she turned to announce this to the class, an intensely loud alarm bell sounded. Everyone stood up. A voice came over the intercom.

"THIS BUILDING IS NOW ON LOCKDOWN! REMAIN IN YOUR SEATS AND FOLLOW LOCKDOWN PROCEDURE! DO NOT ATTEMPT TO LEAVE! FURTHER INSTRUCTIONS WILL BE PROVIDED!"

The message repeated itself. Rather than heed the announcement, in a panic the class emptied itself out into the hall, where every other class on that side of the building had done exactly the same thing. A generalized sound of shouting filled the hallway outside and came faintly from the surrounding buildings as well. Emma turned around. She and Dr. Li were the only two people left in the room. Their eyes fixed on each other momentarily, and then Dr. Li shuffled over to her right and dropped heavily into a chair, digging into her purse for her phone.

"Well, so much for closing the blinds, shutting the door, and turning the lights out," she said as she found her phone and began scrolling through whatever information the administration had sent about the lockdown.

Pop! Pop! Pop! Emma heard the sound again, and there could be no mistake about what it was now: gunshots in or somewhere around Wheeler Hall, across the tree-lined courtyard outside Emma's window. The shots sounded insignificant compared to the huge booms she'd heard in movies. She heard movement behind her as Dr. Li came over to gaze out the window with her. People continued to stream out of Wheeler Hall, though the flow looked thinner. Emma turned to Dr. Li.

"I wonder if they're locking down Wheeler as well?"

"It's probably the entire campus."

"Do they prepare you for stuff like this when you're hired as a professor? What are we supposed to do?"

"Emma, I don't think anything can prepare you for this."

They stood in silence, leaning over the small counter space in front of the open window. The stream of people slowed to a trickle and then stopped altogether. A crowd had formed outside the building, but well away from it. Emma couldn't tell the size of the crowd because of the trees in the way. Both of them had questions that would have to go unanswered at this point, so there was no point in bringing them up. Who was doing this? Why? Had there been any warning? Had someone been killed? Would they (whoever *they* were) be able to stop it?

"Look!" Emma cried.

A window in the top left corner of Wheeler Hall had opened. Emma could see a figure leaning out the window. He or she might have been shouting down at the crowd, but Emma could hear nothing with the racket of the alarm bell and the constant lockdown message.

"Where?" Dr. Li asked.

"Over there," Emma said and pointed, screaming "No!" as the person's intent became clear.

Dr. Li saw the figure just in time to witness him or her begin shooting into the crowd from the window. It struck her that from this distance, the three shots sounded thin and hollow. With a speed that only panic can produce, the confluence of people below the shooter dispersed in all directions like a drunken swarm of bees, not without leaving a few behind on the ground. From this distance, neither Emma nor Dr. Li could tell if they'd been trampled or shot.

"My God," said Dr. Li, putting a hand over her pounding heart.

With that, behind them the door to the classroom opened, and they both whirled around. A terror-stricken girl entered.

"Dr. Li! It's Chris! He's been trampled!" With all the commotion outside the classroom, Dr. Li wasn't surprised. The shouts and yells from the hallway had quieted down over the last few minutes; at least, it had become harder to hear outside noises over the din of the alarm.

The professor turned to Emma while walking quickly toward the door and the girl, who hopped up and down in worry. "Stay here, Emma; it's safer than going out there."

"Okay, I will."

Dr. Li left the room with the girl. Emma barely knew Chris; he wasn't in any of her other classes, and she didn't know the girl at all. She hoped he'd be okay, but the professor was right: at only five-feet-two and 95 pounds, her diminutive form made her more likely than most to be caught up in the mob and trampled. She turned her gaze back out the window. As she did so, one fact that had escaped her attention suddenly blazed up in red letters in her mind.

Jenny had a class now in Wheeler Hall.

Suddenly the scene unfolding outside the window became all the more terrifying. She squinted her eyes, trying to make out the features of any of the victims lying—wait! Jenny didn't go to class today! Emma breathed a sigh of relief, tinged with guilt. The injured people out there were worthy of the same concern, even if she didn't know them. She also felt bad for Jenny's dad, but glad that Jenny had been kept out of this mess.

Movement outside the window caused her inward thoughts to turn outward. A group of black-uniformed men (a SWAT team?) approached Wheeler Hall, armed with rifles and body armor. With a speed she hadn't thought possible, they entered the space where the crowd of people had been and then dispersed: a group of them broke off and went around one side of the building, and another group went around the other. One who remained had a megaphone and began shouting into it, but Emma couldn't hear what he said. She wished the alarm would stop; everybody by now knew they were to stay put until the emergency ended, so there was no need to continue blaring the message into everyone's ears until they became deaf.

There was a pause, during which presumably the person with the gun responded, and then she could hear the blare of the megaphone again. The figure in the window disappeared inside the building while Megaphone Speaker said whatever he had to say. In what must have been mid-sentence, Emma unexpectedly heard another *pop!* sound, while Megaphone Speaker kept right on talking. After another pause, Megaphone Speaker resumed talking.

The door opened behind her again, and students from the class began trickling back in, directed by a black-uniformed officer. Tina, her friend from down the hall where she and Jenny lived, came directly over to her and before Tina could speak, Emma did.

"Where did you go?"

Tina looked surprised. "Well, I tried to get out, of course!" Tina was heavyset and could hold her own better in a mob of people than Emma could.

"Why?"

"I don't know, actually." Tina looked confused. "Partially because everybody else was doing it, so I figured somebody knew more about what was going on than I did. The stairwells were completely blocked up and the doors were locked, so there was no getting out anyway. And then *they* came and made us come back." She indicated the black-uniformed officer. Looking outside, she asked, "What's going on?"

Emma brought her up to date, and as a result, Tina whistled "Whew! Who do you think did it? And please don't say, 'a terrorist.'"

"I honestly have no idea."

"It could have been a disgruntled employee. I can't imagine it was a student," said Tina, matter-of-factly.

"Why?"

"Because a student wouldn't have the resources to get a gun. And if he did, why would he go shoot up Wheeler Hall?"

"People have shot up their schools before."

"That's high school. All the unbalanced ones are supposed to have been weeded out by the time they get to a place like this." Tina's obvious pride at being a Berkeley student seemed to be clouding her judgment. Emma began to suspect that Tina's reality filter needed adjustment. Maybe hers did too; they were both only second semester Freshman students, and she felt numb and unable to process these events.

Without warning, the alarm suddenly stopped, revealing a squeal of vehicle sirens coming from outside. Megaphone Speaker had disappeared, replaced by medics tending to those who had been left in the stampede of the crowd.

"ATTENTION! THIS BUILDING IS STILL ON LOCKDOWN! THE INCIDENT, HOWEVER, HAS BEEN CONTAINED. PLEASE REMAIN WHERE YOU ARE. IF YOU SEE ANY INJURED PARTY, PLEASE REPORT THE INJURY BY DIALING EXTENSION 4911 FROM ANY CAMPUS PHONE! FURTHER INSTRUCTIONS WILL BE PROVIDED!"

The message repeated five more times and then stopped. The relief from the lack of noise was palpable, though Emma knew her ears would be ringing for the rest of the day. As things stood, the sirens from outside provided plenty of noise to mask that, and she turned her attention to the scene outside. Emma looked down toward the group of medics and was glad to see movement from some of the victims.

Several ambulances had arrived, and teams with stretchers entered the building. This made Emma's heart sink. Tina watched beside her, silently now except for the sound of her phone snapping pictures as the rest of the scene unfolded. All told, five stretchers came out, two of which were covered completely. Emma hadn't noticed before, but most of her class had now returned and crowded the window on her left and Tina's right. When all of the ambulances had whisked themselves away and there wasn't anything else to see, another announcement came over the intercom.

"ATTENTION, PLEASE! LOCKDOWN HAS BEEN LIFTED. THIS BUILDING IS NOW OPEN. CLASSES ARE CANCELED FOR THE REST OF THE DAY. YOU ARE FREE TO LEAVE. PLEASE CHECK CALCENTRAL FOR FURTHER INFORMATION, INCLUDING COUNSELING SERVICES."

CalCentral was the University Intranet, the information portal where every student had an account. Again, the message repeated about five more times, but nobody waited that long. Emma along with Tina and the rest of the class gathered their things and left. A uniformed officer stood outside the classroom and beckoned them to another officer who pointed everyone toward a stairwell. Otherwise, it almost seemed like the ordinary time between classes, except for the unusual quiet. Hushed conversations whispered sporadically around them, and everyone seemed turned inward. Emma and Tina proceeded down the stairwell and when they left the building, began to go in separate directions. Black-uniformed officers were everywhere, motioning people toward various walkways back to dorms and apartments.

"Where are you going?" Emma asked Tina.

"To get lunch, what else?" Tina replied.

Emma was surprised. At just after 11:00 AM, it was a little early for lunch, though not so early that it didn't make sense. Lunch, however, hadn't even occurred to Emma.

"Oh, okay. I'm just gonna go home and check on my roommate."

"Why?"

"She normally has a class in Wheeler right now, but she said this morning she wasn't going to go. I just want to check."

"Why don't you just call her?"

"My phone's dead," Emma lied. In truth, she wanted to see Jenny physically and personally make sure that she was all right; plus she thought she should be the one to tell her what had happened if she didn't already know.

"I can call her. What's her number?"

"I don't know; it's in my phone."

"Oh. Okay, well I guess I'll see you later then."

"Yeah, see you."

Emma began the trek back to Stern Hall.

16
∞∞∞∞∞

1:30 PM

Greta Stratton-Foster finished her late lunch. She'd been told that she couldn't see Gerald until his surgery was over, and that wouldn't be for a few hours. She'd waited anyway, until she'd been informed that the surgery had gone longer than expected. She figured she might as well pass the time by getting herself something to eat, so she'd come down to the first floor café. The food had been passable: probably more passable than what the patients got, and she now felt full. She pushed back her plate, wiped her mouth, and leaned back in her chair.

The café had mostly emptied out by the time she got her lunch, except for one other table where three men and one woman conversed as though they'd known each other for years. One man and the woman looked to be in their late 50s or early 60s; the other two were younger, one of them portly and on his way to balding, the other trim, with dark hair. The men looked like professionals of some kind: two of them wore ties, and all had sport jackets. The young, trim man (she hadn't seen him stand, but he had that tall, dark, and handsome look) placed his hand on the woman's as he spoke, and she smiled. His head turned toward Greta's and caught her eye, and only then did she realize she'd been staring. She looked back at her empty plate.

In truth, she'd been famished. Was this wrong? Weren't you supposed to pick at your food at times like this? The morning's experience had drained her considerably, and she'd needed fuel. Not knowing the outcome was the worst part. She felt if she knew how the surgery was going and whether Gerry would be all right, she'd know what to do; she could begin making plans and thinking about what the future would be like. Without that knowledge, however, she found herself lost in a sea of waiting, wondering, and hoping: a dangerous state. Waiting meant helplessness until something happened, instead of taking action yourself. Wondering lacked initiative; a dream state where possibilities reigned instead of firm, concrete decisions. Hopes could be dashed; in fact, often were, and in spectacular fashion. No, she didn't want to be in the position of waiting for others, wondering what would happen, or relying on hope. She needed control, information, and concrete plans: solid ground beneath her.

Unfortunately, all she could do for the moment was wait. She had no new information; she couldn't even call Jenny and let her know anything. It made her feel coerced, forced against her will into a mode of operating she assiduously avoided: the mode of the weak-minded, of those who lived by faith instead of reason.

Her thoughts, in an attempt to escape her current situation, invariably turned to her research. She'd titled her work *The Role of Religion in Intergenerational Transmission of Mores and Values in a Cross-Cultural Society*; academic-speak for *Why the heck is religion so important to America's poor minorities, and why, if it's the main vector for teaching kids right and wrong, do they still get so messed up, generation after generation?* The issue wasn't with minorities in general: only poor minorities. Poor minorities lacked resources and had religion shoved down their throats by a grandmother or grand-aunt or some program that gave them assistance, because most of the non-governmental help for them came in religious form. Religion didn't seem to help them much if at all. What they needed were resources they didn't have. To Greta, religion was an unnecessary trapping, an accoutrement to actual, physical help like food, clothing, job training; an add-on that didn't offer any real help at all.

She realized that her current situation might provide some insight on this. She tried filtering today through her projection of the religious thinker. If she believed in an all-powerful being who could just fix everything that had happened this morning, she'd certainly have spent time this morning asking him to do that. Of course, that would be giving credence to fairy tales and wishful thinking. People wanted to believe that because it shielded them from the obvious truth: you're on your own; your decisions are yours, and what happens in your life happens. No deity would swoop in and save anybody from anything. People inhabited this planet because they beat astronomical odds, and their lives were squarely in their own hands. The question then became, what happened to these people when the deity failed to answer their prayers? When random tragedies hit them without warning? When their loved ones suffered and died? Was the resulting disillusionment a part of the cause of the social problems of the poor? Greta thought so.

In her case, she had no illusion about reality. Gerry's life sat solely in the doctors' hands. If they could save him through skillful repair and the knowledge that the study of the human body gave them, then they'd save him. If not, he'd die, be disabled, or worse: his personality or intelligence could be affected. And that meant a much more difficult life for her—a life she didn't want. She hadn't even been sure she wanted the life she already had. Hadn't her actions of this morning proved that?

David had been persistent, of that there'd been no doubt. What had changed today that caused her to give in? What would have happened if that phone call hadn't arrived? She suspected she knew, and she didn't like that knowledge. If she decided to break up her marriage, having an affair first would not be the way she'd want to do it. It's not like she was unhappy. Instead she'd call it non-happy, she supposed, and the way to change her situation would be to change it, not create some scandal. She'd gone down the same road as the religious—living by feelings and emotions, rather than by analysis and logic—and there'd been no rational reason for it.

Maybe that was the problem. She'd lived for decades in a professional world of study, scientific inquiry, and academic rigor. Had she merged her professional persona with her personal one? Had she lost or suppressed a part of herself that had been awake and alive earlier in her life, only to have it come roaring back this morning? It wasn't like her marriage had gone horribly wrong; instead, she and Gerry had just grown apart. They'd "fallen out of love," as they say. It happens. No, there wasn't anything wrong with her, and she wasn't suppressing anything. Their lives were so different now that it would take effort to try to recapture the magic, so to speak, and her actions this morning gave evidence that maybe her heart had already moved on, having tired of waiting for her head to catch up.

She knew Gerry inside out and backwards by now. His foibles had been on display for her every day; in fact, his foibles seemed of late to define him. A guy who could build a computer out of spare parts surely could fix a faucet? Not Gerry. When approached with the idea, he was reluctant to try. One time she made him get up on the roof and clean the gutters: a normal home maintenance task that every other male homeowner she could think of achieved successfully year after year. Gerry fell off the roof and broke his leg. When their dining room chairs began to get loose, he attempted to tighten the screws that held them together and stripped them all. He'd injured himself trimming branches. One time he came in having nearly sawed off half his finger—not with a chainsaw, but with his bow saw. The blood hadn't oozed or trickled; it had poured. Jenny had cried immediately when she'd seen it, and Greta had had to wrap it in a towel to get it to stop hemorrhaging, and then they all made the trip to the emergency room.

For some reason, however, when it came to a new experience or an adventure, he thought he knew everything. He became Gerald the Expert. Once they tried kayaking down some stream in the bowels of South Jersey. That one didn't go all that badly, actually, because they'd had individual kayaks. There'd been a small drop in the level of the water (she refused to call it a waterfall, but Gerry did when he told the story). Everybody else navigated it successfully, bow pointed straight. Gerry hit it sideways, of course. Over he flipped, and he scraped his forehead on something as he hit bottom. It didn't bleed too badly; his suffering that night (and the following week) came more from the patch of poison ivy he'd blundered into.

The next year's trip—the one he'd brow-beaten and guilt-tripped her finally into going on—had been the one to which she'd been the most diametrically opposed: a pheasant shoot. He'd assured everyone that he knew all the gun safety rules; he'd done this before with his dad as a kid and wanted the experience for Jenny; they'd have fresh meat for dinner; yadda, yadda, yadda. And then he almost shot the guide. The guide took his gun away, and the only pheasant they ate that night was given to them by another man in the group who'd looked at Greta with a sorry expression on his face.

She'd vowed she wouldn't go on any more adventures after that.

She didn't believe he was accident-prone, though. During normal, everyday life, he never hurt himself. And he was one of the safest and most careful drivers she knew. In fact, *she* made *him* nervous whenever she drove and he sat in the passenger seat. She smiled. She knew exactly what to do to make him either grab the door handle or press his foot down on an imaginary brake pedal.

That was the result of marriage, wasn't it? The knowing: knowing how to make him nervous in the car, how he liked his steak (medium rare), that he'd laugh at the same part in *The Naked Gun* every time he watched it, that if he couldn't find his shoes, she'd already put them in the closet for him, and countless other things. There were two clichés people used to define people in their situation: *absence makes the heart grow fonder* and *familiarity breeds contempt.* Every day they absented themselves from each other at their separate jobs. Indeed, they probably spent more hours of each day apart than they did together. But it didn't make them miss each other. When they came together again, they stayed in their own separate worlds, thinking about the concerns and problems of their individual days. Was that because familiarity had bred contempt? Was it simply not worth it anymore to include each other, to get into a world they could share, or to spend some time on a project they could do together? Was that how things had worked at the beginning, when everything was new?

Greta didn't know, and she wasn't used to this sort of introspection. Normally, she had no time for it. But today had given her opportunity to form some new ideas. She might be beginning to understand at least one reason why the subjects of her research so readily turned to religion.

She could see how it would be tempting right now to want to put the problems of her life in the hands of an all-powerful being who could fix them. When your life went out of control, didn't you want to be rescued? Her subjects didn't understand, however, that belief in mythical fairy tales made them vulnerable. Those in charge of religion used those mythical fairy tales to control people. They could promise those who knew no better everything and keep them holding out hope forever, while taking everything they had. If they kept people's focus on some mythical god, no one would ever notice. No wonder religion entrenched itself among the poor and disadvantaged. It promised much, but delivered very little. She always came back to this, and it drove her life and her research.

Well, she wasn't going to solve the problems of her research or her own problems just sitting here. She should—

"...-versity of California at Berkeley..."

The phrase spoken from the cable news channel on the TV in the corner of the café caught her ear, and she looked up. The words BREAKING NEWS emblazoned the screen in all caps, and the scene from a helicopter's vantage point depicted a large, white building surrounded by a SWAT team.

"...just coming in, but what we do know is that the shooter entered the building at approximately 10:15 AM local time. There are unconfirmed reports of fatalities, and as you can see from this footage, several individuals were treated at the scene and taken to safety. No motive or identity of the shooter is known at this time. The campus remains on lockdown..."

BREAKING NEWS shrank and became the prefix to a larger headline: BREAKING NEWS: *Shooting at UC Berkeley*. Greta's heart leaped in her chest. She stood up suddenly, her chair sliding violently backward into the wall behind her. The people from the other table looked over in surprise. Again, her eyes locked with the younger man, and she could tell he had read the shock and fear in her face. Without a further word, she grabbed her purse and started fishing for her phone while her legs, suddenly shaky, automatically took her out the door.

Her heart pounding, she frantically fumbled for the phone and finally found it. She had Jenny on speed dial, and she raised the phone to her ear expectantly. Instead of a ring, she heard the three-tone error, and then this message: "We're sorry, all lines are busy. Please check the number and try again later." She barely stifled a curse and dialed again. Same result. In frustration, she tossed her phone into her purse, only to have it bounce back again and nearly topple to the floor before she caught it. This served only to frustrate and now embarrass her, and as the tears began to flow, she ran into the restroom.

Quickly, she found an empty stall, dropped her purse to the floor, and leaned against the stall's wall, sobbing. First Gerald and now Jenny. Would she lose her whole family in one day? Showers of regret from her previous thoughts washed over her: regret over time spent on her own projects instead of with her family, regret over sharp words, a quick temper, rampant impatience, frequent selfishness. The real possibility that she could never redeem this, that her former predictable and now, she admitted, rewarding life had disintegrated completely out of her control, blanketed her with despair. Loss and sorrow squeezed the breath out of her, and she sobbed in great gasps, as perhaps she had not since she was a small child. She knew her sobs could be heard by anyone else in the restroom, but she could no more control them than she could grow wings and fly herself out to Berkeley to check on Jenny personally.

She cried in the bathroom stall for a long time, until she surrounded herself with spent toilet tissue filled with tears.

17

∞∞∞∞∞∞

10:30 AM

Brick Johnson used his phone to trigger the explosives hidden in the alleys on both sides of his house before he even reached the kitchen. Gliding into the backyard, he checked for movement from either alley and found none. Hyper-aware of his surroundings, he heard the sound of gunfire coming from the house. Good; the idiot was shooting at the cops.

He reached into the compartment under the seat of his Kawasaki and grabbed the wallet he knew contained the credentials of Brent Jenson, leaving the gun there in its place. He ripped his current wallet out of his pocket, pulled the cash out of it, and stuffed it into the new wallet, which he then jammed into his back pocket. Both wallets were made of canvas sealed with velcro. He tossed his now useless wallet and his phone into a coffee can filled with gasoline on his back porch, lit a match, and threw it into the can. A burst of flame assured him that soon his phone and the wallet would be destroyed.

He opened a trunk next to the burning coffee can and extracted three Molotov cocktails. Lighting all three at the same time from the coffee can, he threw one of them down the hall past the kitchen, one into the kitchen, and then backed up and fired one up through the bedroom window. All three locations burst into flame immediately.

He could have used fuses and explosives for this too, but he believed firmly in Occam's Razor: the simplest solution really was best.

With a quick, practiced movement, he mounted and started the motorcycle, adjusted his backpack, and took off toward the chain link fence in his backyard. He'd previously cut through the fence and nearly through the horizontal pole at its top, so it burst apart when he hit it. He sped through the parking lot on the other side of the fence and then up Broad Street. Soon he was through Woodbury and heading up the ramp to I-295 North. In all this, no stress showed on his face; in fact, he felt nothing. He'd simply executed a plan he'd long ago prepared and practiced.

As he accelerated onto I-295, he checked his mirrors and found no pursuit behind him. He'd expected that, actually; the whole point of preparing all this in advance had been to evade and escape. He'd done this before, and he'd never been caught. Now, as before, he'd find someplace safe, check in, and await further instructions. He knew those to whom he reported probably already knew he'd been found out and that they'd be hearing from him soon.

In truth, he felt ebullient. He didn't like this life he'd been living for the past few years anyway. Impersonating a high school student? He hadn't thought it possible, and yet it had worked. Creating a drug ring? Interesting: he knew much of his organization's finances came from the illicit sale of, well, many things, but he'd never been part of that end of it before. His job did not include, however, asking questions, making value judgments, or introspection of any kind: he did what he was told, and he did it as efficiently as he could. He'd always done things that way, and for that reason, he knew there'd be no repercussions for how this particular assignment had ended. No, as before, he'd be thanked and tasked with something else to do. He'd do that something else with as much efficiency as he'd already demonstrated until another thing came along. His life was simple, and he liked it.

Rather than continue up I-295, he exited onto Route 42. He'd heard about a traffic accident earlier today, but it was further south from his current location, and indeed, there seemed only to be normal traffic now. He wanted to make sure that no one had followed him. So far, he could find no evidence of any pursuit. Still, making many turns made it harder to be followed, so he jumped off Route 42 onto Route 130 North. After passing through a few lights, he turned right onto a side street into a neighborhood in West Collingswood. It presented a stark contrast to busy Route 130 behind him: tree-lined streets, old but still well-kept houses, the sound of dogs barking as he passed them. A small, white church stood among the houses, its simple architecture blending in with the neighborhood. It had no parking lot, but he could see a grass-covered lot behind the building. He pulled up onto the sidewalk, turned into the lot, and cut his engine.

Now that he knew he hadn't been followed, he had to do one more thing he hadn't had time for earlier. He opened the compartment under his seat and retrieved new plates for the motorcycle. Using a screwdriver he also had in the compartment, he quickly removed the plates currently on the bike and replaced them with the new plates. He dumped the old ones into a trash can behind the church, which thankfully seemed deserted at this time on a Monday afternoon.

Now to check in. He knew there was a pharmacy just down the street on the other side of Route 130, on Collings Avenue. Time to go get a burner phone. He restarted his motorcycle, cruised very slowly out of the grass lot so as not to leave any trace of himself, and headed around the block. Making a left onto Collings Avenue, he went straight through the light across Route 130 and pulled into the pharmacy on the left. The contrast between the one side of Route 130 and the other side struck him. It was as though the road contained an invisible wall blocking the obviously poor neighborhood on the one side from the nicer, middle-class neighborhood on the other side. He got off his bike and entered the store.

Five minutes later, he exited the store, already pulling apart the carton containing the phone. He knew the phone likely shipped with enough battery power to make his call immediately. As he re-mounted his bike, he jammed the SIM card he'd purchased with the phone into its slot, booted the phone, and made his call from the parking lot. After two rings, someone picked up.

"Yes?" A male voice, low. Obviously software-filtered.

"The cat's at the vet." He hated this week's code phrase.

"What's his prognosis?"

"They think he'll make it."

"Very good." The phrase had been accepted.

"175 checking in," he said.

"Status?"

"Clean."

"Good. One moment, please." There was a pause of about 30 seconds.

"Proceed to checkpoint 86, passcode 1908101293847. 15:00 hours." He'd have to use the phone's browser to look this up.

"Got it." He'd only need the passcode for the next minute or so; he could keep it in his head for that long.

The call dropped.

Next, he enabled developer mode on the phone, which enabled him to side-load applications. He accessed a website that looked like a technical support site for various models of phones. He entered his phone's make and model into a search box and tapped *Submit*. In response, the phone downloaded a file. He tapped on it, and the phone's operating system asked if he wanted to install the software. He tapped *Yes*, and a new icon—a simple globe—appeared in the phone's menu. He tapped that, and after the cache of the phone's original browser was overwritten fifty times with random data, a new, secure browser launched and automatically accessed a website. He had no idea where this site was, because the browser never showed him an address, it connected through an onion network for anonymity, and it changed every day anyway. Using this site, he entered the passcode, looked up location 86 in his area, and an address in Pennsauken appeared. After quickly memorizing the location, he exited the browser. He waited, knowing that now the browser was busy deleting itself and then overwriting its former location fifty times with random data, completely removing any trace that it had ever existed on this phone. When the icon disappeared, he put the phone to sleep again, started his motorcycle, and looked up.

Two cars crawled slowly down Collings Avenue in front of him. A few people walked the street, meandering as though it didn't matter how fast they got to wherever they were going. A man wearing an ancient, stained, olive green army jacket shuffled across the parking lot: probably homeless.

"Hey."

The man looked up.

"Merry Christmas," he said and tossed him the phone. Before the man could reply, he took off for Route 130 again, headed for Pennsauken. *Brent Jenson*, he reminded himself. *I'm now Brent Jenson.*

18
∞∞∞∞

12:00 PM

Sal Fuchetti arrived home once again, having replenished his supply of pipes. He'd just finished an odd phone call. He'd called the guy who had wanted him to do this job, saying he could still get to work on it today, but he'd been told not to bother and to come back tomorrow. The guy was an absentee landlord who lived in Florida. Wouldn't he want the job done as soon as possible? It didn't make any sense. Now he had nothing to do, and he'd have to get on the phone and try to reschedule a couple other jobs he had lined up for tomorrow for today, if possible. What a mess.

He couldn't understand what had happened to his pipes. He'd just secured the new ones exactly the way he had last night, which was exactly the way he'd been doing it since forever, with the same plastic ties he'd used for years. PVC pipe didn't weigh much, and the ties were strong: plenty strong enough to keep his pipes secure. One tie went around each end of the bundle, one went in the middle, and two each hooked around the two end ties and secured the bundle to his pipe rack (which he'd built himself 15 years ago, out of old galvanized steel pipe) mounted in the bed of his Dodge truck.

He jumped out of the truck and went back to check the pipe rack. Everything looked perfectly secure, just as it always had. It didn't make sense. Why, after doing the same thing for so long, would his system suddenly fail today?

He turned and surveyed his neighborhood. He lived in a row house (*town house*, he corrected himself) just off exit 48 of Route 55, in Glassboro. This was a new neighborhood, not completely filled yet, and he was glad to be here. Fresh air, farm markets nearby in the summer, and what he hoped would be nice neighbors as the development filled out made his new home preferable to city living.

He turned to head into his house, and his right steel-toed boot crunched on something. He lifted his foot.

A plastic tie.

He reached down and picked it up. The normally smooth surface had roughened from grinding on his boot, but it looked pristine except for one thing: it had clearly been cut through. The realization hit him hard, and his heart began to beat rapidly. He leaned against the side of his truck, staring at the tie. Had someone sabotaged him?

A thousand things went through his mind at once. *Who could have done this? Why would someone do this to me?* He looked up. *Was it one of my neighbors?* Mrs. Feldman lived in the unit next to his, and the next ones over were empty (he had the end unit). Across the street were mostly empty units, with a few families newly moved in like himself: he didn't know them real well, except to wave and say hi. *Could it be somebody from another part of the development? What could I have done to them? Well, at least I could use this as evidence for my insurance claim so my rates don't go up. Maybe it was an accident?*

He looked down at the tie and ran his thumb over the edge where he believed it had been cut. Smooth. He ran his thumb over the other edge, where the tie should have been attached. Also smooth. If it hadn't been cut, it had been a clean break, and those ties weren't under any kind of stress that would make them break; he was sure of that. But maybe he should make sure.

He pocketed the damaged tie, went to the back of his truck, dropped the tailgate, and climbed in. Crawling to the toolbox mounted at the back of the bed against the cab, he unlocked it and found a bundle of ties. He pulled one from the bundle and examined it, running his thumb and forefinger down its length. It seemed perfectly smooth on the non-grooved side. He grasped one end in each hand and pulled with all his might. As expected, the tie slipped out of his right hand without breaking. He put this one aside and performed the same test on a few more. All of them seemed fine. Maybe he should test more thoroughly, however.

Rummaging through his toolbox, he found two needle-nosed pliers. With one in each hand, he used them to grasp the ends of one of the ties and again pulled with all his strength, trying to break it. No matter how hard he tried, even twisting it violently, the tie wouldn't break. No, it seemed the ties were fine. He turned and sat in the bed of his truck, his back against the toolbox. What was going on here?

He decided to call the cops. At the very least, if he reported it right away, he might get out of that big insurance bill that would likely be arriving. It was worth a shot, anyway.

He packed everything back up and went into his house.

19
∞∞∞∞

12:30 PM

Mary Simmons tried to smile as someone swept aside her privacy curtain. She felt dizzy and drowsy, and she wanted to go to sleep. Of course, they wouldn't let her do that. First came the tests, then the lunch tray, then the nurse with pain medication. She didn't have much experience with hospitals, but apparently you weren't allowed to sleep in them. The most she could manage, therefore, didn't even qualify as a wan smile. She couldn't be sure, but she may have managed something between a frown and a grimace.

A small, balding Italian man greeted her. He had a kind face behind barely visible, frameless glasses.

"Hello, Ms. Simmons. I'm Dr. Angelo. How are you feeling?"

"Call me Mary, please. Tired and groggy, and my head hurts. How are you?"

The doctor smiled. "Thank you for asking. As far as I can tell, I'm doing better than you are."

"I'll bet you are."

"Well, Mary, I'm afraid you have a concussion. Tell me, have you ever had a concussion before?"

"No, Doctor, this would be my first."

"That's good. Your concussion isn't too serious. I didn't observe any swelling of the brain or anything like that. But based on your symptoms, I'd like to keep you here for a few hours just to see how you're doing."

"Oh, Doctor, I'd really like to go home. How long do you think I'll have to stay?"

"A hospital isn't a prison, Mary. And unlike Hotel California, you can check yourself out at any time." He smiled at this, but turned serious again when it became obvious the joke was lost on Mary. "Of course, I'd prefer it if you would stay for a few hours for observation. Don't worry; I'm not admitting you. You'll stay right here, just for a little while."

"Why? Do you have to make sure I don't fall asleep?"

"Actually, no, that's a common myth about concussions. As long as you're able to hold a conversation as you're doing now, you should get some rest. What I'd actually like to watch for is dizziness, disorientation, or nausea. Any of those things can make you a danger to yourself. Is there someone at home who can watch for those things?"

"No, I live alone."

"Okay, then I'd really like you to stay, just for a few hours, so we can make sure you're recovering normally. Is that okay with you?"

She thought for a moment. A picture formed in her head of her empty house and her bed and hours before her. What did she have to do today anyway, at this point? Better to be safe than sorry.

"Okay, I'll stay."

"Thank you. I'll be back to check on you periodically, probably about every hour or so. If everything looks good, I'll have you out of here by dinner time, I promise."

"All right. Thank you for going the extra mile, Doctor."

"Thank you for being such a good patient. I'll see you in a little bit."

And with another sweep of her privacy curtain, he left. She closed her eyes. All the sounds of the hospital—carts going by, beeps, boops, dings, and dongs of medical equipment, hurried speech in medical jargon—became more prominent, as if the shutting off of one sense somehow automatically heightened another. Someone—a woman—in the next compartment was having a boot fitted. Mary felt a bit disoriented with her eyes closed, and the room did seem to rotate on an axis mostly perpendicular to the floor. She supposed that meant she'd made the right decision.

She sighed. What a day. *I should probably call my mother*, she thought, but then decided against it. She didn't have the stamina at this point to sustain a conversation with her mother, and it would make her worry anyway. Plus, Mom wasn't good under stress; she could say anything, and often did blurt out whatever came to mind. And where Mary was concerned, all she ever seemed to think about was her daughter's unmarried status. She'd probably just ask if she'd met any cute doctors at the hospital.

Was it so bad still to be alone in your mid-thirties? And who got to define *alone* anyway? She had friends; she had co-workers: successful relationships with people. Did she really need anything more than that at this point? Of course not. She had just as much value—perhaps more—as herself alone than she would in being half of a married couple. She had complete freedom to do what she wanted when she wanted, and nobody could place any restrictions on her. If she wanted to sit down and read a book all night, ignoring the dirty dishes in the sink, she could. If she wanted to go to the store and buy a new coat, she could go right out and do it. If she decided she wanted to fly to Paris tomorrow, she could book the flight, and no one could stop her.

Of course, she'd be terrified to do something like that. She'd never done anything like that in her life. And that really was the point, wasn't it? A person is only as free as her circumstances and personality allow her to be. Did that make her truly free? Was she really free to fly to Paris? Maybe not. For one thing, the fare would probably bankrupt her if she booked the flight for tomorrow, plus she just couldn't see herself doing something so, so—reckless. It would be like jumping off a cliff without first checking to see how far you'd fall. She knew no one in Paris and could barely speak the language. She would have to use those minimal communication skills to get transportation, eat food, and find a place to stay. And then when she finally got to her hotel room and put all her bags down and sat on the bed, what would she do? She'd still be alone. In Paris. Free to do as she wished, of course, but with no idea what *to* do. She wasn't all that great at defining adventurous activities.

Okay, so she wouldn't do that; she'd instead do something else, something more fitting to her personality. She just didn't know what yet. What mattered most, however, was that she had total control over her life. She didn't have to go to Paris, or Rome, or anywhere to prove that. Mom wanted her to follow a particular path: the one she had followed. And who knows? She still might. But Mom needed to understand that she'd do it on her terms. Why did Mom persist on this issue so much? And why did Mom's persisting on it occupy her thoughts so much? She might as well have called Mom; she couldn't avoid the topic in her own mind anyway.

An idea began to dawn on her. Maybe Mom wasn't so worried about her love life. Maybe instead she worried about the direction—or lack thereof—her life was going. If Mary continued down this path for another ten years, what would her life look like? Suddenly she could see herself in the mirror in her bedroom at home. As she watched, she began to age ten years into the future. The few gray hairs she'd noticed recently became a shock of gray above her forehead. Her still trim but plumping form widened a bit, and the result, while not fat, did not fill her with pleasant feelings. Her bright, green eyes dimmed a bit and a darkness appeared beneath them. To hide this, she wore larger, rounder glasses. Her cheeks sagged ever so slightly, and her teeth bore the yellow color and stains of her daily tea habit.

She saw herself turn and head out her bedroom door, down the hall past the bathroom and into her living room. A cat sat curled in each of her two sitting chairs, and two more stretched out on the couch. The TV sat where it usually sits, and everything looked as neat and tidy as it had when she left the house this morning. She went through her day: to work first, a day of handling patrons at the library for eight hours. After that, she'd come home to her cats, feed them, and scoop their litter boxes. After this, she'd make herself dinner and eat it while watching TV. She'd then curl up on the couch with a good book, browse the Internet on her laptop or tablet, or talk to Mom or one of her friends on the phone, perhaps to make plans to do something on Friday or Saturday night.

What struck her was how little would change in ten years. She'd likely have the same job, about the same pay, be in the same house, and have the same, limited social life that she had now. What would she have accomplished in those ten years? She'd have had some fun with her friends; she'd have done more work at the library, curating, cataloging, and recommending books. She'd like to think she'd have grown as a person through the casual reading and study she did. But if she wanted to be honest with herself, the only difference ten years would make is that she'd be ten years older, ten years fatter, and have ten fewer years left to live her life. She'd still be totally free to do whatever she wanted, but did the evidence show that she'd so far been a good arbiter of what was important about life? Not so far, no. If she were ninety-something-years-old and on her death bed looking back at her life, would she be satisfied with what she'd accomplished? Would the world be any different because she'd been in it for a lifetime?

If she continued down her current path, the result seemed fairly empty. She'd do some work; she'd have some fun, and then she'd die, and maybe be replaced by someone else who would do the same. Did those experiences have value in and of themselves? They had value to her in the moment, for sure. Was there, however, any lasting value to them? Was any part of those experiences of her life something she could pass on to others? She had to admit: no, not really. They would die when she would, forever lost to the rest of the world, and even if they weren't lost, there'd been nothing unique about them. Lots of people worked, went to parties, took care of animals, had fun with friends, experienced literature's mind-opening effects. So then came the next obvious question: was her absolute control over her life, to do whatever she wanted, actually giving her the full and complete life she'd always dreamed of? No, she had to admit, it wasn't. In fact, it was quite possible that the iron control she'd developed, designed as it was to give her the most satisfaction, would actually cause her to miss out on life.

She was no revolutionary. She would not, through force of ideas or personality, change the world like Martin Luther King Jr., or Mother Theresa, Plato, or Jesus. What, then, was left to give her life meaning? She had no one to impart her accumulated wisdom to, no one to listen to—and help her carry out—her dreams, no one who would miss her if she disappeared tomorrow into a hole in the universe. She'd been living this way for the last ten years, wasting it, wasting life. All she had, the most precious resource given to her, was time, and she'd been letting it go by.

It came crashing down on her like the proverbial ton of bricks. Mom was right. She was *actually* right to be concerned about her. If she wasn't the type to go out and change the world through force of personality, business, or rhetoric, the only way to leave a legacy was through charity or family.

Her eyes snapped open. The brightness of the hospital's emergency area stabbed like a dagger through her skull. She quickly closed her eyes again, and the room resumed its slow rotation. She smiled. It had taken a nasty bump on the head to knock some sense into her. She would be making some changes in her life, most definitely. The only thing she needed to decide was what she would change first.

20

∞∞∞∞∞∞

1:00 PM

"Well, that looks pretty good, even if there's no art to it anymore," said Dr. Reynolds, putting the final adjustments on the Velcro straps of her brand new boot.

"Art?" Gloria asked.

Dr. Reynolds stared off into space, seeing something that only existed in his mind. "Yeah," he said. "I used to really enjoy making casts."

Well, Gloria thought, *if I'm going to get a random orthopedist at the hospital, it may as well be one who's a fanatic about what he does.*

Dr. Reynolds had a faraway look in his eyes. Gloria couldn't tell if her boot reminded him of something, or if he truly felt nostalgic. Eventually, he looked up and smiled at her. He had a kindly, if absent-minded face, with wire glasses perched precariously at the end of his pointed nose. A gleam from his hairless head reflected from the harsh fluorescent lights above. He'd brought a laptop into the room, and he began tapping on its keyboard to update whatever needed to be updated in her medical records, smiling and humming to himself.

A man this much into his work surely would have trouble managing home and professional lives, yet Gloria had checked: a wedding ring had practically embedded itself into his left ring finger. Had this eccentric man at some level been able to balance his personal life with his clear obsession with the topic of his work?

Why is that such a surprising idea, she wondered. Just because her marriage hadn't worked out didn't mean others—even geeky others—couldn't make theirs work. She sighed. This wasn't a helpful train of thought. Better to focus on the task at hand.

"So can I walk in this thing?" she asked.

"Yes," said the doctor. "You should be able to get around normally, without pain. I would advise, however, that you try to stay off it for today if you can."

"I'll try," she said unconvincingly.

He paused, possibly deciding whether to reinforce his advice. "Well, that's it then. You should make an appointment with my office in three weeks, and we'll see how it's healed." He handed her his card. "I'll have them call you to set it up."

"Thank you, doctor."

"Do you have any questions?"

"No, I don't think so."

"All right then, I'll get the paperwork started to get you discharged."

"That's fine, doctor, but I came in with someone else who was also injured. How can I find out how he's doing?"

"Is he still here in the emergency room?"

"I don't think so. He had a stab wound. They took him away almost immediately, and I don't think he ever came back. His name is Jameel. Jameel Jones."

"They probably brought him right into surgery, in which case he's either still there, in the recovery room, or in a room of his own at this point if it was bad enough that they want to keep him."

"He was bleeding pretty badly. I saw it happen."

"Oh my, you have been through a lot today."

"Yes, considering how my days usually go, that's something of an understatement."

"I'll see if I can find out anything for you. HIPAA regulations being what they are, I may not have any success. In that case, I'm afraid you'll have to go to the front desk and pretend you came in off the street to visit."

"That's what I was afraid of. Thanks for giving it a shot."

"It's no problem. I'll be right back."

He got up and left. Gloria assumed, however, that she wouldn't see him again. If she did, she'd be pleasantly surprised. She looked down at her legs, at their lopsidedness. The left one was perfect, except for a missing shoe and torn hose. The right one sported an unwelcome black bulge that—Dr. Reynolds's nostalgia notwithstanding—years ago would have been white and eventually covered with signatures. A teacher cannot get out of the public eye though, and the boot would still make her the center of attention that she did not want.

Thoughts of her students made her wonder how class had gone today. It was after lunch now, and there was no point in going back. She'd missed the whole day. In a sense, missing the whole day gave her some relief. She was tired. It would be better to start fresh in the morning. She'd have time tonight to figure out what she'd say to her students to get the day started tomorrow. Maybe even some of them knew about Jameel; the rapidity with which news got around to the students could boggle her mind. At least she'd be coming home today in relatively good shape. Other people involved in the accident this morning may not have been so lucky.

A thought struck. She wondered if anyone who'd been injured this morning happened to be here, right now, in this emergency room. She'd been so concerned about finding Jameel when she came in that she'd hardly noticed anyone else. As a math teacher, she liked to put things in math terms. She had a filter she used whenever she looked for someone specific in a crowd; she called it the *not* filter. It worked as she scanned a room looking at faces, and in this case the filter had been set for Jameel's face. For that reason, as she'd scanned the room, she filtered each face as *not Jameel*, over and over, to the point where she couldn't remember what any of those faces had looked like, because there were all *not Jameel's*. She couldn't process the whole room and look for Jameel at the same time. She sighed. She really should be more observant. She decided to try while she waited, using her ears instead of her eyes.

Someone came to check on whoever occupied the next compartment. The noisy emergency room interfered with her perception, and she could only hear the compartment's activity in bits and snatches. She could tell that the person asked the patient—a woman—several questions, most of them designed to elicit answers regarding how dizzy, disoriented, or nauseated she was. Sounded like a head injury. That's a candidate right there: someone could easily get a head injury if they'd been in a car accident. Could another accident victim be in the compartment right next to her?

This, she realized, could be a fun—though a bit morbid—game, and certainly passed the time better than feeling sorry for herself about her loneliness, her injury, or her desire not to be made a big deal of when she revealed her boot. If she did find somebody else who'd been involved in the accident, what would she do? Should she try to talk to this person about her experience this morning? She suddenly had an intense desire to do that; it would help her process such a powerful experience if she knew someone who had shared it. Could the woman in the next compartment be such a person? Gloria didn't know; this person's injury could've come from the accident or anything else. She could just as easily have fallen down some stairs at her home and bumped her head.

No, it wouldn't be right to pry into a stranger's life like that, and she'd be too embarrassed to slide the curtain back nonchalantly and talk to her anyway. Instead, she decided she'd try listening to what, if anything, transpired in the compartment on the other side of her. She closed her eyes, which heightened her awareness of the conversation she'd already been listening to.

"...see you turn your head." A pause. "How's that feel?"

"Not great, but better than it was an hour ago."

"Can you describe it?"

"Sure. When I turn my head and my head stops, the room keeps going in the same direction I turned my head in. Instead of spinning all the way around, though, now it figures out what's wrong, stops, and goes back—as long as I don't keep moving my head."

"Okay. How about your neck? Is your neck bothering you at all?"

"Not so far, no."

"And you say you banged your head on your steering wheel?"

"I *think* I banged my head on my steering wheel. I don't exactly know, though. It all happened before I knew what was happening, if you get what I mean. My airbag should have deployed, but I don't think it did. It's all very foggy. I already told the other doctor all of this anyway; why are you asking me again?"

So she'd been injured in her car. Gloria started to feel excited. Maybe it was *the* accident! Maybe she could compare notes and find out what happened!

The other doctor ignored her question. "All right, Mary. Let's wait a little longer, if you don't mind, and see if things become more clear. I'll check back with you in another hour."

"Okay, doctor. I'm so tired. Can I sleep?"

"Certainly. Go ahead and take a nap, and I'll be back in an hour."

"Okay. Good night."

"Sleep well, Mary."

The doctor left. Gloria checked her watch. Not anywhere near night. Mary must've really whacked her head. It didn't sound like she was in any shape to talk anyway. Gloria would just have to console herself with the fact that she *might* be next to somebody else from this morning, but she couldn't be sure.

She sighed and looked around. She could see through the gap in the curtain various hospital employees going to and fro up and down the hallway. Everything seemed a bustle of activity for everyone else except for her. Why did everything having to do with health care have to take so long? She wanted to go see Jameel, to find out if he was all right, and then maybe get home for some much needed rest. The Captain—her dog—would be happy to see her, and she could do with some cuddling, even if only the doggy kind.

21

∞∞∞∞∞

1:30 PM

Lunch—hoagies all around—had been good, if not overlong. It turned out that Sean and Dan had some things in common. Besides being pastors, they'd both been educated locally; Dan had gone to Biblical Seminary, Sean to Westminster Seminary. Sean appreciated Dan's seminary degree. Not all Baptist ministers had them; the minimum requirement, as far as he knew, was a Bachelor's from a Bible college. They'd gone for different reasons: Dan's interest lay in the original languages (Hebrew and Koine Greek), while Sean had his passion for counseling. Margaret remained mostly quiet, following the conversation as she ate, but she seemed happy to listen and not to have to carry the conversation anymore. Colin asked many questions about Sean's ministry at the hospital. He was a newly-ordained deacon and thought he might want to spend some time in the hospital on a regular basis. Sean believed volunteering was limited to full-time clergy, but he told him he'd check for him.

As the lunch hour progressed into the afternoon, the café had become nearly deserted. Only one other table was occupied, and only by a single customer. The table sat directly across the room from theirs, and the woman seated at the table faced mostly in the same direction as Sean, toward the TV, which she ignored in favor of her cheeseburger. She ate voraciously. During the course of his meal Sean had noticed her presence, but only as part of his natural inclination to be aware of his surroundings. At one point, Margaret turned to him.

"I want to thank you for taking the time to listen to my story," she said.

"Margaret, that's what I come here for."

"I know, but I wanted you to know how much it meant—still means—to me."

He placed his hand on hers and looked down at the table. "I'm just a servant, trying—and failing sometimes—to do what I can to encourage God's people. Most of the time, like today, I'm the one who gets encouraged." He looked up at her and smiled. She smiled back.

Out of the corner of his eye, he noticed the woman at the other table eyeing him. He glanced over and caught her eye, and she quickly looked down at her now empty plate. From this distance, he couldn't see her features in any detail: she seemed thin, dressed professionally, and had curly blond hair. Her body language—the business-like way she'd eaten, the quickness of her movements—suggested that she had somewhere to be. Because of that, he surmised that she'd probably only been looking in his direction, and not at him directly. Maybe she'd been daydreaming or preoccupied. Whatever occupied her thoughts, he wasn't involved. He said a short prayer for her, asking that God would intervene in her situation and use it for her good, and then turned back to his own plate, on which the last few bites of his sandwich lay. Colin was speaking.

"...back to work today. It's already heading toward two o'clock."

Sean felt he should try to diffuse the impression that he'd been lost in his own thoughts rather than listening to the conversation. "Where do you work, Colin?"

"Insurance," Colin said, stating what he did rather than where he did it. "I review possible cases of fraud. Basically, it's a lot of report reading. Various investigators write the reports, and I am on a team that reviews the reports and makes a recommendation."

"Wow, that sounds like an interesting job."

"It is, though it's not as interesting as being one of the investigators. I used to do that. I was promoted last year."

"Yeah; I'll bet. Is it safe to say it's a good possibility I have insurance with the company you work for?"

"It's a good possibility. I don't want to say who it is, though. If you've ever had a dispute, there are legal and liability issues."

"He'd tell you, but he's afraid someday he'd have to sue you," Pastor Dan added with a smile.

"I get it, I get it," said Sean. "So tell me, what are some of your most interesting cases?"

"Oh," said Colin, "I don't want to give you any ideas."

"I can't believe you said that, Colin!" Pastor Dan said mockingly. "He's a fellow man of the cloth!"

"'There but for the grace of God, go I,' eh?" Sean said, smiling.

"Exactly." said Colin. "But now that I've given you some warning, there have been some real doozies."

"I'm all ears."

"There was one car accident scam that made this guy a huge profit before we caught on to what he was doing. Note that we had a team of investigators, yet I had personally looked into three of his incidents, and I know some of my colleagues had also had some dealings with him."

"So this guy was frequently getting into car accidents, or what?"

"Yeah; he was constantly getting rear-ended and getting his cars totaled. Then he'd get stuff for pain and suffering too, because of course he always had whiplash or something like that. Now you know that if you rear-end somebody, it's almost always your fault legally, right?"

"I've heard that, yes."

"Well, this guy had evidently built a business on it. He would find some two-lane highway, and then he'd go exactly the speed limit, or maybe just a little bit under."

"In New Jersey? Not a good idea."

"Right. So it wouldn't take too long until somebody—or maybe several somebodies—tailgated him. Then he'd make sure there were cars in the other lane coming in the other direction before he'd just slam on his brakes, and of course the tailgater wouldn't be able to stop. Blamo! Instant profit. Of course, he'd make sure he'd turned the wheel slightly to the right so that when he was hit, he'd get pushed onto the shoulder instead of into oncoming traffic."

"Smart."

"Yeah. I estimate he collected an insurance settlement at least ten ti—"

A screeching sound of metal on tile from across the room interrupted the conversation, and they all turned as one to see the woman from the other table stand up so forcefully that her chair slid backward, tipped, clattered onto the floor, and hit the wall behind her. She wasn't looking at them, however; her gaze was fixed on the TV. She seemed to feel their eyes on her after a few seconds, and then looked over, directly at Sean, a look of horror on her face. Without a word, she gathered her belongings and quickly left the room. Sean looked up at the TV.

"...shooting at the University of California at Berkeley this morning. There are several confirmed dead in Wheeler Hall at the center of campus..."

The screen showed an aerial helicopter view over a white, columned building surrounded by trees. Several small figures in black in front of the building bustled with activity.

"Another school shooting," said Margaret with sadness.

"Yeah, and I bet she knows somebody there," said Dan.

"We should pray about it," Colin said.

"Why don't you start?" asked Sean.

They prayed.

22

∞∞∞∞

2:00 PM

Greta's phone rang at the wrong moment: when her hands were full of soap. Her heart leaped, and she immediately shut the water off, wiped her hands on her jacket, grabbed the phone, and answered it just before it went to voice mail.

"Hello?" She spoke much more loudly—and more shakily—than she'd intended.

"Mom?"

"Oh Jenny thank God! I've been trying to reach you as soon as I found out!"

Mom's intensity surprised Jenny. Not much usually got through her iron control. It left her both puzzled and touched. Then the source of Mom's concern dawned on her.

"I'm all right, Mom. I didn't go to class, remember?"

Their conversation from this morning—it seemed like days ago—came flooding back. "Yes, I remember." Greta realized she didn't know where on campus the shooting had occurred: whether it had been in a dorm or a classroom hall or a lab or a cafeteria or a music room or what. Something primal and protective, something she thought she didn't have anymore, had asserted itself instead, and she'd slavishly followed its lead without further thought or reflection. She didn't like that at all, and she realized something else.

That was the second time today she'd gone completely out of control.

She realized these thoughts had taken her away from Jenny, and she shook herself. She hoped the inordinately long pause hadn't seemed too awkward.

"I'm so glad you're safe, Jenny," she said now, with more poise. She decided a little humility might also be in order. "I'm so glad you didn't listen to me."

"Wow, Mom, I can't remember you ever admitting you were wrong before."

"Don't get used to it. I'm still your mother, and I reserve the right to tell you what I think is best." A warning pierced her chest; she couldn't remember so often second-guessing her own words.

"You always have, Mom."

She decided to let that slide. They'd both already been through enough today and didn't need to be picking at each other. She decided to change the subject. "Do you know what it was all about?"

"No, I have no idea. It happened, though, in the building I was supposed to be in."

"Wow, I'm so glad you didn't listen to me," Greta reiterated.

Jenny cleared her throat. "Yeah, I'm glad too. Hey, I actually didn't call you to talk about this. I wanted to find out about Dad. How is he?"

"I don't know, Jenny. He was in surgery when I got here, and they said it would be a while, so I went and got some lunch. The shooting was on TV, which is why I tried to call you."

"When did you find out he was in surgery?"

"When I first got here."

"Why didn't you call me?"

"Because there was no news, Jenny. I don't even know what his injuries are; no one has talked to me about it at all. It's very frustrating."

"Yeah, but you could at least have told me what you did know."

"But I didn't know anything."

"You knew he was in surgery! That's something!"

"Jenny, it's obvious he would be in surgery. He—"

"It's not obvious! He could've been pronounced dead when he got there! He could've woke up and talked to you! All kinds of things could have happened!"

She realized Jenny was right. The idea that Gerry might already be gone without any warning, taken from her against—no, beyond—her will had not occurred to her as a possibility. Gerry had been an axiom in her life; his non-existence unthinkable. Such an obvious thing, however, *should* have occurred to her, so she couldn't admit that it hadn't. She had to come up with some other explanation.

"Jenny, listen—"

"No, you listen! If you hear anything, *anything* about Dad and how he's doing, you have to call me! I don't care what it is! I want to know! I'm sitting here on pins and needles—"

"You could've gone to class, you know." As soon as Greta said it, she knew she'd made a mistake. Her chin dropped to her chest. Why did she so often blurt exactly the wrong thing?

"What!"

"I'm sorry, Jenny, I shouldn't have said that. I don't even know why I said it." She sighed. "I've been under a lot of stress today—"

"Excuses, Mom. Always excuses. The problem is always with something other than yourself." Jenny sounded cold. Quieter. Then she shouted. *"Look in the mirror next time! You'll find the source of all your problems there!"*

"That's not fair, Jenny. I—"

"Call me if something happens with Dad."

"Jenny—" Too late. She'd hung up.

Greta dropped the phone in her purse. Breathing in great gasps, she leaned on the counter with both heels of her hands to steady herself and try to stop the shaking. She stared at the sink, where the leftover suds slowly dissolved into the drain's filter holes. The clarity of the soap bubbles struck her. The harsh, bright light in the bathroom showed every detail as each tiny bubble popped; the silence broken by a tiny *tic!* sound. It occurred to her that clarity like this eluded her when she looked inward at herself. A sickness festered inside her; she knew that much. She hadn't set out today to create a mess, yet that's what she'd done. Had the accident really changed anything? Hadn't she been on the verge of losing her family anyway? It seemed inevitable now: Jenny hated her, and Gerry? Gerry'd been presupposed, a rock: always there, but—if her conversation with Jenny could be believed—part of the background, so much so that she barely noticed him anymore. He was like the floor under her feet: a foundation of support rarely thought about, but circumstances could now force her to notice his absence. Gerry could die. Gerry might now be a vegetable. If either of those things happened, all avenues for repairing anything vanished like smoke. The thought left an empty, twisted, hollow feeling inside, centered in her chest, dragging her down with its weight.

The unfairness of it wrapped her like a suffocating net, and she suddenly realized how fragile, how precarious, her life—one she thought she'd controlled with an iron fist—had become, and maybe had always been. Instead of running her own life, it seemed she'd been given a measure of responsibility which had now been yanked out from under her, sending her into a spiral of uncertainty that left her surprised—shocked, even—at how badly she managed when things weren't under control.

Having Gerry suddenly cut off from her with no opportunity to resolve anything was bad enough. But why did the possibility of something happening to Jenny hit her so hard, when the possibility of Gerry's demise seemed so improbable and remote—and certainly not to be taken seriously? What did that even mean? She shook her head; she couldn't even understand her own thinking.

Another woman entered the bathroom and disappeared into a stall. Time was up. Now she needed an information update, and maybe that would help her find answers to her own thoughts. She would try to take Jenny's words seriously, face her issues head-on, and not blame her circumstances for her problems. *Hm. Now Jenny's giving me advice*, she thought. *She really is an adult now.* Gathering herself, she looked up into the mirror, breathing deeply. She let the breath out slowly, through pursed lips, and she realized she needed to touch up her lipstick. Even if she didn't have it all together, at least she could look like she had it all together. After doing that, she gathered her purse, straightened her blazer, and headed out the door, back to the surgery waiting area.

As she rounded the corner and the row of chairs came into view, she saw a doctor, still in scrubs, coming down the hall on the opposite side of her. They both entered the waiting area at the same time.

"Mrs. Foster?" he asked. He was big-faced, with a squarish head and red cheeks that were well on their way to becoming jowls.

"*Dr.* Foster," she corrected automatically. She wanted him to know not to talk down to her. After all, the Ph.D was a higher degree than an M.D., wasn't it?

"Excuse me," he said quickly. "Medical doctor?"

"Sociologist."

"I see." She could tell he'd talk down to her anyway. "I'm Dr. Marsden. William Marsden." He held out a hand, which she shook briefly. "I've just come out of your husband's surgery."

Greta bit her lip and looked down at the floor and immediately hated herself for it. She raised her head again and defiantly decided to push through this.

"So tell me what's happening." Businesslike and professional.

Dr. Marsden blinked. "As you know, he was in a terrible accident—"

"Actually, that's all I know. I don't know the details."

He cleared his throat. "Well. Whatever happened resulted in multiple fractures of the cervical, thoracic, and lumbar spine. The good news is that the cervical and thoracic fractures only exhibited the flexion fracture pattern, which has a low chance of spinal cord disruption, and we didn't observe any disruption in those regions. The bad news is the lumbar fracture, which exhibited a rotation fracture pattern."

"What does that mean?"

"In simple terms, it means your husband was subjected to very high-energy trauma. His upper spine has fractures, but only in a straight pattern of compression, and this pattern is unlikely to disrupt the spinal cord. However, his lower spine shows a rotation pattern, as though his lower back twisted due to the trauma. This pattern is much more likely to disrupt the spinal cord. He was unconscious when he arrived, and for the surgery we induced a coma. I applied spinal instrumentation to stabilize the affected vertebrae, but I'm afraid the MRI did show spinal cord disruption in that lower, lumbar region."

Clearly, he wasn't talking down to her as Greta had expected. She had no idea what he was saying, except that Gerry had spinal injuries and was unconscious. She couldn't figure out, however, how both to get him to speak more colloquially and to preserve her hard won respect as a scholar. In the end, though, she decided getting accurate information was more important than her reputation before this man who had tried for the last few hours to save her husband's life.

"I'm sorry, Doctor—" A moment of panic: *what was his name again? Ah, forget it; it doesn't matter right now.* "—I've had a very difficult day, and my medical jargon is a bit rusty even for a good day."

"Of course; I apologize." The doctor looked sympathetic, almost sorrowful. "Your husband suffered a severe trauma that resulted in spinal injuries in multiple locations."

A feeling of dread began to creep over her, starting at her kidneys and spreading up her back. She gripped her purse strap more tightly and blinked.

Realizing she meant for him to go on, Dr. Marsden continued, "The injuries to his upper spine are what we call flexion fractures. The spine is compressed. Something forcefully pushed down on his head, compressing his spine such that it fractured."

The dread spread immediately from her back to her whole body, and Greta's left hand went to her mouth. She uttered one word, at barely a whisper: "Gerry."

"Excuse me?" said Dr. Marsden.

"His name is Gerry." Her hand now uncontrollably shook.

"Would you like to sit down, Mrs—Dr. Foster? There are chairs right here." He indicated a row of chairs in the waiting area to her right.

Suddenly, scenes from their early life together flooded back: meeting in college, laughing with friends, kissing at the top of the Ferris wheel on the Wildwood boardwalk, passion in Greta's apartment off campus—passion that had resulted in Jenny and a quick, small wedding with only parents and close friends. Gerry's injuries sounded bad, and she needed a break; she wasn't sure she could hear more right away. A thought occurred to her as a tear slipped down her cheek and she looked down at the floor.

"Actually, it's Stratton-Foster."

"Pardon me?"

She looked him in the eye. "I never fully took his name. I didn't want to lose my identity, even though there was no academic reason for it since I hadn't published yet. Everybody assumes it's because of my academic career, but of course he knows it's not, and I think it hurts him a little every time I'm introduced that way. Or at least it used to." Her eyes went to the floor again. The tears flowed freely now, and Dr. Marsden looked at her with concern and care on his face. He stepped forward and took her elbow.

"Why don't we sit down and finish our discussion," he said. "Unless you have any more names you want me to know."

She gave a little snort, which made her realize she needed a tissue. She visibly shook now, and she wasn't sure she'd make it to the chairs without help anyway. "Yes, I think that would be wise."

He guided her expertly to a chair, where she sat heavily. She rummaged through her purse for a tissue while he grabbed one of the adjacent chairs and spun it around so he could sit facing her. She cleaned herself up as best she could, thinking all the time about her surprising behavior. She never thought she'd ever be this emotional. Other women did this, women still trapped in a mindset brought about by generations of patriarchy. She'd thought she'd thrown all that off long ago, but here it was, rearing its ugly head and making her seem foolish to this man who was only trying to inform her of the results of the surgery he'd performed on Gerry and then get on with his life. Did he *really* care, or was the concern on his face an act that he'd performed many, many times? She couldn't tell.

Putting the tissue away, Greta raised her eyes to him and said, "Please continue; I won't interrupt again."

Dr. Marsden seemed to gather himself. "Your husband—Mr. Foster, to you, Gerry—had the best diagnostic care. From what the neurologist told me, he doesn't have a significant head injury. A concussion, perhaps." He smiled. "I would say your husband has a hard head."

Greta smiled in spite of herself.

"Okay, so let me get back to the spinal issues," continued Dr. Marsden. "I did most of the work on his lumbar region, here." He turned sideways and leaned forward, pointing to his low back. "Mr. Foster has what we call a rotation fracture here, which can only be caused by severe trauma. We think that Mr. Foster was out of his seat at the time of impact—"

"Wait a minute; you think he wasn't wearing his seatbelt?"

"Oh, no, no, not at all. In fact, if he hadn't, he'd probably not be with us. No, the seatbelt kept him from 'floating,' shall we say, too far out of his seat. But he did float some, and the impact upside down—we think—caused his torso to shift violently sideways, causing the fracture."

"Okay, I'm with you so far."

"All right. Now, this type of fracture, as you can probably imagine, is the one most likely to cause spinal cord disruption. This is a technical term for any kind of interruption in the spinal pathway. What I—well, really, the team—have done is build a structure, which we call instrumentation, around the injury so that it can heal."

"Makes sense." For some reason the more she talked, the more the feeling of dread she'd had dissipated, and this gave her more courage. She hung her head for a moment, took a deep breath, and faced him. "You've given me all the details except one: will he be all right, or is this—" She struggled for the right expression, then finally got it: "—life changing?"

Dr. Marsden had been leaning forward; now he sat back. "The truth is, we don't know. The injury could heal. The injury might not heal. If it doesn't, it's low enough that it should impact only his legs. We'll have to wait and see. We've done everything we can to promote healing. Now it's up to his body."

She sighed. "Thank you. Thank you for giving it to me straight, and not trying to spare me the details."

"You're welcome," he said. "Now, I'm sure you have some questions?"

Greta's mind blanked. She knew she should have questions, but she was drained emotionally and physically, and she couldn't think of any. "Give me a moment," she said.

"Of course."

Her gaze went down again to the tiled floor. She could think better without looking at him, and she did her best to lose awareness of whether or not his eyes were on her. She closed her eyes.

What happened next? She'd spend the day in the hospital of course, grieving over Gerry, grieving over their lost lives. What about tomorrow? She had no idea what to do. Did she come back here all day or part of the day? Was that even helpful or worth it? What about the day after tomorrow and the day after that? What if weeks, months went by, and Gerry didn't wake up? And if he did wake up, would he be disabled? She had a life beyond Gerry: a career, goals, dreams. Were they all gone now? What would happen to her students, her research? Was she to spend the rest of her life nursemaiding an invalid? She wasn't sure she could live with that.

At least thinking about all this gave her the questions she needed to ask.

"How long do you think he'll be out?" she asked, raising her eyes to meet his.

"One thing we know is that the nervous system has its own way of protecting and healing itself. In the case of a severe trauma like this one, it shuts the body down in order to do repairs. The coma we induced should last only a day or two. After that, it's really up to Mr. Foster's body."

"Can you give me an estimate?"

"Oh," he said with a sigh, "that's hard. I'm not a neurologist, of course. In my experience, though, it could be anywhere from a week to as long as a few months." Greta's sharp intake of breath caused Dr. Marsden's eyes to widen almost imperceptibly before he got them under control. "Of course," he said quickly, "those are the outliers. But you must understand the terribly severe trauma your husband went through. He's very fortunate to be alive."

Greta nodded as the tears threatened again. Looking down at the floor again, she fought to maintain control. "Can I see him?"

"Yes, of course. He's in intensive care, just for a few days, to make sure he's stable. It's down this way." He rose from his chair, and she rose with him. He turned quickly, seeming grateful their conversation seemed to be winding down. She followed him down a hall and through double doors he used a key card to get through.

Once inside, everything became more technical. The electronic beeps and chirps of medical equipment played their song, like a strange cricket-cicada symphony from a parallel universe's forest. Nurses—and possibly doctors, she couldn't be sure—strode in and out of rooms and around corners with purpose. Dr. Marsden led her up the corridor to a central station and then off down another corridor to the left, toward the patient rooms. They didn't have to go far; apparently the room he sought was fairly near the station, an ominous circumstance to be sure. Greta looked at the floor as he held the door open for her; she wanted to be in control of the rate in which she'd take in the scene. As the door closed behind her, she slowly lifted her head.

Nothing could have prepared her. Gerald lay flat, covered in plaster. It went from his hips all the way up his back, behind his head, across his chest, and under his chin. A thin headband of plaster crowned him. Two metal rods were attached to this at the one end and to his upper chest under the plaster at the other end. Wires snaked into the hole in the cast between his hips and his lower chest, presumably up to his chest area. More wires connected under the headband. An IV drip sat next to him, affixed to his left arm, while screens displayed various bits of data. His eyes were closed; he looked peaceful. In fact, it hardly looked like him at all: the huge cast and maybe his deep coma had the effect of rendering his features smooth and generic, like a mannequin or a poor computerized model. It was Gerald, though. She recognized the small scar on the side of his nose (a fish hook accident when he was a boy) and the mole on his forehead.

Recognition brought shock. She'd just seen him this morning. He'd been so full of life, frantic even, because he'd been late for his presentation. He'd run around like a maniac trying to get out the door, lamenting his oversight in forgetting to charge his watch. The last she'd seen him, he'd given her a quick peck on the cheek and run out to the garage, one arm in a jacket and the other shouldering the bag containing his computer. The door had slammed shut with finality. He was gone, replaced now by this husk of a human being, this lump of flesh that could only breathe regularly. How could a person, a live person, with thoughts, dreams, feelings, loves, hates, and desires be reduced to this so quickly?

Worse still: what would she do? How could she handle this? The weight of it crushed her with a force so powerful she began to heave. As she struggled to take in enough air to stay conscious, Dr. Marsden quickly took her elbow and led her to the room's only chair, where she sat heavily. Black spots dotted her vision and obscured the corner of Gerald's bed—the only thing in her view at the moment. As she got her breathing under control, the spots cleared and eventually she made the effort to look up helplessly. No words would come to her mouth.

Dr. Marsden spoke. "Can I get you anything? A bottle of water perhaps?"

Her throat was dry. "Yes, that would be fine," she croaked.

"I'll be right back." He turned and left.

Greta put her head in her hands and sobbed. She sobbed not just for the loss of Gerald, whose life-altering injuries were inescapably on display; she sobbed for herself, for the foundation of her life that had been wiped away in a moment. How sure of herself she'd been, just hours ago! She'd had all the power she needed to live a fully self-actualized life: a position of respect and authority at the University, a research project to enhance that and also be a powerful influence in her field, students who hung on her every word, a man who pursued her with a passion she hadn't felt in years, and who, until today, she'd believed she had wrapped around her finger.

Gazing at Gerald, helpless to do anything but breathe, showed her that likely her past life was gone. Now she'd have to play the part of the longsuffering but faithful wife of an invalid who'd once been a vibrant human being, even a hero—if not to her, to Jenny—but had become a shadow of his former self. Her life was ruined, all because of Gerald and his obsession with his work, with his life. She hated him. She hated herself for hating him, because she'd loved him once. She would be trapped now, in a nightmarish world of menial caretaking, polite conversation with people who had no interest in her interests, nor the ability to understand them, and endless days that were all the same.

Dr. Marsden returned with the water bottle. Greta ignored him. If she'd now taken possession of a meaningless life, she'd at least use all the time she needed to accept that. After a minute or two, it dawned on her that she'd already begun to change, to transform into a different, lesser person. She'd forgotten to care that this man she'd just met had witnessed her weakness. No, she could not allow that. She needed to remain true to herself, and weakness could not be tolerated. She reached into her purse and her dwindling supply of tissues and began to clean herself up. Dr. Marsden just stood there, water bottle in hand. Finally, she finished and looked up. He handed her the bottle of water.

"Thank you."

"You're quite welcome. Is there anything else I can do for you?"

"Are you his doctor now? Will you be checking in on him from time to time?"

"Yes, I'll be doing exactly that. Monitoring his progress and making any corrections necessary."

"Thank you. I'm sure I'll have more questions later, but right now I just want to be alone."

"I understand. If I don't see you again today, I'll be back tomorrow."

"Okay. Thank you for all you did to save him." She wasn't sure the words were quite sincere, but she didn't care anymore.

"You're welcome." Without another word, he turned and left.

After the door closed, Greta took a deep breath and stood up. She walked over next to the bed and stared for a while, listening to and watching Gerald's breathing. Dark thoughts threatened, but she determined not to despair again. She knew she had to replace the despair with action in order to get rid of it. What did you do when you faced an insurmountable problem? The answer came. You break the problem into smaller parts that you can handle. Fine. What was the next step? Again, the answer came.

Jenny. She would call Jenny.

23
∞∞∞∞∞

2:00 PM

Jameel found an opening. He faked right, then drove left around the opposing player, only to discover the massive tree trunk leg of the opposing team's power forward in his path. He dribbled the ball one more time as he stepped over the leg, twisted around behind the player and leaped upward, ball in his right hand ready to spring off his first two fingers backward into the basket.

Instead, the power forward simply twisted in place, hands in the air, blocking both the shot and Jameel's upward momentum. Jameel and the ball, instead of soaring gracefully through the air, bounced off the forward and fell awkwardly to the court as the ref's whistle blew. Well, at least he'd drawn the foul.

He'd landed harder than he'd anticipated, and he sat on the floor collecting himself for a moment while the other players lined themselves up. Matt Francis, a teammate, reached down to help him up, and Jameel gladly took his hand. The crowd was strangely quiet. He took his position at the foul line, and the ref tossed him the ball. He dribbled the ball a few times, lining up his shot, but something wasn't right. That fall had knocked the wind out of him a little; he felt pain when he tried to straighten up. And where was the sound? He could see classmates in the stands cheering him on, but no sound came out of their mouths. Instead, he could hear only a faint beeping noise.

He shook his head, dribbled the ball a few more times, eyed the basket, and as he began to take his shot, he saw Freddie Dietrich standing out of bounds behind the baseline, staring at him. The ball clunked against the backboard, next to the rim. The ref tossed him the ball again, and now Freddie began mouthing words at him: *where's the money, Jameel?*

He shook his head and tried to concentrate on his shot. The beeping sound grew louder. He dribbled the ball again to help himself focus, but each time the ball hit the floor, he heard an unsatisfying beep, beep, beep instead of the gratifying pound, pound, pound of the ball echoing off the floor, walls, and ceiling of the gym. As he raised his head to line up his shot, he saw Freddie again, and this time he held a knife. *I need the money now, Jameel*, he mouthed, and Jameel noticed blood on the knife. Other sounds now intruded on the beeping, a rhythmic whooshing sound, like air flowing through a tube, the echo of voices far away, and other electronic noises. He tried to dribble again but as he looked down, he saw his shirt soaked with blood. Dropping the ball, he flattened his left hand against his stomach, and it became slick with red, sticky wetness.

Raising his eyes only brought Freddie back into view. *I'm gonna take it from you*, he mouthed, and everything came flooding back all at once: the meeting, the argument, the knife. The familiar surroundings of the gym dissolved away, and he could feel again the cold, alien metal of the knife invading his body when he lost his grip on Freddie's wrists after his back slammed against that tree. What had happened afterward? Ms. Williams, the cop, the hospital. Awareness shot through him: he remembered where he was! Now he knew what those sounds were!

His eyes shot open.

At first, the brightness blinded him. Rather than standing on a basketball court, he found instead that he lay prone, with ceiling lights shining in his eyes. His eyes watered from the light, and he blinked to clear them. His vivid dream still mostly real, he instinctively flattened his left hand against his midsection, expecting it to come away wet. Instead, he felt only dry bandage and no pain. An IV snaked its way out of his right arm to somewhere behind him. As his eyes adjusted, he remembered more: he'd ridden an ambulance to the hospital; Freddie had fled. He must be just out of surgery. They'd patched him up. The beeping sound he'd heard came from something next to and behind him, something he couldn't quite crane his neck far enough to see. He tried adjusting himself, to sit in a more upright position so he could look around, and it was then that a nurse seemed to appear from nowhere. She placed a gentle hand on his chest.

"Lie still. You're just out of surgery, and you don't want to break any of those nice, new sutures Dr. O'Malley worked so hard on."

Jameel relaxed. No, he didn't want to break any sutures, and getting all worked up wouldn't help him anyway. "Who are you? Where am I?" he asked.

The nurse smiled. "I'm Rosa Ramirez. You're in a recovery room at Cooper Hospital in Camden. I'm here to take you out of the recovery room because you're awake."

Only then did Jameel realize that he wasn't the only patient in the room. The nurse went somewhere behind him, made the beeping noise stop, unlocked the wheels on his bed, and pushed him past at least three other patients out into the hallway. They turned left and went down the hall past a nurses' station and down another hall to silver elevator doors.

"Where are you taking me?" Jameel asked, his voice surprisingly scratchy.

She smiled at him, her dark eyes flashing. "I'm checking you into Hospital Hotel, where the accommodations aren't always great and the food could be better, but the service is top-notch and done with a smile."

Jameel raised an eyebrow. "Do you have that line prepared and ready for all your, uh, guests?"

Again, she looked surprised. "Why yes, actually. It didn't sound natural?"

"Maybe just a little too cheerful."

"Hm. I'll work on it."

The elevator door opened, and she wheeled him inside. Thankfully, no one else entered. She pressed a button with her thumb, and the doors closed. Suddenly, Jameel thought of something. "What happened to all my stuff? My clothes?"

"Your 'stuff,' as you put it, sir, has already been delivered to your room by the concierge. As I said, the service is top-notch."

Jameel began to understand the game. It was meant to help him feel better about his circumstances. Well, she deserved an A for effort. He decided to play along. "I'll have to remember that when I leave my tip."

"Oh, no tips necessary, sir."

The elevator door opened, and she wheeled him out into an almost identical hallway, except the walls and floor seemed less yellow and more white. After traveling through a maze of corridors, she finally arrived at an open door. She pushed him through the doorway and stopped, leaning over him so he could see her.

"Since you're the first one here, I took the liberty of assigning you the window position. I assume that's all right?"

Jameel looked into the room. There were two beds and two beefy men dressed in white, seemingly waiting for them. "I'm getting a roommate?"

"Probably. No one has been assigned yet, though."

Clearly, the hotel charade had broken down. It had to eventually, he supposed. "Yes, the window bed is fine. Thank you."

She pushed him over next to the bed, locked the wheels, and stepped back. The beefcakes took over, one at the head and one at the foot of his bed. They did something with the sheets, counted to three together, and heaved him over to the other bed. After adjusting the sheets, the nurse thanked them, and they left.

"How do you feel?" she asked.

Surprisingly, Jameel felt perfectly lucid. He wasn't groggy at all. "Actually, I feel great. I'm not even in any pain."

"That's temporary," she said. "Once the anesthesia wears fully off, the pain will come, but we'll take care of that."

She removed the IV from its temporary hook on the chair and hung it on a pole next to the bed.

"The doctor will be in shortly to check on you," she said when all was done.

"How long am I gonna be here?" Jameel asked.

"Probably just a day or so. See that IV you're attached to?"

"Yeah."

"That's an antibiotic drip. We want to make as sure as we can that you have no infection when you leave. When you do get home, you'll probably have a nurse come out and help get the wound cleaned every day for a couple of weeks. But I'll let the doctor give you all the details."

"Will you be my nurse?"

"No, I'm sorry. I work downstairs. But I'm sure the service up here is every bit as good."

"Okay. Well, thanks for everything."

"It's my pleasure." She smiled at him, turned, and left. He was alone.

He looked out the window and found he had a great view of the hospital's roof. Spinning air vents dotted the gray landscape, along with mechanicals that he couldn't identify. He turned his head back to face front, looking down at his body—broken now—and sighed. What was he going to do now?

He'd never in his life intended—*ever*—to use drugs. He'd been driven by his circumstances—no, tricked—to try them and even then, the drugs had been just a temporary thing to get him through the rest of basketball season, while he both worked to bring in some extra cash for Mom, and made sure his grades stayed high to win as many scholarships as he needed. Something had to give, and it wasn't going to be him. He had to keep all this stuff going, no matter what. Everything counted the most now: his senior year. If he had any chance of being the first in his family to "make it," this was it. He couldn't fail.

Freddie had found him a few weeks before Christmas asleep in the locker room. Everybody else had already changed and left, and Jameel had been so tired. He'd worked late at the restaurant the night before, and after that he'd had to finish a paper due that day. He knew he could catch a few Zs during gym, and Coach wouldn't mind. He'd sat on the floor with his back to the wall of lockers and had been asleep almost immediately.

Freddie frequently tried skipping gym. One of his methods was to hang around the locker room for so long that class was half over by the time he finally emerged. Jameel knew there'd been the possibility of an encounter, but he'd been too tired to care. Some time after he'd drifted off, he'd been shocked awake by somebody kicking the bottom of his sneaker. Jameel's immediate reaction had been anger, but he stayed cool.

"Hey man," the soon-to-be-dead kicker said.

Jameel's eyes opened halfway, enough for him to recognize the speaker. "Freddie. Man, if I weren't so tired, I'd kill you right here." He closed his eyes again.

Freddie had ignored the threat. "Whatcha doin', sleepin' in the locker room?"

"I'm tired. Beat it."

"Mr. Dorsey know about this?" Mr. Dorsey was Coach. Only kids who didn't play sports called him Mr. Dorsey.

"Yeah, he knows. It's cool. Now get outta here."

Freddie persisted. "Why you so tired?"

Jameel opened his eyes fully and gave him a hard look. "I'm *busy*. Look man, this is my only chance to catch up on some sleep. Leave me alone, and get *outta* here, now. I'm not gonna say it again."

Jameel, at six-foot-five and 190 pounds, easily out-sized Freddie.

They'd been friends years ago when they were little, because they both lived in the same neighborhood. As they'd gotten older, though, they'd followed different paths and had grown apart. Jameel still had some fondness and affection for Freddie, and he assumed Freddie felt likewise. This kind of threat would have worked on Freddie's friends, but not on Freddie himself. Freddie continued undaunted. "I think I can help you, man."

Jameel sighed, closed his eyes, and leaned his head back on the lockers. He highly doubted Freddie had any resources or advice that could or would help him. "How can you help me, Freddie?"

Something dropped in his lap. He'd opened his eyes and looked down at it. It was a sandwich bag, zipped closed. Inside was a small quantity of what looked like a clear, crystal, almost glass-like substance.

"What's this?"

"Crank." The word was lost on Jameel.

"What's that?"

"It'll give you energy, all you need. You won't need to sleep in the locker room."

Jameel picked it up and threw it back at him. "I'm not buying drugs from you, Freddie."

Freddie threw it back. "I'm not selling it to you. I'm giving it to you."

"Why?"

Freddie shrugged.

Jameel knew the Freddie of the past; he didn't know much about Freddie now—just that he'd become one of the "bad" kids, the kids he wanted nothing to do with. He knew their path wasn't the way out of his—or his family's—predicament. He didn't trust him—and now, of course, he knew that his instincts had been right. He should have thrown the bag back at Freddie and kicked him out of the locker room. Instead, he'd said, "There's gotta be a catch."

Freddie had spread his hands, palms open wide. "Yeah, there's a catch."

When Freddie didn't volunteer the information, Jameel had been forced to ask, "What is it?"

And then he'd said the words that eventually had haunted him: "You want more, it'll cost you."

He remembered the warnings that had flashed in the back of his mind. But his mind had been dull; he couldn't remember being this exhausted in a long time. His awareness, normally clear, had been thick and mushy, and the warning flashes hadn't been able to penetrate the fog. Instead, he thought *hey, what can it hurt? I'll never use the stuff anyway, and if I take it now, Freddie will leave me alone and let me sleep.*

He'd taken the bag. After Freddie had shown him how to use it orally or nasally (the thought of snorting brought drug movie images to his mind, and he shook with revulsion at the idea), he'd left. Jameel had been free to sleep away the rest of gym class, and after putting the stuff in his bag, he'd done just that.

The nap had helped. He woke up when everybody else started filing back into the locker room, got dressed, and went back to class. When he got home that afternoon, he'd taken the bag out of his backpack and stuffed it in his bottom dresser drawer. As usual, Mom was at work, and his brother Daryl had been watching TV. He'd gone to work and forgotten about it.

A few days later, however, he'd been in a similar predicament. He'd had a basketball game, and then he'd had to study for a Calculus test. He'd been up late the night before busing tables at Charlie Brown's, so he'd started the day at a deficit. At least it had been a home game, and they'd won it. By the time he'd gotten home at 10:30 PM, Daryl was sound asleep in the other bed, but when Jameel had cracked the books, the words and symbols blurred on the pages as his eyes became heavy. He couldn't cram anything into his brain, and this test would be hard. Mr. Valdez gave no leeway for students involved in sports; in fact, it seemed to give him perverse pleasure when a player's grades dropped low enough to prevent the student from playing.

That had never happened to Jameel, and he wouldn't let it happen now, close to the last half of his senior year. He shook his head and tried to concentrate. When that didn't work, he paced the floor and came back to it. He tried squats. He did a few push-ups. Each strategy would help for a minute or two, but eventually his body started shutting down, until he'd found himself opening his eyes, the side of his face mashed into his book, drool on the pages, at 3:00 AM.

This wasn't working. He had to focus and concentrate on the material so he could reproduce it on the test in just a few hours. How would he get through this?

That was when he'd remembered the bag in his bottom dresser drawer.

No, bad idea. Not something to be thought of, much less considered as an actual possibility. But he had a full day of school ahead of him, then basketball practice, in addition to the test. Plus he had to work again tonight. How could he get through all of that, with the way he felt now? Something would give, and it would probably be that test. He couldn't let that happen.

He'd pulled the bag out of the drawer and thrown it on the white, lined pages (college ruled, always college ruled) of his notebook. In the light of his desk lamp, the crystals shone with an eerie purity. He'd selected a small piece and turned it over in his hands. It looked harmless enough. He broke off a chunk about the size Freddie had shown him and put the rest of the piece back in the bag. Placing the chunk on his notebook, he'd stared at it for a while. It looked so small and insignificant, smaller than the Advil he took when he had a headache, smaller even than the allergy pill he sometimes needed to take in the summer. Surely such a tiny chunk couldn't hurt him.

He'd taken the chunk quietly into the bathroom, grabbed a cup of water, and without further thought, swallowed it. The deed was done. For good or for ill, he'd now find out if it would help him or kill him. He'd gone back into his room, put the bag away, and sat down at his desk again to work.

He didn't know how long he'd been studying when he'd suddenly felt a surge of energy. It had been like something outside of him had *pushed* it into him, as though he were a balloon that could feel the rush of air making it take a shape it had never taken before and could never take by itself without the air. His heart had begun pounding. He looked up from his Calculus book and stared straight ahead as the sensation traveled from his core out to his limbs, his fingertips, his toes, and bounced back again, rising in intensity. Sleep had become the furthest thing from his mind. It was working!

Apart from his unintended nap, he never slept that night.

His mother had awakened to find him just finishing cleaning all the dirty dishes in the kitchen sink. She gave him a wet, sloppy kiss on the cheek in appreciation before heading off to the shower. After cleaning up, he'd left early. He'd gotten to school early that day, aced the test, attended basketball practice, and gone to work, where everything had fallen apart.

He'd kind of felt like he'd been running out of steam when he got to work, but he'd pushed through. Somewhere around an hour after he'd started, he'd become overwhelmingly tired. He'd grabbed a rack of clean water glasses from the kitchen to restock his busing station and misjudged the location of the shelf. The entire rack of glasses had fallen to the floor, shattering most of them. He'd apologized to the waitresses and the hostess, cleaned up the mess, gone to get another rack of glasses, and dropped the second rack in the same exact way. Restaurant patrons distracted from their conversations pointed at him and whispered to themselves. This time, the manager had come out and pulled him aside.

"Hey Jameel, what's going on? You don't look so good." Jameel just stared at him with droopy eyes. "Jameel? You with me?" He'd snapped his fingers in front of his face a few times.

Jameel shook his head, trying to clear the fog. "Yeah," he croaked. "I don't feel so good."

"All right, man. Go home. We'll be okay."

"Need the money." Jameel's salary helped Mom make the rent.

"Yeah, but you're in no shape to work. Look, gimme a call tomorrow if you're feeling better, all right?" He knew Jameel was a good kid who had a lot of pressure on him.

Jameel had no energy to argue. "All right. Thanks, Mike."

"No problem. You take care of yourself."

And with that, he'd been ushered out the door. Jameel couldn't remember how he'd gotten home that night, but by some miracle, he had. He'd woken up the next day at noon, having missed a half day of school.

He'd vowed never to take the stuff again. He'd told Freddie so, and Freddie had just laughed at him.

"You didn't do it right," he'd said.

Jameel's eyes narrowed. "What do you mean?"

"You're supposed to take another hit *before* you crash like that. That way, you never crash."

"Yeah, and then I run out of stuff and come crying to you for more."

Freddie had spread his hands magnanimously in his now familiar—and annoying—gesture. "Not necessarily. Just time the crash for when you can get some rest. You crashed too early. Crash when it's convenient."

"How do I do that?"

"Well, you know what it's like now. Wait till you start getting that feeling like the wind's going out of your sails." He'd gotten that phrase from Brick and was very proud of it. "When you start feeling like that, take some more."

"Thanks for the tip, but I'm still not using any more of the stuff."

"Suit yourself. I was just trying to help you, but you know, screw it now. That stuff cost me fifty bucks, and you just disrespect me. Fine. I don't have to put myself out for you. I'm done with you, man." He turned and began walking away, in his usual Freddie swagger.

Jameel instantly felt bad; he hadn't expected Freddie to turn on him so suddenly. He couldn't make fifty dollars most nights at the restaurant—usually only on weekends. Freddie might be misguided, but maybe he'd really tried to help him the only way he knew how. Jameel caught up with him; they were both going the same way anyway—Freddie to his car, Jameel to a stroll home. "Hey Freddie, wait!"

"What?" he asked, not turning around.

"I'm sorry. I didn't know how much it was worth. I'll give it back."

"I can't take it back now," Freddie lied. "I don't know where you kept it or if it's still pure or what. Do whatever you want with it."

Jameel had caught up with him by now and slowed to walk next to him. "It's exactly how you gave it to me, except for what I took that one time. You can have it back."

Freddie stopped and turned on him. He stuck a finger out and poked Jameel in the chest. "I can tell you don't trust me anymore. Fine. I don't trust you. I'm not taking jack back from you. Did anybody else come through for you? Any teachers give you a break 'cause you're Mr. Big Shot? Coach let you skip a game? No. I'm the only one who gave you somethin' to help you keep up. We grew up together. You wanna throw my fifty bucks down the toilet, then I'm done. Don't come cryin' to me for help, ever." He began walking again toward the parking lot.

"I'm sorry, Freddie."

Freddie had kept walking. "Later, man."

Jameel had watched Freddie disappear down the path to the parking lot, and then he'd gone home. He'd skipped practice that day because he had a paper coming up for English class and he had to work that night. Christmas break was in two weeks, and he'd been looking forward to abandoning himself to the holiday, the basketball tournament, and work, with no school. But he'd had to get this paper done first.

The same thing had happened. After a few days, he'd found it difficult to balance school, sports, and work. Before long, he'd taken more of the stuff. This time, he'd let it carry him for three days, from Wednesday to Friday. By the time he'd gotten home from work late Friday night, he could feel that roughness at the edges of his consciousness, that feeling that he was losing it, that he was losing himself. He didn't like that feeling, and he almost wanted to take more of the stuff to avoid it. But he figured he really needed to get some sleep.

Instead, Mom had been up waiting for him on the couch.

"Jameel!"

Jameel looked up. "Oh hi, Mom."

Mom's eyes had widened. "Jameel, you look awful! What happened?"

Jameel remembered his surprise. "What? Nothin'. Why?"

"Take a look at yourself in the mirror." She marched him down the one hallway in their duplex, into the bathroom, and switched on the light.

Dark circles—almost bags—sat beneath his eyes. Something had happened to his cheeks: they were sunken, as though they were missing some flesh. It made his face look thinner, almost gaunt. Had he lost weight? He didn't know. He didn't feel different—just tired; very tired, and getting tireder by the minute. He decided to follow that tack with Mom.

"Yeah, Mom, I'm really tired."

"Are you sure? Do you feel sick?"

"No, Mom. I've just been really busy lately."

"Yeah, I've noticed." She switched off the light and led him back into their living room, where she sat on her easy chair. Jameel took off his jacket and put it in the closet, and then sat opposite her on the couch. "Are you sure you haven't bitten off more than you can chew?" she asked.

Talk of biting and chewing had suddenly made him feel very hungry. "No; I'm okay," he said. "I'll be glad for Christmas break, though."

"You're almost halfway there. I feel like I've hardly seen you this fall; we've both been so busy. I wanted to stay up to catch up with you. I just wanted to let you know how proud I am of you. You're working so hard. You're gonna make it; I just know it."

Jameel smiled weakly as his stomach growled. "Thanks, Mom."

She stared at him for a while, and he didn't say anything. "Well, I can see that you really need some rest. I'll let you get to bed." She got up, and he got up with her. She kissed him on the forehead. "I love you."

"I love you too, Mom."

She had turned and gone off to her room. Jameel watched her go and then followed closely after. It had been all he could do to get his shoes off before he collapsed into bed. He'd been so hungry, but he didn't care: his tiredness overwhelmed his hunger. As he drifted off, he'd searched his memory of the last few days for the time of his last meal. It came to him just as he'd been slipping into unconsciousness: he hadn't eaten in three days.

Oblivion took him.

He'd awakened around 2:00 PM on Sunday afternoon. He'd found his mother had called him out sick from work the night before, and as soon as he'd gotten up, she'd made him a big pancake breakfast. She'd even stayed home from church—her only social and spiritual outlet—so she could care for him. All he heard about all day from her was how proud of him she was and how she believed he'd go far.

It made him feel horrible.

She didn't know he'd now turned to drugs to keep up—illegal drugs most likely, though he'd long since decided not to find out exactly what Freddie had given him. He knew nothing about illegal drugs, and he didn't want an education on the topic. He couldn't be sure this would actually help him if he got in trouble, but the term *plausible deniability* had crossed his mind once or twice. Anyway, he'd started to realize that if he needed drugs to keep up with life, then life had gotten too complicated for him, and maybe he really wasn't up to the task of excelling, of being the first in his family to rise up out of simple subsistence. Maybe he was destined to be a deadbeat drunk (*addict*) like his now-deceased father or a laborer like his mother. Maybe he wasn't good enough to reach for something higher. He had realized by now that he *liked* how it felt to be high, and he knew just as well that he *shouldn't* like it. Using drugs was cheating, and no way to rise up and do better than his forebears. But no matter how many times he told himself these things, some other part of him said the opposite. Even now, he felt that if he could just take some, he'd be able to do anything. That's what it felt like.

He shook himself as he came back to the here and now, in his hospital bed. Staring back out at the gray rooftop, he actually felt thankful for what had happened. For better or for worse, the long roller coaster ride was over. He'd of course sworn off taking any more of the stuff, Christmas break had come and gone, and of course his circumstances had dictated that he needed to take it again. And of course he'd run out of what Freddie had given him and had had to buy it from him, twice. Meanwhile, he'd become more and more emaciated, less able to perform well either at basketball or at his job, and certainly less able to hide what he was doing. The straw that had broken the camel's back was when he'd had a choice: give his last dime to his mother so she could make the rent, or buy some more from Freddie.

In the end, he'd decided to try the fabled third option: give the money to Mom and beg Freddie to give him more now, and he'd pay him double at the end of the week. He'd been surprised when Freddie had agreed, but then Daryl had gotten sick over the weekend, and he'd had to take care of him instead of going to work. He'd done everything he could to avoid that confrontation this morning, because he knew he could make the money by Wednesday. But Freddie hadn't let him.

He shifted position in the bed and felt the first twinge of pain in his abdomen. There were drugs for everything, to solve every problem: drugs to deaden pain, drugs to rev you up, drugs to calm you down. He'd believed once that humans were different from animals, not so subject to the whims of every instinctual need. Now he knew differently: people *were* animals, animals smart enough to find a way to scratch every itch, satisfy every urge, or if that was impossible, descend into blissful oblivion to make the futility of their meaningless lives go away or seem unimportant. Anything that could take away awareness of that meaninglessness had value; nothing else mattered. Now he understood. He understood why his father drank, why Freddie sold drugs, and why many of his friends cared about nothing except the next party. He'd thought he was different, but he wasn't.

He was just like them.

He found the remote control wired to his bed and pressed the button to call the nurse. It was time for more drugs.

24

∞∞∞∞∞∞

2:00 PM

Sal went back into his house and sat down on his couch. The interview with the cops had been interminable. He'd been surprised himself, actually, at what he didn't know. *Do you know the individual who owns the property you were headed to?* No, Officer. He called me out of the blue, said he found me on Google. *Have you ever done business with him before?* No. *How do you know the guy would pay you?* He gave me a credit card number; I ran it and it said he had enough credit to cover my estimate. *Do you have the credit card number?* Yeah; I can get it. *Have you ever been to the location before?* No, I used my GPS this morning to get me there. *Can you think of anyone who would want to do this to you? Someone who doesn't like you?* No, I honestly can't. *Can you think of anyone who has something against your customer?* I don't know the customer; we've only spoken on the phone. *When did you last speak to him?* Today, after I replaced my equipment.

They'd examined his broken plastic tie—and berated him for contaminating the evidence by touching it. They'd examined his truck. They'd tested his current setup. The process had taken so long that he'd ordered lunch—Chinese, normally reserved for dinners—while they'd pored over his truck and his driveway. Finally, in the middle of his General Tso's Chicken, they'd decided to interview him again. They double-teamed him, not with good cop and bad cop, but with neutral cop and silent cop: a big guy with sandy blond hair and a mustache, and a short, balding but muscular guy. At least it was only an interview; they'd let him sit on his couch and eat while they stood. Short Guy did most of the talking; they'd started with a not-so-neutral question.

"What made you jump to the conclusion that this was an act of sabotage?"

"I've been doing this for a long time, Officer—" he looked at his name tag, "Ferrelli. I've never had this happen to me before. I also tested my plastic ties before I called you by trying to break them myself."

"Okay. So let's go over everything from the beginning. You got a call a week ago from this guy, uh—"

"Roger Blackfield," put in his partner, looking at his notebook.

"Yeah," said Sal. "He called me and left a message on my machine because I was on a job. I use my cell for my calls, but all my advertising uses this land line, and I let it go to the machine if I'm not here, which I'm usually not. When I got home, I called him back." Sal paused, looking up at them. Since they didn't respond, he figured he should continue. "He said he owned this building, a row of townhouses that he rents. One of them's vacant, and he has a possible tenant, but he needs the plumbing fixed. He lives in Florida in the winter, but in the summer, he stays in Ocean City. He owns a bunch of properties that he rents, he said."

"And you've never worked with him before?"

"No. He said the guy he was using retired, and that this was my chance. If I did a good job on this one, he'd have lots of other work for me."

"Okay, so that was your motivation, right?"

"Yeah. Usually I go look at the job so I can give an estimate. But he's not there; he's in Florida. He wanted the estimate on the spot from his description."

"That's unusual, isn't it?"

"Yeah."

"So why'd you do it?"

"I didn't do it, really. I told him I could only give him a ballpark figure. You know, it could be this much, or it could be this much more."

"What did he say?"

"He said it sounded reasonable. He gave me his credit card number and I checked to make sure he had enough on there for the big number, and he did. So I figured, hey, this could be good for me, and there didn't seem to be much risk. I'll give it a shot."

"Okay, so what was the job?"

"Can I ask you a question?"

"Sure."

"What's this got to do with somebody vandalizing my truck and my stuff?"

"Sal, you've given us nothing to go on. You have no idea who could have done it, and you say you have no enemies. So either it wasn't vandalism or sabotage, or maybe somebody doesn't like this Blackwell guy."

"Blackfield," said his partner.

"Yeah, him. So just tell me everything you can about this guy and the job, okay?"

"All right," said Sal. "Like I said, I only heard about it on the phone; I ain't seen it yet."

"That's fine; just tell us what you know."

"The guy said he was there at Christmas last year. Something about visiting family for Christmas. While he was up here, his tenant called with a busted pipe in the kitchen. He went there and shut the water off, and I think he tried calling his other guy, but he got the runaround. Finally, he tried to fix it himself, but he didn't get nowhere. Said it was his worst Christmas ever."

"I'll bet."

"Yeah. Anyway, he said the unit next door was empty, so he had the tenant move into that one, and he just left it vacant, with the water shut off. It's been that way for a year now."

"A year?"

"Yeah; he said he just left it vacant. He had other stuff to do or something."

"Did he actually say that?"

"No, I guess I'm assuming that. I didn't ask why."

"Why not?"

"The guy's asking for my business. And his business is none of my business, you get me? I just need the information for what I need to do, you know? The facts."

"Okay, so what happened next?"

"Nothing much. I told him I'd do the job, and I scheduled it for this week. He told me where to find the key to the place, and I got supplies on Saturday, 'cause I wanted to start first thing this morning."

"So what happened this morning?"

"Well, there was a traffic jam. It's Monday, you know? I got off 55 and tried to go around it. I was on 47 in Westville, and I hit a pothole, a big one. When that happened, all my pipes just fell off the truck. I couldn't believe it. I caused at least one accident. The Westville cops were there; there's got to be a report."

"Yeah, we're looking into that."

"I know one lady had to go to the hospital. I feel real bad about that. I couldn't understand what happened."

"Okay, try to focus on just the facts. What did you do next?"

"I went right back to the supply place and re-bought all the stuff I thought I'd need for the job."

"You did that first, before calling this, uh, Blackdown back?"

"Blackfield," said his partner.

"Yeah. I figured while they were getting my order, I could call him while I waited, you know?"

"Okay, what did Blackburn say?"

"Blackfield!" said his partner.

"I didn't want to tell him everything that happened, you know? So I just said I'd been in a car accident this morning, but I was okay and that I'd get on the job this afternoon instead of this morning. He was expecting me to give him a more firm estimate, see, once I got there, so I had to call him."

"What did he say?"

"He said 'come back tomorrow.'"

"Really? That's what he said?"

"Yeah. He said the job could wait another day, that I should recuperate."

"You told him you had all the stuff and all you had to do was go back there?"

"Yeah."

"That doesn't make any sense."

"I know, right? He don't know me; this is business. I got all day; I probably coulda still finished the job. I told him that."

"And what did he say?"

"He said the job had waited this long; it could wait another day."

"What did you say to that?"

"Well, now I can think of all kinds of stuff I coulda said. But I'm not so good on the spot. I just said 'okay.'"

"And that was it."

"Yeah, that was it. I guess I'm going there tomorrow. And now that this happened, I probably lost the whole day, because I don't know if I can move one of my other jobs up. It's gonna screw up the whole week."

"Can you think of anything else he said that seemed out of place?"

Sal thought for a moment and then said, "No, why? Are you gonna call him?"

"Yeah, if you want us to look into this."

"Actually, no, I don't."

"*What?* Why?"

"'Cause if you call the guy, maybe he doesn't want to answer a bunch of questions. Maybe he doesn't want the cops calling him. He ain't done nothing wrong. And he may not want me to do the job no more. It could be more trouble than it's worth. He can just get another guy."

"Wait, so you're saying now that you don't want us to look into this?"

Sal thought a moment, his head down. "Yeah, forget it. Not if you're gonna call the guy and ask him a bunch of questions. I don't like the way this whole thing went. I thought you could test the tie or find a hair with DNA or something."

Officer Ferrelli sighed. "That's TV, Sal. That's not the real world." He and his partner looked at each other, and some silent communication passed between them. "You've just basically wasted our time and yours if you do this. What if something else happens? What if you or somebody else really gets hurt this time?"

An image of Mary sitting in her car, with that goose egg forming on her forehead, rose vividly in his mind. It felt like a smack in the face.

"Somebody already did get hurt," he said, "and it wasn't me. No, maybe this was just a random thing. If somebody had wanted to hurt me, they probably woulda done something else." He looked up at them. "I'm sorry for wasting your time. It's probably nothing."

"You know we're still going to have to file a report."

"Yeah, I know. But that report will get filed, and then nobody will look at it again, right?"

"Maybe. If something else happens, and it becomes a criminal investigation, they will. And then you won't be able to say anything about who's calling anybody, get it?"

"Yeah, I get it. But nothing's gonna happen."

"Okay, Sal; if that's the way you want it. No guarantees, though; we may still follow up on this."

"Please don't. It might affect my livelihood."

"No guarantees."

The partner closed the notebook he'd been writing in, and both officers showed themselves out without a further word. Sal looked at the cold Chinese food sitting on his coffee table while he listened to them pack up and eventually drive away.

It *was* weird. Why would the guy not want him to just do the job today, if he was willing to do it? He looked at the clock: 2:15 PM. There might still be time to get the job done. He didn't want the cops calling Blackfield, but surely Sal could call him and discuss it, right? He wouldn't get offended by that, would he?

Time to find out.

He pulled his phone out of his pocket, scrolled through the numbers in his recent calls list, and dialed the one he recognized as Roger Blackfield's. The phone rang twice before he answered.

"Hello?"

"Hey, Mr. Blackfield, this is Sal Fuchetti."

"Hey, Sal! How's it going?"

"I'm good. Hey, you remember I called you earlier, right?"

"Yeah, you said you'd been in a car accident and you couldn't do the job today. You gonna make it tomorrow, or are you calling to cancel that too?"

Sal saw stars, like he'd been punched in the eye. That wasn't what he'd said—not at all. Blackfield had told him not to come; he knew that, as sure as he knew his own name. There was absolutely no way he'd ever said he couldn't make it. But how could he communicate that? He had no idea.

"Uh, yeah, um, I don't remember saying that," he mumbled.

"Yeah, that's what you said. You said you had a car accident, that you hit your head, but it wasn't bad, and you thought you'd be fine to do the job tomorrow."

"There, uh, must be some misunderstanding."

"Yeah, and there must be some kind of mistake. Don't quote song lyrics to me, man. What's going on?"

Sal decided to be frank. "I was actually calling to tell you I was still ready to do the job *today*, because I thought you said to just come back tomorrow."

"No way I would've said that. I want this done. And I remember you

147

explicitly saying to me that you couldn't do the job today."

"I'm sorry, sir, but there's no way I would've said *that*. I'm perfectly fine; I didn't hit my head."

"What is this? Are you screwing around with me? I don't really need you, you know. There are, like, a hundred other plumbers I could call. I have a schedule to keep! I already have a call in to my contractor to reschedule him for later in the week!"

Sal thought furiously. How could he salvage the situation? "I don't know what happened, Mr. Blackfield, but I do good work, and I stand by it. I was in a car accident this morning, but I wasn't hurt. I called you after, to let you know why I'd be late in giving you an accurate estimate for the work, and what I remember you saying is not to worry about it, to rest up, and do the job tomorrow."

"And I'm telling you, there's no way I ever said that. I've got somebody who wants to rent that apartment next week. I needed the plumbing fixed today, because I've got a guy tomorrow—wait a minute; I'm getting another call."

Click. Just like that, he'd been thrown into the abyss of *on hold*. Sal couldn't believe this. How could he have had one conversation, but the customer had had a completely different conversation? It made no sense. Could they have talked past each other to such an extent? He didn't think so. Something else was going on; this was too weird.

Click. "Okay, I'm back. It appears that you have a reprieve. That was my other guy who's replacing the drywall and floor where there's water damage. He can do Wednesday. Unlike you, *he* is a guy I've done business with for years, who I can trust. The jury's still out on you, and now you have one strike. Get there tomorrow, and get it done."

"That's all I've wanted to do since you hired me. I really don't know what happened."

"Yeah, well, I don't have time for games or any other nonsense. I can be your best friend or your worst enemy. I've got, like eight other properties that need work. You treat me right, I treat you right, get it?"

"Yeah, I get it. I'm sorry for what happened. The job will get done; you can count on me." He lamented his words as soon as he said them. Now he sounded like some kid's cartoon. He wished he could say the right thing in the moment, but his tongue always seemed to get tied up.

"Yeah; we'll see. Gimme a call when you know how much it's gonna really cost."

"Yeah; okay. Thank you." Was he really thanking Blackfield for chewing him out? Yes. Yes, he was.

"Yeah; I'll wait to hear from you. Later."

Blackfield didn't wait for Sal to say goodbye; he hung up.

Sal threw his phone onto the coffee table and hung his head in his hands as it clattered across the surface and then dropped to the carpet below. Wow; he'd almost lost the guy's business. How could he have been so far off? In all his years as a union plumber and now a union contractor, he'd never had a conversation go so wrong like this before, not in all his years of experience.

He closed his eyes and began to replay his earlier conversation, the one from outside the plumber's supply store, in his head. It had been noisy with traffic from outside, and he'd been trying to avoid the cigarette smoke clouds from other guys who had been waiting, but he hadn't thought he'd been all that distracted.

The conversation had been different, almost cordial. Blackfield had actually shown concern for him—unwarranted concern, but concern nonetheless. Sal had tried to convince him that he really could do the job today. And then it hit him. He sat up, straight as an arrow, eyes wide.

The voice wasn't the same. It was similar, but the Blackfield he'd spoken to earlier today wasn't the same Blackfield who'd just hung up on him. He'd spoken to two different people. And then suddenly, another realization hit him so hard he stood up.

Blackfield could have spoken to a different Sal Fuchetti.

25

∞∞∞∞∞

2:30 PM

Pastor Sean Peterson checked his watch. "It's late; I only have a short time before I start my real shift, and I want to pass through intensive care first." He pushed out his chair and gave his mouth a last wipe with his napkin.

"Real shift?" asked Dan.

"Oh yeah. It was totally coincidence—" He decided to correct himself. "—or *providence*, I suppose, that I'm here at all. I'm just filling in for someone else. I'm not usually here at this time. I usually volunteer in the afternoon."

"*What?*" exclaimed Margaret.

Sean smiled. "It's true." He threw his napkin on his tray and stood, reaching into his pocket. "Here's my contact info," he said, handing them each a business card. "If you need anything, please call me."

As they exchanged handshakes—along with a hug from Margaret—Colin asked, "Hey, uh, I hope this isn't imposing or anything, but would you mind if I tagged along? I have the rest of the day off and would enjoy the opportunity to see your ministry personally. I promise I'll be quiet and unobtrusive."

"I would like that very much. In the multitude of counselors there is safety, after all."

"Proverbs 11:14. But I'm not sure I get you."

"Let's just say that religious ministrations are offered, but not always accepted. I won't confirm or deny that I've actually had things thrown at me, but, uh, vigorous rejections of my services are somewhat common. It would be nice to have someone else with me; it may reduce the chance of being pelted."

"Ah, got it."

They said their goodbyes. Margaret and Dan went one way toward the lobby and outside, while Sean and Colin went the opposite way toward the elevators. As they rode up, they had the car to themselves.

"I don't know what we'll find when we get up there," Sean said. "I'm sure a lot of people were affected by that car accident. There may be some distraught families. You sure you're up for this?"

"No, not really. But getting out of your comfort zone is really the best way to grow."

"Wise words," Sean said as the elevator door opened.

They passed through the waiting area. The hallway in Intensive Care was narrower than everywhere else. Fewer voices could be heard as well, because the machinery was louder. Unlike everywhere else in the hospital, he heard no voices except at the station, where Sean checked in with a nurse to see whom he might visit. As they proceeded down the first hallway, the difference in activity made it seem ominous.

"Right here," Sean indicated an ajar door. Knocking three times, he poked his head in.

A woman, blond, probably in her mid-to-late forties, sat next to a bed containing a figure bound up in many contraptions. She'd had her head in her hands, but looked up. His eyes widened: the woman from the café.

"Yes?"

Sean recited the line he'd prepared for this moment: "I'm Sean Peterson, a minister on staff with the hospital. Would a pastoral visit bring you comfort at this time?"

26

2:45 PM EST/11:45 AM PST

Jenny ended the call with her mom just as Emma walked through the door. Relief washed over Emma's face as she sprinted over to give Jenny a hug. Words no longer worked for today; too much had happened. Both girls simply held each other and sobbed. They cried for themselves; they cried for each other, and as they cried, they realized that this day was a marker. For the rest of their lives, they'd measure events by whether they happened before today or after today. Today had irrevocably altered them. The people they were yesterday had disappeared, transformed into the people they were now, and now every day would be different. The world would not be the same place it had been, and no matter how closely their future lives resembled the patterns of their former ones, they would never be the same people they were yesterday.

When they finally disengaged, they saw the drain of this day in their faces. Hollowed, red eyes and runny noses replaced the freshness that used to be—should have been—there. But the tears had somehow been cleansing. They hadn't cleared away the burden of the future, but they had washed away the immediacy of its overwhelmingness, leaving space to examine the events of the day.

"I'll get us some tissues," Jenny said, getting up to retrieve some from the bathroom.

"Maybe neither of us should've gone to class today," Emma said.

Jenny let out a small chuckle. "At least your class wasn't in the same building as the shooting." She paused, looking at the floor, then looked up. "Do you know who it was?"

Emma shook her head. "No. I have no idea. From where I was, you could hear the gunshots but you couldn't see anything." She grunted. "I bet Tina is already getting the whole story."

"What do you mean?"

"She went to lunch early. She said she was hungry."

Jenny sniffed. "I was surprised they lifted the lockdown so quickly."

"There's nothing worse than a bunch of people trapped in a building they don't want to be in. Multiply that by the number of buildings on campus, and I think they did the right thing. They let us out as soon as they had the situation under control. If they had waited, more people would've been hurt."

"I guess you're right."

"I know I'm right. You weren't there. People were packed into the stairwells. They were screaming, crying—" Emma's voice broke and she stopped. "It was awful."

"This whole day has been awful." Jenny began to cry again.

Emma came over and sat down next to her. "Did you get some news?"

"Yeah. Dad's had multiple spinal injuries. They've done surgery, repaired what they can. But they won't know how he is until he wakes up. He could pull through, or he could be paralyzed; we just don't know."

"That's it? That's all they could tell you?"

"Yeah, that's it. I know he's alive, but whether he's—" Jenny's voice caught, and she paused, fanning air into her eyes, as though that would really dry them. She sniffed so hard her ears popped, and she tried to continue. "—whether he's the same Dad I grew up with—" The flood spilled over; despite her best efforts, she couldn't continue. She sobbed again, her head in her hands. Emma put an arm around Jenny, and she leaned on Emma's shoulder.

Emma tried to think of something to say, but nothing came to mind, though she desperately wished for the right words. She sat and held Jenny for a while—long enough to get lost in her own thoughts. It hadn't occurred to her that she'd ever go through what she went through this morning. School shootings happened in far away places, to other people. And Jenny's dad, in the same day: what were the chances of that, of both happening on the same day? One in a thousand? One in a million?

Just then the door burst open, startling both of them.

"You're not gonna believe this!" Tina yelled, her mouth half-full of something she was chewing.

Jenny turned to Emma, "We really need to learn to lock our door." Emma managed a wan smile, but it wasn't enough to break the additional tension Tina had brought into the room.

If Tina had noticed any tension, however, she didn't give any indication.

"Oh fine; I'll just go somewhere else then," she said, swallowing, as Emma observed the object in Tina's left hand: a half-eaten hot dog. "You two clearly can't appreciate news like this."

She made as if to turn and leave the way she came when Jenny said, "Stop! I'm sorry, Tina; it was a bad joke. What do you have to say?"

That was all the encouragement Tina needed. She spoke quickly. "I went to the cafeteria, and of course they weren't ready for us. I don't know what I was thinking going in there, but they didn't have anything ready because they were all on lockdown just like us. Some lockdown, by the way. Isn't everybody supposed to stay in the classroom and not panic and try to get out like they did?"

Emma chose not to remind Tina that she also had tried to flee with most of the class. Tina continued, "Well anyway, the staff was just getting back to making lunch, but excitement like that makes me hungry, so I got one of the workers to make me a hot dog." She held up the remains of the hot dog that she still held.

Jenny felt impatience rising within her, and she tried to tamp it down. "Nice," she said. Tina was Emma's friend; Jenny didn't really like her all that much. Tina's self-importance knew no bounds, and she tried too hard to insert herself into everything. And here she was, doing it again, proving Jenny's assessment of her character. Jenny wanted her to leave. Now.

"Yeah, score, right? I mean, people were starting to trickle in, and they were probably hungry too, right, or they wouldn't be in the cafeteria, and here I was with the only food in the room!"

"Nice," Jenny said, a little more impatiently.

"Well, I was planning to just sit down and hang out there, you know? I figured somebody would come in, somebody who'd had a class in Wheeler Hall— Hey Emma, didn't you say Jenny had a class there this morning?"

"I didn't go," Jenny said with some tension.

"Oh yeah, right, right. Something about your dad." She paused a moment, her eyes toward the ceiling, reflecting, and then blurted, "Your dad! Right! How is he?"

Emma noticed Jenny's balled fists and intervened. "She doesn't know very much yet. He's alive, but he's in a coma."

"Oh, that's terrible. I'm so sorry to hear that." Being sorry seemed also to fuel her hunger, because she popped the remaining bit of hot dog into her mouth and began chewing slowly. Jenny's face began to take on a pinkish hue.

Emma stood and faced Tina. "So that's it? That's your story?"

"Of course not!" she said, still chewing. "I was just getting to the good part." She took her time, finished chewing, and swallowed hard. "It's hard to tell a story on an empty stomach. That was one of the best hot dogs I ever had. Do you think the intensity of an experience can somehow make everything else—like a hot dog—seem more real or alive somehow?"

A small, not so nice growl escaped from Jenny's throat. "I don't know," Emma said. "Why don't you continue with what you were telling us?"

"Right, right." She produced a napkin from her pocket and wiped her mouth. "Well, after I got the hot dog, I turned around and ran right into Vern!"

Jenny looked confused, and Emma explained, "Veronica Stapleton, or Miss Stapleton, I guess. She tells us all to call her Vern. She's the English department clerk. The English department is in Wheeler Hall." Emma and Tina were both English majors. "I don't believe half the stories she tells, but she's been here a long time."

"She doesn't look that old," Tina said.

"Trust me; it's all as fake as the pound of makeup she puts on her face." Emma's father was a successful plastic surgeon. "Vern likes to tell all kinds of crazy stories about the English department, stories about professor-student relationships, wild parties, you name it. She also mothers the students a lot, so most of them like her. I don't."

"Oh, Vern's fine," Tina said. "She puts on a good show, that's all. I'm sure she gets a kick every year out of shocking a bunch of freshmen. I bet most of those stories aren't even true, but when she's done telling them those kids are putty in her hands."

"That's manipulation!" said Emma.

"Works for her," said Tina. "She could stay quiet and just do her job and go home, or she can make it a little more interesting by providing a little intrigue. Whether it's fake or not doesn't matter. It's the experience that counts."

"Whatever you say," said Emma. "So what did she tell you?"

"She was there!" Tina exclaimed. "I got it all from the horse's mouth!"

"Well, spit it out!"

Tina didn't need further encouragement: she responded in a torrent of words. "It was Donald! You know, Dr. Maitland's graduate student?" She paused while Emma shook her head. "Oh, come on! The betting pool guy! You don't know about the betting pool?" she asked as Emma shook her head again.

"See, that's what you get for *not* talking to Vern. You're just out of the loop." Tina paused to let that sink in, and it seemed to, because Emma looked away. She continued, "Okay, here's the deal. Vern's been running a betting pool on this guy. Everybody knows Dr. Maitland is retiring at the end of the year, and he's got this one lone graduate student left. He's been working on his dissertation for, like 10 years or something like that. I don't know what the topic is, but I do know that he and Dr. Maitland disagreed on it. Maitland thought the topic was too broad and needed extensive research using original sources in England; Donald thought differently. Maitland let him pursue it to let him learn the hard way or something like that, and they've been going back and forth on it for a decade.

"Vern says that Dr. Maitland expected this guy to drop the topic years ago and do something else, but he's been tenacious. So when Maitland announced his retirement, Vern started a pool for people to bet on whether this guy will finish before Maitland retires. You guys know the stakes, right? If he finishes, he gets his Ph.D and all is well. If he doesn't, he has to find another adviser and basically start over. Ten years of his life wasted and gone."

"I'm guessing this guy figured he wasn't going to make it?" Jenny asked.

"Actually it gets better than that. Apparently last week, Dr. Maitland informed him that he'd be retiring a semester early."

"Oh no," said Emma.

"Oh yes. He's got heart issues or something, and his doctor told him to get rid of stress, and I guess Donald topped the list."

"Oh no," Emma said again.

"Apparently, he just walked out without saying anything. That was Friday. He must've just snapped over the weekend, because he came into the department this morning with two handguns, one in each pocket, like it was the wild west or something."

"Oh no!" Emma said for the third time.

Tina ignored her, as her story gained momentum. "Vern said he came in, and she knew right away something was off. Wild eyes, or something. He had both hands in his pockets, and she knew they weren't empty. He was looking around a lot, his eyes darting back and forth." Jenny could see Tina was really getting into it now, and she began to talk faster. "He asked her if Dr. Maitland was in, which also sounded off to her because she knew that he knew his schedule. I mean, he's been working with the guy for 10 years; he's gotta know when he's in because he's gotta meet with him on a regular basis, right?

"Vern said she initially thought maybe he had doubts or didn't want to go through with it or something, but when she told him yes, Dr. Maitland was in, he started heading for his office right away. And this is the scary part: you know what he did next? Can you guess? You're not gonna be able to guess."

"No idea," said Emma. Jenny stared ahead, eyes vacant, incredulous at Tina's ability to put aside the horror of the shooting to try to get the most out of telling the story. She clearly enjoyed telling it, and likely would enjoy telling it all day.

Tina continued. "Okay, don't try to guess. She said he turned back, looked her in the eye, and said, 'I know about the pool. I'm gonna want to talk to you after I talk to him.'"

Emma gasped. "No way!"

"Yeah, can you believe it? But Vern watched him as he went into Dr. Maitland's office: he had to take his left hand out of his pocket to open the door, and she saw the gun."

"What did she do?"

"She said she screamed. He went in and closed the door anyway, and then she heard the shots."

"So he killed Dr. Maitland?"

"Apparently. Vern didn't wait around to find out. She said she started screaming, 'Gun! Gun!' and got the heck out of there. She heard more shots after she left, but she was down the hall by then and into the stairwell. She said she just kept screaming 'Gun!' over and over and started a stampede of people leaving the building."

"I saw it," said Emma.

"You did?" asked Tina. "How?"

"I stayed in the classroom like I was supposed to, and Dr. Li and I watched from the window. Of course, I was too far away to see who anybody was."

"Oh. Well, between you and me, all those lockdown drills where they tell you to stay put are a bunch of crap. You stay in the room and you're a sitting duck."

"Whatever." There was no point in debating her on a side topic in the middle of the story. "So what happened next?"

Tina spoke again, at first a little off-balance, but she recovered quickly. "Vern ran outside, and people came streaming out of the building with her. She said she just kept running and running and running."

Tina stopped.

"That's it?" asked Emma.

"Yeah; pretty much."

"Does she know what happened after that?"

"She didn't say anything. Why? Do you know what happened?"

"I was watching everything from the window, remember?"

"Did something happen after that? What is it!?"

"The guy—Donald, I guess—leaned out the window and started shooting into the crowd outside the building."

"No way!"

"Yes, he did. Do you think he was trying to find Vern?"

Tina's mouth clicked shut. Her eyes tilted up and to the left as she tried to remember the details of her story, and then she spoke, "You think he was trying to make good on his threat? To get her next?"

"I can't think of what else it could be."

Jenny broke in. "Wait, wait. We don't know that. A guy who thinks it's a good idea to shoot his adviser is obviously not thinking rationally."

"Unless it was all in cold blood," Emma said.

"What do you mean?" asked Tina.

"Well, think about it. He's fighting with his adviser for what, almost a decade? Then the adviser quits on him? That's a lot of pent up anger and frustration right there. Add that to his knowledge that Vern was running a betting pool on him. He hated them. Hated them both. He set out to murder them both in cold blood, and the only reason Vern survived is that he wanted to do Dr. Maitland first." Emma's words chilled Jenny, and she shivered.

"No, he wasn't like that," said Tina. "I thought he was nice."

"Nice!" exclaimed Jenny. "How well did you know this guy?"

"Well, we went out a couple times."

"*What?*" Emma said.

"He's, like, ten years older than you!" Jenny said at the same time.

Tina continued, unabashed. "It was no big deal, really. Casual. I wasn't even sure if they were dates. The first time was coffee; the second time was burgers, because he wanted to introduce me to In-N-Out. We went Dutch the first time; he paid the second time. I never saw where he lived, and he knew I lived on campus. Nothing ever got serious or even romantic, really."

"*Really?*" Emma asked, her right eyebrow raised.

"Really! Okay, he kissed me when we said goodbye the second time, but it was just a quick peck on the cheek. Nothing to write home about. And it was all before the break."

"Did he call you when you were home? To wish you a happy Hanukkah or something?" Jenny asked, interested now.

"No."

"Text?"

Tina rolled her eyes. "No, nothing, nothing like that. No contact since last semester. I swear!" She added that last sentence because of Emma's glare.

"Tina, I think you need to go down and see the cops," said Emma.

"Why?"

"Because you knew him! Certainly you can add something, some detail about this by being a witness!"

"Oh, that's ridiculous! I barely knew the guy. We had a couple conversations over coffee and burgers, way before all this happened. It has nothing to do with what happened today."

Jenny broke in, not necessarily with real concern for Tina, but wanting to pile on. "How do you know? He could've told you something—some detail—months ago that would point to some reason for this!"

"But he didn't! I would remember!"

"Are you sure? Cops are trained to interrogate you and ask you questions all sorts of different ways, to help you remember details you'd never remember by thinking about it yourself."

"Oh, please; give me a break!" Tina groaned.
"You have to go to the police," said Emma.
"You have to go," said Jenny.
"Nope. No way. I'm not going."

The argument went on for about ten more minutes, and eventually Jenny and Emma prevailed.

27
∞∞∞∞∞

2:45 PM

At first, Greta thought the doctor had come back, but this man was younger, handsomer. It took a second, but then she recognized him from the café. After he spoke, though, her heart sank. This man was not here to help. This man represented everything that she opposed: the merciless, dishonest preying upon the weak-minded or those at their weakest. This man stood for an entrenched, male-dominated hierarchy that had taken advantage of the weak and helpless for generations. Promising help and comfort, they offered nothing of substance, siphoning money, service, devotion, and respect from those who knew no better.

She'd devoted her life and her research to opposing them.

The timing, of course, was terrible, but typical. She should've expected something like this to happen, when she was at her lowest. That's when they came. That's when they took advantage. Up to now, she'd never interacted with one of these guys directly; they'd always found some way to weasel out of an interview or a questionnaire. But now she had one, and she could tell him exactly what she thought of him.

But she was so tired. It had been an exhausting day, and she was physically and emotionally drained. This would not be the thing she'd choose to do right now. In fact, she'd come close to dozing off a few minutes ago. Yet as she thought of the life ahead of her, the truncated life of a care-giver, she realized this might be her last—her only—chance to actually talk to one of these guys who had been avoiding her attempts at interviews for her research. If she couldn't be involved in the day to day analysis of her work, David would publish, even though this was her project, not his. Because he'd be free to lecture, to present at conferences, to be *in her world*, he'd wind up with all the credit. When a reporter wanted a quote or a fellow researcher wanted to discuss the comparison between faith-based and secular initiatives in addiction, child care, and crisis pregnancy, they'd go to him. When religious people, because they could not ignore her work, finally did want to talk about outcomes, they'd contact him, not her.

This could be her only chance to test her point of view firsthand. Despite her exhaustion, she decided to go for it.

He'd just asked her if a visit would bring her comfort. She thought the best strategy was to be coy at first: "I don't know, sir, what would you say?"

"May we come in?"

"How many are you?"

"Just myself and a colleague."

"Sure."

They entered. The first—the handsome one—was tall, with dark brown hair, piercing blue eyes, and professionally dressed, with a jacket hooked over his arm. The second was shorter, portly, balding, with glasses. Both men, of course.

She decided to take charge immediately. "I'm sorry; I already forgot your name."

The taller one, concern in his face, immediately stuck out his hand. "I'm Sean Peterson, a chaplain on staff here at the hospital and pastor of Living Waters Independent Reformed Church."

She almost snorted. The names of these organizations were an incomprehensible mix of the poetic and impenetrable. How could anybody pick a church when their very names made no sense? She realized her thoughts had interrupted her for too long, and she—very late—took his hand. He shook hers gently, grasping only her fingers.

The other man spoke. "I'm Colin Donnell. I'm just a friend of the pastor's here." He stood back and didn't offer his hand. He seemed uncomfortable.

She went all out. "I'm Greta Stratton-Foster; *Doctor* Greta Stratton-Foster. Rowan University Sociology department. I have to say, I'm not a religious person, and so I'm not optimistic you'll have anything to say to give me comfort." Getting back into the world of logic and debate felt better; more familiar. She sat up straighter.

Sean smiled. "Why did you agree to visit with us then?"

She decided to remain coy. "Curiosity."

"Fair enough."

He shifted his jacket to the other arm, and Colin shuffled his feet uncomfortably. She couldn't blame them: the bed dominated the room, leaving little space for anything else. She had the only chair. Gerald's equipment chirped and beeped.

Sean indicated the bed. "What happened?"

"My husband had a spectacular car accident this morning. He broke his spine and is in a coma. The doctors aren't sure when he'll wake up, if he'll be paralyzed, or how bad it could be. My life, for all intents and purposes, is in limbo." She snorted for real this time. It was unbelievable how much religiosity permeated the English language. "I suppose that's a religious term. Do you believe in limbo, Pastor?"

As she spoke, his face filled with amazement, then with concern. She couldn't tell it from real concern or an act. When he spoke, he spoke matter-of-factly: "No, I don't believe in limbo—either the theological limbo or the limbo of life."

"Well, I don't know anything about the theological limbo, but the limbo of life, as you say, now seems to be my reality. Thus, our first area of disagreement. Your move, Pastor." She crossed her arms across her chest.

"Move? Like a chess game?" A warning stab hit his low spine.

"Isn't it?"

"Not on my part. I volunteer here; this is not a paid position. I see and hear horrific things every week, and I try to offer hope and help to people going through traumatic situations. It is most definitely not a game to me."

"Okay; proceed. Enlighten me with what you could possibly do or say to 'help.'"

Colin looked uneasy. Sean cleared his throat uncomfortably and asked, "Can you tell me why you believe your life is in limbo?"

"Isn't it obvious? I'm a professor and a researcher. My work is important to me. I have many students. I'm about to publish an important study, incidentally, one that compares outcomes of so-called faith-based non-profits with those that simply try to help people without all that baggage. Now my husband, because he was late for a meeting, went and did something stupid, and because I'm the spouse, the wife, I'm expected by society to nurse him back to health, regardless of the circumstances to my own life. It isn't fair to me."

"What would be fair?"

"I was just thinking about that before you came in. As usual, a socialist solution would work: if there were a provided service, I could send him there to be cared for by professionals. I could continue my work and visit him. It would be the best of both worlds, really."

"Does that thought give you comfort?"

"Yes it does. Unfortunately, such a system doesn't exist in this country."

"The services exist; you just have to pay for them."

"And therein lies the problem. It's part of why we need change, and why my research is so important. I must be able to continue my work, and yet because I can't afford those services, this responsibility falls on me. Yet I am not a skilled caretaker, and taking this on means the skills I do have to offer society, that I have spent my life developing, now must go to waste."

"I'm no expert on medical service, but I'm sure there are home health aides and other services your insurance provides that'll be there to help."

"Oh, for sure, but those things won't prevent putting a hold on my life."

"Don't you love your husband?"

She almost reeled. That was the question of the day, wasn't it? This morning, Gerald had been almost a non-thought, a far away and sometimes convenient, sometimes inconvenient truth. He didn't interfere with the part of her life that mattered most—her professional life—and she didn't interfere with his. She had married him, so she knew she had loved him once.

Greta paused, struggling with what to say without making herself vulnerable. She already hated this guy for derailing what she wanted to talk about and making this about her. "Honestly, I've been thinking about that a lot today, and I'm not sure. I think I did once. But we don't have a lot that connects us anymore. We sort of live separate lives under the same roof. He's very focused on his job and so am I."

"Do you have any children?" he asked. Again, he was making this about her. She had to figure out how to turn this conversation to where it was safe and knock him down a few pegs. If she could get him to talk about himself, she might be able to turn the discussion to what she wanted to talk about.

"Yes. A daughter. She's a freshman at UC Berkeley," she said.

"UC Berkeley. The one on the news?"

"Yes, the very same. She's all right, and thank you for asking. Right now, she's not pertinent to our discussion."

Sean paused, struggling to balance sensitivity with frankness. He decided, since she claimed to be so logical, to go with an examination of the facts. "Okay, so let me summarize. You're obviously a very intelligent person, focused on your career and work, so I'll try to be analytic about this. You and your husband have successfully raised a daughter who is now off to college. You find now that that's done, you don't have much in common anymore, and so you're both focused on your areas of interest. Your husband was in an accident this morning due to his focus on his work. You're angry about this because of its effect on you. He was solely focused on himself without regard to the possible consequences to you. You are reluctant to make career sacrifices for him, since he was unwilling to sacrifice his career to keep the family status quo. This shows that perhaps his love for you is also not what it once was. Because you're not sure if the foundation of your marriage—love—is viable anymore, you can't find motivation to forgive his terrible mistake of this morning and share in its consequences. Is that about it?" Sean stopped, not sure if he should say any more.

A flash of anger welled up, reddening her face. She hated giving people cues to her inner thoughts like this, but she couldn't help it: he'd made her angry. Sean saw this and immediately worried if he'd gone too far.

Greta almost stood, but settled for putting the heels of her hands on the chair's sides. "No, that's *not* it. I don't believe anyone should be forced into a lifestyle that prevents their self-actualization. Gerry wouldn't either, if the roles were reversed."

"So the solution is that society should in some way shoulder your burden?"

"That's the thing: I don't believe it's my burden to shoulder. I didn't sign up for this. Gerry didn't sign up for it either. It isn't fair."

"You are certainly experiencing a greater tragedy than most people expect when they take their marriage vows, but we still promise to be there 'for better, for worse, for richer, for poorer, in sickness and in health,' and so forth."

Excellent. Now Greta could see a way to turn the conversation to more constructive topics. The last thing she wanted was to have this religious oppressor attempt to psychoanalyze her. "We made our own marriage vows. We preferred that over vows from traditions steeped in patriarchy and oppression that we didn't believe anyway."

"Okay, then, it's true. You didn't sign up for this. On that point we agree."

"Yes." The tension seemed to release. "So what would be your solution?"

"I appreciate your asking, even though you said you're not a religious person."

"So I imagine, then, that your solution involves speaking to an imaginary friend in the sky?"

Smiling, Sean said, "God is not an imaginary friend, but if you're referring to Him, yes."

"Sorry, not interested. So that's it? It's that simple: make empty promises from an imaginary god. That's how you comfort people? You don't actually *do* anything?"

"I sincerely believe that God is real and His promises are true, and that also translates into action."

She paused. "I highly doubt that, but okay, I'll bite. Give me your spiel." She really wanted to hear firsthand whatever it was that made these people so compelling to the poor.

Sean smiled again. "Given the preponderance of TV evangelists spouting the lies of the prosperity gospel, I understand your skepticism. At the very least, let my volunteer status here speak to my sincerity. I hope you'll hear the difference between what I have to say and what you've heard."

"That remains to be seen."

Colin shifted on his feet uncomfortably. Sean took a deep breath and said, "Okay. I have good news and bad news."

"I can't imagine how bad news would comfort somebody," Greta said.

"It isn't supposed to, but the good news depends on first understanding the bad news."

"From your perspective."

"Yes, we all have our worldviews, but I'm speaking in universals."

Greta crossed her arms over her chest. "Not sure I believe in those either, but okay."

"The bad news is what you see all around you." He spread his arms, holding his Bible in one hand, indicating the room. "God created the world to be perfect, with no disease, suffering, or death. In our innocence, He defined for us what is universally true, beautiful, and good. Yet humanity spurned that and attempted to define reality for ourselves, leading to chaos. Creation fell, bringing every manner of suffering upon the human race: violence, corruption, disease, racism, death. There's something wrong with the human race, something that results in all of these things. We're born bad. No one escapes it, not even the morally upright ones, the accomplished, or the successful. Not you, not me. We Christians call this thing *sin*. The Bible teaches that human beings have a sinful nature, that we're corrupt, from birth to death. It's this internal corruption we all carry that causes every problem that's occurred from the dawn of time to this very second.

"As you noted, things just don't seem fair. You are a hardworking and loving person, but now through no fault of your own, your life is turned upside down and you are so far separated from God that you don't even believe in Him. There is nothing we can do to change our natural-born sinful nature, fix the world, or return to perfect fellowship with our Creator."

"Wow," Greta said. "Yes, that's pretty bad news." She decided to summarize, to make sure she had it right—a pedagogical technique she used in the classroom. "So you're saying not only that I'm bad personally, but so is everyone else. And I suffer both because of my bad decisions which are my fault, and because of other people's bad decisions, which aren't my fault. Like Gerry's decision to get in a car accident this morning." She indicated the bed, but kept her eyes fixed on Sean. Sean glanced over at Gerry, covered thoroughly in his body cast, the incessant beeping and the readout on his monitor the only indicators that he lived.

"What happened this morning might not have been Gerry's fault," he said.

Greta felt his words like a slap across the face. He was right. So far, all day—from the police officer's phone call onward—she realized she'd been angry partly because she'd made the unconscious assumption that through will or negligence, somehow this accident had been Gerry's way of messing up her life, at the moment she approached real success and recognition in her field. Why had she thought that? For the first time, she turned and gazed—really gazed—at Gerry's motionless form. He'd never held any animosity for her. And he certainly wouldn't have wanted to end up like this.

And somehow, this pastor had turned things back around to her again.

Greta took charge of the conversation once again. "Okay, so everybody makes bad decisions. That doesn't mean we're bad at our core. I don't believe I'm all that bad."

"That's why it's so insidious. Nobody believes it. It takes a lot of convincing for people to realize the problem isn't just outside of ourselves. It is ourselves."

"So you're saying we're all running around, living our lives, and we're all what's wrong with the world, but we don't know it?"

Sean nodded. "Either that or we deny it. If we really think about it and examine ourselves honestly, we might see it, but most people don't want to do that. And even if we do see it, we can't do anything about it."

"Okay; that's pretty bad news. I don't agree with it because I think you've missed a huge thing called random chance, but I'll let you finish. What's the good news?"

"Oh, I'm not done yet. So far, this is mostly a position on human nature. We've barely reached the religious part."

She wanted him to get to the point. "Then get on with it."

"Okay. God isn't pleased with our sin. In fact, He's already judged us and found us wanting. So by nature, we're born corrupt; that corruption follows us throughout our lives, and God has us earmarked for destruction."

"Is that hell?"

"Yes. But there's also good news."

"If we're corrupt and worthless and God is against us too, how could there be good news?"

"God didn't leave us in that helpless estate. Because God loved us even though we were unlovable, He sent His Son as a man, Jesus Christ, to represent us. Jesus obeyed God perfectly and never sinned. Then He took all our sin and corruption upon Himself and was punished for it in place of those who would surrender their lives to Him. All anyone has to do is trust Him to pay the penalty for their sins, commit their lives to Him, and they can be saved. God accepts Jesus's perfect obedience on our behalf and His punishment in place of ours, and He gives us His Holy Spirit as a guarantee that we are saved."

She smirked. "Saved? From what? Do saved people stop making bad decisions?"

"No, though as I said, we do have the Holy Spirit who helps guide us through God's Word, to make better decisions. We're saved from eternal punishment for all the things we've done wrong in our lives. We're saved from our sins, and are no longer in bondage to them. We're freed to, as Jesus said, 'go and sin no more.' We may not always succeed at that, but it becomes possible for the Christian to more and more every day put off more of his sin and put on Christ's righteousness."

"That's the good news?" she asked, an eyebrow raised.

"Yes, that's the good news. Our relationship with God can be restored through Jesus, opening up a host of promises He has made to us in His Word. We are all lost and we cannot save ourselves. We need a savior, and God has provided that savior in Jesus."

"So let me get this straight. I'm trying to deal with a tragedy in my life, and you tell me that I'm lost and corrupt, but I can be saved from that by committing my life to Jesus. How does that help me?"

"I grant you that it doesn't solve all your problems. But it solves the biggest problem of all, the one you didn't even know you had. You become God's child, and then God is with you through your trial and promises to work through it for your good."

She crossed her arms again. "He's with me? What's He going to do for me? Make it all better somehow?"

"We don't know what God's will is. But He will help you through it, not just spiritually, but also through His people. If you're His, God has promises for you, like the one in Romans 8:28 that says all things work together for good, for those who love God and are called according to His purpose."

She closed her eyes: he'd spoken too many words and jumbled too many concepts at once. "Can you repeat that again? That quotation."

"Sure. All things work together for good, for those who love God and are called according to His purpose."

She couldn't believe what she'd just heard. She opened her eyes, and blue lightning flashed from them. She stood. "What a load of crap! Do you really believe that? Or is that something you tell people so you can control them?"

"Yes, I really believe that," Sean said quietly. Though Greta stood, Sean towered over her; yet somehow he seemed to shrink beneath her fury.

"I don't believe you," Greta said. "I think you use this cockamamie story—that you people have always used it—to string people along, so it seems like deliverance is always there, just around the corner, if they only continue to pray, believe, and do what you say. And meanwhile, you strip them of everything they have: their individuality, their time, and their money. You are the ultimate parasites on society, and you always have been. You offer nothing, and you leech everything good from everybody else."

"I'm sorry to hear you say that. I believe I've just told you the most important information there is to communicate. I can't speak for everyone who claims to be a Christian, but I will say that most Christians would be the first to admit they're not perfect, and that they're still struggling. And there are some in our midst who don't truly believe anyway. I believe Christianity is the single most important feature of Western society. Christians started the first hospitals and universities. Christianity gave rise to science, technology—"

"Oh, come on! Christianity represents everything that's wrong in the world, and we're still trying to correct it. Christianity gave rise to science? I've never heard anything so ridiculous. Christianity created universities and hospitals? Sure, maybe in this country, but the concept of the university goes back to Plato. And it's good they've been wrested from you and freed to pursue knowledge without baggage. You and everything you represent are a relic, a dinosaur. The world is passing you by, because your true colors have been revealed. You don't represent anything good."

The pastor looked sad. He looked down at the floor and took his jacket from over his arm, as though he would put it on. "I'm sorry. I've upset you, and that was not my intention. Obviously, now is not the best time to be discussing this, but I would love an opportunity to speak with you further."

"Why, so in the name of comforting me you can make me feel worse again? No, sorry. I'm on to you and what you represent. I have been for years. What you do is wrong, pure and simple, and I want no part of it. You offer hope and help but deliver very little, and expect too much."

"Dr. Foster," Colin said, "how do you know what Christians do is wrong?" Both heads swiveled to Colin, who up to now had been silent.

"What kind of question is that?"

"You've charged Christians at large with doing wrong, and the pastor here has admitted that yes, wrong things have been done in the name of Christ even if that isn't what Christians are supposed to represent. But what I don't understand is how you can know what 'wrong' is."

She paused in thought, vertical lines appearing on her forehead. "I suppose I know because I inherit that knowledge from society."

"But society can't universally, definitively say what's right and wrong. There are societies of cannibals who wear the shrunken heads of their victims as jewelry. We would judge that as wrong, but they believe that's right."

"Well, that's wrong because it devalues life."

"Yes, but how do you know devaluing life is wrong?"

"Because society can't exist without life, without the life that makes up the society."

"And what's so great about society? If the universe is meaningless and we're all bags of matter and neural impulses, what does it matter if one bag of matter destroys another?"

"Because—because we are everything. We give meaning to the universe." Her head whirled; how had she gotten on the defensive again?

"But we disagree. Your view is one in a sea of endless worldviews. Some say what we experience isn't reality, and that all individuality must be eradicated in favor of universal oneness. Others say they're reincarnated into castes that define their value. Some have begun to think this isn't even reality, and we're in a simulation. What makes yours the right one? How do you know so definitively that Christians are wrong that it upsets you?"

Greta paused, struggling for words. "Because you—you manipulate and control people through lies, lies you know are false because you don't believe them yourselves. You say out of one side of your mouth that people should be married to have sex, and then you molest little boys and girls in your ivory towers. Your leaders live in palatial houses, extorting money from devoted followers. You do all this and you get away with it, because there's no oversight; nobody is watching you."

"You speak as though Christians are this unified, organized block that deliberately and diabolically does these things. I condemn these things along with you. No one who does these things represents biblical Christianity. But I know why all the things these people do are wrong, because they go against what God has said in His Word. But how do you know?"

"I just know." The adrenaline from an opportunity to put these people in their place was wearing off, and Greta could feel fatigue threatening her clarity of thought.

"Yes, you do. You know because God's law, as the Bible says, was written on your heart, as it has been for everyone in the world. You know instinctively and intuitively that murder and rape and extortion and stealing are wrong, because you are made in God's image. But please consider this: you suppress that truth, the truth that these things come from God, because you don't want to be associated with Him or with people who follow Him."

"No, I don't. I'm a sociologist. I believe in rational thought, not superstition."

"And yet you could give me no rational reason for why you believe anything is right or wrong. You just know."

"Yes, I know. I know because society knows. I know because there is consensus on these things. Society is growing and evolving, and with it comes a clearer picture of ethics and morality."

"Are you speaking of Western society, Eastern society, liberal, or conservative society? I'm sure you know our current cultural and political climate is a battleground. So the question then becomes *whose* ethics and morality win out? I ask you again: if morality—right and wrong—is defined by any group of human beings, what gives that group of human beings the right to force their morality on anyone else?"

"No one has that right. That's part of why I oppose you and all you stand for. That's what Christians do."

"It's what everybody does. I'll demonstrate. Do you believe in a woman's right to choose abortion?"

"Yes."

"Okay, I don't. Society has not come up with a way to resolve this for decades. Why do you think that is?"

"Many reasons. An entrenched patriarchal system that has repressed and controlled women's behavior for so long that it's taken generations—and will likely take a few more—to get its influence out of our collective consciousness. A political system that bounces back and forth between ideologies, delaying progress. An inconsistent system of education that fails to impart scientific knowledge. I could go on."

"We have so many points of disagreement there, but I want to stay focused on the morality question. We share this, though, this knowledge that our position is the right one and it must be defended. Do you feel that?"

"Yes. What's your point?" Greta considered sitting back down; she was getting really tired now.

Colin, however, became more animated and took a step closer to her as

Sean stood aside. "Before I make it, I just want to say that this is our first point of connection. We both feel the same thing: a righteous indignation that the other is wrong, that we must persuade, defend, oppose, convince. We feel it so strongly that it can drive our emotions, our behavior, our words. But we're diametrically opposed. We're both convinced that we are right, but in opposite directions. To make it worse, you have a group of people with your beliefs, and I have a group of people with my beliefs."

He went on, "I asked you how we can resolve this, and you mentioned systems of philosophy, politics, and education. But I have my own systems of philosophy, politics, and education. There was something else behind your answer; do you know what it is?"

"I'm getting tired of this; please enlighten me."

"Power. Your power against my power. That's where your version of morality leads: one human system against another human system. With no way to say universally which one is the right one, your worldview devolves into might makes right. Whichever system has the most power oppresses the others. No one is free; we're always at war. No one is right and no one is wrong. And on down into history it goes, just like the Pastor here described. By trying to define meaning and morality for ourselves, we find we don't actually have knowledge of meaning and morality; we only have different opinions, and we make war over them. We make life meaningless and immoral. And I can tell from what you've said that you attach significant meaning to your life, and that you fear this accident will strip that meaning away. We are here to say no, your life has intrinsic meaning, no matter what happens, and that God has made a way for you to know that and to know Him."

Greta sat heavily in her chair. This conversation had fatigued her more than she had anticipated. She couldn't come up with a response; maybe exhaustion had begun to shut down her brain. If she'd been sharper, she knew she'd think of something. At this point, though, she wasn't sure that her current mental state allowed her to analyze what he said thoroughly. It was time for them to leave. "So you're saying there's no solution if I just want everything in my life to go back to the way it was before. That works for me; I'm back to where I started. I'm tired, and I think I'd like to rest now. I'm not sure I'm convinced, and I'm certain now is not the time to be making big changes in my life."

Sean broke in. "Of course. But let me say that this is one reason why we believe in God: if you don't believe in Him—and I mean the Christian God, not some nebulous god-idea—you can't know anything. You destroy knowledge itself. This is only one example: without God, we can't know morality. We can't know what's right and wrong. We have only groups of people fighting against other groups of people over power, and none of those groups has the universal authority to dictate morality to the other groups. They can only fight. And I think we can both agree that that's wrong. The difference is that I acknowledge that God's word tells me that it's wrong, while I believe you get it as a legacy from the Judeo-Christian influence on the Western culture you come from."

Greta sat back and looked up at him. "Maybe. I'll have to consider it. But right now, I have too much to deal with."

"Yes, I understand. Will you allow us to help you shoulder your burden?"

Greta's eyes narrowed. "What does that mean?"

Sean wiped the corner of his mouth with the back of his hand. "Uh, when I took on this ministry, I didn't do it alone. My congregation wants very much to be a part of it. We agreed to, as we say, 'come alongside' people I come into contact with here at the hospital, to help them with whatever they need."

"For a small donation, I suppose."

Sean looked horrified. "No, not at all! No strings attached. We want to show the love of Christ to people; that's it."

"And how do you do that?"

"Many ways. It depends on your needs and your comfort level. Do you have a dog that needs to be walked while you're here at the hospital? Do you need somebody to take your car to the shop, go grocery shopping, clean your house, cook some meals? Would you like someone to sit with you and keep you company; someone more low-key than me? Though I do intend to come see you again, if that's okay."

"I'm not sure I trust people I don't know to do those things."

"I understand. The offer is there, and you're not putting anybody out if you accept help. We *want* to do this for you, if you'll let us."

"Let me think about it."

"Okay, that's fine. Do you mind if I stop by tomorrow? Maybe I can bring you some nice, home-cooked, non-hospital food?"

"You can stop by, but I may send you away."

"That's fine too." He reached into his pocket and pulled out a business card. "Here's my contact information if you need it. Please feel free to contact me if you need anything, at any time."

She took the card and without looking at it, stuck it in her purse on the floor next to her.

Sean asked, "Do you mind if we pray?"

"Can you do it somewhere else? I need to be alone now."

"Certainly," he said and reached out his hand. She shook it tiredly. "It was very nice to meet you, Dr. Foster. Please know that we will be praying for you and your daughter as you weather this storm, and for your husband's healing."

Colin waved. "Glad to meet you."

"Good-bye," she said to both of them.

They walked out.

28

3:00 PM

Brent Jenson, formerly known as Brick Johnson, pulled into the driveway of the dilapidated-looking row house in Pennsauken. The nondescript house looked identical to the rest up and down the block. He hadn't expected the driveway to be unoccupied—clearly people were home at other houses in the row. As he scanned them, he noticed empty driveways on both sides of this house. Warily, he parked his bike and since the street was quiet, pulled his gun as he approached the front door.

He knocked.

The door opened a crack. "What do you want?"

"175."

"Yeah, we got the call a few minutes ago. Get your bike out of sight, around back."

Brent shoved his gun in his pants immediately and went to his bike as the garage door opened. He wheeled it in past a large van and out the back door into the unkempt back yard, infested with once overgrown and now dead weeds. The back door opened, and a hand waved him up the steps and into the house.

He found himself in a dimly-lit dining area. A small, round table sat at his left, where a neatly manicured man in a dark suit sat alone. The house bustled with activity: figures in white clean-suits with masks over their faces moved quickly, some taking down the remnants of equipment, some with carpet cleaners, vacuum cleaners, or air paint-sprayers coating the walls in light blue. Whoever had let him in had already disappeared; the man at the table motioned him to sit. He complied.

The man spoke first. "175, status?"

"Compromised by civilian. Clean escape. No witnesses, evidence destroyed by fire."

"Excellent, as always." The man indicated a tablet in front of him, its screen illuminating his chest in blue. "Your report checks out: drone report says the house burned to the ground." He paused, sighing. "We were bringing you in anyway. As you might suspect, this is the lab where all your meth came from. We're evacuating."

"Another assignment?" Brent contained his curiosity.

"Yes, but not this again. We're moving you up. Giving you more responsibility. You've proven yourself over the past four years. We can use you for higher-level projects than financing."

Brent's heart leaped, but he kept his relief and excitement off his face. Finally! He'd been doing this so long he'd started to wonder who were the good guys and who were the bad guys.

"Sounds good, sir."

"You've done well. Not many make it past this trial period. We have to be sure our operatives are loyal, and this is a good way to weed them out. Some are sloppy and get caught. Some get restless; others find their morality. Those who fail are easily dealt with, since they're engaged in criminal activity anyway. Those who succeed move up to the real work."

"Looking forward to it, sir."

"You'll leave your motorcycle here; the team will take care of it. I'll have a car take us down to Washington, to headquarters. There, you'll get a full briefing and your new assignment. Any questions?"

"How long, sir?"

"Not long. A week at most. There's much to do. Like I said, we were bringing you in anyway. The owner of this property finally decided to do something about it, so we're cleaning up and getting out. This team'll find another abandoned house to set up shop."

"How'd we know?"

"We have ways. You were involved. That plumber we had you visit last night was supposed to come here and fix broken plumbing that we'll have to break again so he can come tomorrow. Creative work, by the way. Nice, clean, neat. That's another reason we're bringing you in; we like your methods. You apply just what is necessary: not too much, not too little.

Too much, and you expose us. Too little, and the mission fails. Ask too many questions, and we're doing your job for you. You're one of the guys who gets it. Too many of these guys—" he indicated the people cleaning the house, "—would've probably shot the guy and made a big mess."

"I appreciate that, sir."

The man checked his watch and stood. "Well, there's no point in wasting time. We're gonna hit rush hour at this point no matter what we do. These guys can finish cleaning up and get out later."

Brent stood and carefully pushed in his chair. The man grabbed his tablet and motioned him with it further into the house.

"This way; the car should be outside now."

Brent followed. He didn't know how his life would change, but he was ready for anything.

29

∞∞∞∞∞

3:30 PM

Mary sipped the last of her overly salty chicken noodle soup. She felt much better—a little woozy still, and everything seemed far away—but definitely better. No more room spinning or dizziness. The food had helped. She looked forward to going home; she now had to decide how she'd get there.

She had Sal's card in her purse. She could also call one of her girlfriends, which would probably be the better, safer idea. Her mind turned to her previous thoughts: better and safer was how she'd been running her life, and that philosophy hadn't gotten her very far. She resolved to do something different, even if it made her afraid.

The sound of the curtain being pulled gingerly aside made her look up. A well-dressed, dark-skinned woman poked her head through the new opening.

"Hello—I'm sorry. I was next door," she stammered. "Am I disturbing you?"

"I'm just lying here," Mary replied. "Are you from the hospital?"

"No, I'm just another patient." She lifted her right leg, showing a foot in a boot. "I was next door," she repeated.

"Oh." This could be interesting. "What do you want? Do you want to sit down? There's a chair right here."

"Thank you." The woman limped over to the chair next to the bed and sat down heavily. "We sure have been through a lot today, you and I."

"We have? I mean, yes, I have, and obviously you have, but we haven't—together, I mean. Like, I don't know what happened to you and you don't know what happened to me."

"Yes—right. I'm sorry." She held out her hand. "I'm Gloria Williams. I'm a school teacher. I came by because I wanted to know if you were in the car accident."

Mary's forehead furrowed. "I was in a car accident, but I didn't know it was *the* car accident. Am I famous or something?"

"Uh, no, not as far as I know. There was a big car accident on Route 42 this morning; it happened right in front of me."

"Is that how you got hurt?"

"No, I managed to do that another way," she evaded. "I saw what happened; it was horrifying. I guess I'm looking for a connection; I just want to find out if everyone was okay."

"Well, I was in an accident, but it was in Westville, not on the freeway. I try to avoid that; it scares me."

"I'm sorry; are you okay?"

"I got a good knock on the head, but I'm feeling better, thanks." Suddenly she had an idea, and before she had a chance to think it through, she blurted, "You said you're a school teacher?"

"Yes. High school."

"You'd be good at giving advice then?"

"Well, I don't know. I can try."

She frowned. Should she really be seeking advice from somebody she just met? She'd never have considered doing that before. But now she had another opportunity to do things differently. She decided to go for it. "I'm conflicted. I was in an accident because I hit a telephone pole trying to avoid a bunch of junk that came off a plumber's truck. After the accident, the plumber was very nice. I don't remember much because I hit my head, but I liked him. He was very apologetic and offered to help me and he gave me his card."

"Did you get a police report and trade insurance info?"

"Yes, we did all that. I don't think he's trying to get out of anything, if that's what you mean."

"So what's your question?"

"Should I call him and ask him to drive me home?"

"Oh, wow." Gloria's hand went to her mouth. "That would be very bold."

"Yes, it's not like me at all, but this knock on the head may have done me some good. I need to make some changes in my life."

"Yes, but do you think you need to start right away?"

"I already am. The old me probably wouldn't have talked to you."

Gloria paused, looking at the floor. She then faced Mary and smiled. "Well, girl, don't let me stop you."

"So you think I should do it then?"

"Life isn't life without taking some risks. But maybe you can make it only a calculated risk."

"What do you mean?"

"Do you have a friend you can text or contact who can meet you at home, in case this guy isn't on the up-and-up?"

"Yes, I do. But she'll probably try to talk me out of it."

"You think she'll be successful?"

"I don't know. Maybe. I can be—I don't know, like a push-over. And I don't want to be talked out of this. I don't want to go through life playing it safe and everything always being the same. I want it to matter."

"Okay, how about this," Gloria said. "Why don't we trade phone numbers, and you can text me?"

"But you hardly know me."

Gloria smiled again. "You're not the only one in this world who can be a push-over. It's my grandma's fault, really. When I was a kid and I was having trouble with somebody, she used to say stuff like, 'Girl, you try to control everybody, you gonna fail. You ain't in control. God puts people in your life, and it's your job to figure out how to live with them. That's how you grow. The only person you can control is yourself. Be better than you were yesterday, and you lift others up with you.' Sounds to me like you're trying to do just that, and I want to help you."

Mary stared at her blankets silently. Finally she looked up, tears in her eyes. "Thank you," she breathed.

Gloria patted her hand. "You are very welcome." She waited till Mary had composed herself and then said, "Let's talk. I've got some time; the student I came in with is probably gonna be here overnight anyway, and I can see him later. We can trade accident stories until the doctor comes back and you can get out of here."

"Sure; sounds good," Mary said.

30
∞∞∞∞

4:00 PM

As the sun disappeared behind the house across the street and the room began to darken, Sal got up from his couch and began pacing. He had to be sure: was the Blackfield he'd spoken to first the same Blackfield he just talked to? The more he thought about it, the more he convinced himself: yes it was. The guy was kind of a jerk, a guy used to being in charge and bossing people around. Not a guy you ever get close to; he sounded like one of those guys who considered people who worked for him a different class, people to be used for their skills, not to know or personally care about. What was the other guy like? He stopped pacing and squeezed his eyes shut, trying to remember. How did the conversation start?

He remembered stepping outside the supply place. A couple other guys were already there, puffing on cigarettes and talking. Not wanting to talk shop and not good at small talk, Sal had whipped out his phone and stepped away from the clouds of smoke so he could make his call and do what he could to salvage the day. A busted pipe didn't take that long to fix; he thought he'd still be able to be in and out of there and then take a late lunch.

He remembered he didn't have the guy's number in his phone; he had to look up the call history and find it. He'd dialed it, and then—what? How did it go?

He thought Blackfield (or whoever it was) had answered with a simple

"Hello?"

"Hey, uh, is this Roger Blackfield?"

How had he answered? Politely: "Yes, this is Roger. May I ask who's calling?"

"This is Sal, your plumber? You asked me to do a job this morning."

"Sal! Yes, wow; are you done already?"

"Naw, that's why I'm calling."

"Is there a problem?"

"Not really. I got in a car accident this morning so I didn't make it. But I —"

"Oh no, are you all right?"

"Yeah; I'm fine. No damage to my truck or anything. I just had to come pick up some more parts, and then I'll get the job done this afternoon."

This was where things got weird. "No. Absolutely not. If you were in a car accident, you should take it easy. The job can wait till tomorrow."

"Thanks, but I'm fine. I didn't hit nothin'. I—"

"No, I insist. Rest up; you can do it tomorrow. I've heard people who get in car accidents sometimes don't feel pain until hours or maybe days later. In fact, if you show up today, I won't want you doing any more work for me. Take the day; I'm sure you're shaken up."

"No, really, I—"

"Not another word about it, please. I want our working relationship to start off right."

Sal had been speechless, backed into a corner without anything to say. After a long pause, he said, "All right. I'll do it tomorrow." Maybe he could shuffle something around and get another job done.

"Very good. Rest up; I hope you feel better."

Sal felt fine. "Uh, yeah. Okay."

"Talk to you tomorrow."

"Okay. Thanks. Tomorrow."

Something bothered Sal at the back of his consciousness, something about the way Blackfield had sounded. The tone was all different between the two calls, but it wasn't that. Something else. Something more basic; easy to pinpoint. A difference between Blackfield number one and Blackfield number two.

Tomorrow!

Blackfield one pronounced it the same way Sal did, the Philly way: "Tomarrah." Blackfield two pronounced it the right way, the school way.

He was certain: he'd spoken to two different Blackfields!

How could he have called the guy back at his own number and gotten somebody else? And who called Blackfield pretending to be Sal?

He wanted to call the number again, to see if he got the same guy, but he knew that was a mistake. If Blackfield one answered—the one he'd talked to twice, the one he suspected was the real one—he'd only get him mad, and that would be the end of this opportunity. He didn't know what the deal was, but he knew whoever had done this had a clear goal.

Somebody didn't want him at that house today.

Whoever did this could both intercept the call Sal made *and* spoof a call *from* Sal. How—

In a moment of sudden realization, Sal yanked his phone out of his pocket. He sat on the couch and stared down at it. Was it hacked? He activated it. How could he tell? Everything looked like it always did. If his phone made a call he didn't make, would that call show up in the call log? He opened the phone app and checked the list. Nope, not there. Admittedly, technology wasn't his thing, but he got enough robocalls to know that spoofing calls from somebody else happened all the time. It probably wasn't the phone. He stuck it back in his pocket.

He thought about calling the cops again, but would they listen to him? Surely they had ways of retrieving call records from phone companies. Would they go to all that effort? Probably not. Calling them again was a hassle and probably also a waste of time.

If he wanted to find out what this was all about, there was really only one thing to do. Go up there, to the house in Pennsauken. Go where somebody didn't want him to go.

He knew his curiosity was probably getting the better of him, but no work would get done today: the darkening room proved that. The least he could do was satisfy his curiosity. He stood and headed for the door.

His phone rang in his pocket, and he jumped a mile. He fished it out and answered it.

"Hey, this is Sal."

"Hi, Salvatoré." A woman's voice, familiar. "This is Mary Simmons. We met this morning, after, uh, after my car met a telephone pole."

His heart jumped. "Mary! Yes, hi." His heart sank; this might not be good. "Are you feeling better?"

"Yes, I am. The hospital is getting ready to release me."

"That's great! I feel really bad about what happened; if there's anything

I can do, you let me know, okay?"

"Well, that's what I'm calling about."

"Oh yeah? Already? What can I do for you?"

"I was wondering if you would pick me up here and drive me home."

This might dampen his plans, but at this point he had no choice. "Absolutely! Which hospital are you at?"

"Cooper." Camden.

"Where do you live?"

"Westville, not far from where the accident was."

"Yeah; I can come pick you up; I'll be there in about 20 minutes." He thought for a second, and then asked, "Do you mind if we make a stop in Pennsauken real quick? It's not far from the hospital."

"Why?"

"Just checkin' out a job site for tomorrow. Since I'll be in the neighborhood, I thought I'd go find it, and that'll make my life easier in the morning. Should be what, five minutes from the hospital, if that."

She paused. "Okay. I guess that's okay."

"Great! I'll see you in 20 minutes."

"Okay, Salvatoré. Thank you."

"No problem at all. See ya."

"Bye."

He hung up and walked out.

31
∞∞∞∞∞

4:00 PM

After spending time in the chapel praying together, Sean and Colin stood up.

Sean checked his watch. "I'm well into my shift now. I don't think that last encounter would've gone nearly as well if you hadn't been here. Thank you for tagging along."

"It's no problem. I like opportunities to get out there 'on the field,' so to speak," said Colin.

Sean sighed. "I'm not used to antagonistic encounters like that, or at least I'm not prepared for them. I need to brush up on my apologetics."

Colin smiled. "You picked up right where you needed to. I'm not so good at the pastoral stuff, but I do like the debates."

"I'm really glad you were there. It's shaky as it is, but I don't think I'd have an opportunity to talk to her again if you hadn't jumped in."

"Thanks, Pastor."

Sean grabbed his coat and began walking out of the chapel.

"One of the things I like to do is go down to the emergency room and see if there's anyone I can pray with. Do you want to come?"

Colin shook his head. "Unfortunately, I need to take off. But thanks for letting me tag along."

"Any time."

They exchanged phone numbers and a handshake, and Colin left.

Sean considered himself a people person. He enjoyed meeting people and talking with them. Much to the chagrin of his wife, it was not unusual for him to strike up conversations with perfect strangers anywhere and everywhere.

Ministry was different from regular conversation: the subject matter had to go somewhere, somewhere specific. Most of the time, he had little trouble directing conversations where he wanted them to go, and once he got there, he found that most of the time he was far more versed in talking about spiritual things than those he encountered. People didn't seem to think or care about their spiritual lives very much. Spiritual matters were easy to neglect, to let die on the vine, so to speak.

Sean ambled slowly down the corridor, thinking. What drove a person with no spiritual side? Obviously, to claim no spiritual aspect was either to lie or to be deceived; Scripture was clear on that point. People simply suppressed spiritual matters for many reasons: to avoid guilt over things they'd done, to perpetuate the illusion of independence and control over their lives, to avoid responsibility to the God who made them. To suppress these things was to suppress the things that made them human, that made them different from animals.

Animals operated on instinct, for self-preservation. Hunger translated into nut gathering, field grazing, foraging, violence. Cold translated into taking shelter, heat into a dip in the water. Animals never rose to anything else until humans became involved and met these needs. When humans created relationships and provided them food and shelter, animals became tame, pets. If you fed your dog, he learned to beg for food —but more importantly, suddenly the dog showed love and devotion. If you provided a home, your cat learned to scratch the door to get in, and more importantly, began to thank you for opening the door with a face-rub on the leg. They rose above their base natures, really, only when people become involved.

Humans, Sean thought, could become like natural animals, but on a higher level. Instead of living their lives for a purpose, to make the world better than it was than when they'd entered it, some decided to act like animals, to operate on instinct and self-preservation. Don't like your life? You can escape from it in various ways: binge-stream a show, play a video game, go out to a bar and drink your life away. Need a relationship? Nah; it's much easier to gratify that need with porn. Then you don't have to deal with that other person and his or her needs.

Many people were lost and operating like animals. And to Greta's point, the church had not always been the brightest guidepost to the truth. That's why it was all-important to be one of the faithful ones, to succeed where so many had failed or were deceived. And by God's grace, he would. He would point people to God, who reached down to create relationships with people, saving them from destruction and empowering them to rise above their self-serving, base natures and join with Him in redeeming the world.

He entered the emergency room area, more noisy than usual, and waved to the staff, some of whom waved back as they busily went about their tasks. A row of curtain-covered compartments to his right receded into the distance and then bent to the left against the back wall of the large area. Saying a quick prayer, he poked his head into the first compartment and recited his line: "Hi; I'm Pastor Sean Peterson, on the ministerial staff at the hospital. Can I pray with you?"

Rejection followed for a while, but he made his way down the line of compartments.

32
∞∞∞∞

4:30 PM

Gloria watched as Mary stood shakily, a young, thin attendant helping her with his arm around her waist. She lost her balance and the attendant stumbled, causing Mary to lean on Gloria's shoulder. The sudden weight made her wince at her own pain.

"Whoa," Mary said, looking at the floor.

"Still dizzy?" the attendant asked.

"No; head rush, I think. Give me a moment."

Presently, her eyes cleared and she looked up. "I'm all right. I can walk."

"Okay, let me see you do it." The attendant watched her closely.

Slowly, Mary stepped around to the front of the bed. "See?"

At that moment, a man's head popped around the corner of the frame supporting the curtain system. "Hi, I—oh, wow; it's crowded in here. Am I interrupting something?"

The man was well dressed; dark blue shirt with red tie, slacks, a jacket slung over one arm. He didn't look like a doctor. Everyone looked at each other, not sure how to respond.

Finally, Gloria said, "I guess that depends on who you are and what you're here for."

"Oh, sorry. I'm Pastor Sean Peterson, on the ministerial staff here at the hospital. I would like to pray and talk with you, if that's okay. If not, that's okay too; I'll be praying for you anyway."

His friendly and cheerful demeanor surprised them momentarily, but Mary said, "I'm right on the verge of getting out of here, and I don't want to stay any longer if I don't have to. Plus I have a ride coming." After a pause, she added, as though she'd just thought of it, "B-but thank you for your prayers."

An idea struck Gloria. A minister on staff at the hospital, going around and talking to people, might have visited somebody involved in the accident this morning. He might even know what happened to them!

"Okay; that's fine," Sean said. "I wish you all of God's grace and will pray for your full recov—"

"Wait!" Gloria almost shouted. "I would like to talk to you."

The man's head swiveled to face her. "Great! Are you, uh, are you a patient?"

Gloria lifted her foot. "Yes; I've just been discharged." She indicated Mary. "We were just talking."

"Oh, so you came in together?"

"No, we just met. I'll explain. First, let's get Mary out of here so she can catch her ride."

"Mary? Nice to meet you. I'm Sean," he said again, reaching out his hand. She shook it gingerly. The attendant ushered her toward a wheelchair.

"No thank you, I can walk. I just showed you," she said.

"I have to offer it," he said.

They made their way out of the emergency room area and into the lobby, where Sal's red Dodge Ram soon pulled up. Gloria turned to Mary and grabbed both sides of her face, looking her straight in the eyes.

"Now you be careful, girl. You got your phone?"

"It's right here in my purse."

"Good. You run into anything you don't like, you call me, text me, whatever."

"I will."

"Do you need help?" Sean asked.

Gloria looked at Mary, and they both smiled. "No, Pastor. I'll be fine," Mary said. Gloria embraced her warmly, and she went out the door to the waiting truck. Gloria watched approvingly as Sal—barrel-chested and rough—assisted Mary as she climbed into the passenger side of the truck. Shortly, they were off.

"Seems like you've had an interesting day," said Sean.

"Oh, Pastor, you don't know the half of it."

Gloria went through her day: her commute, the accident, arriving at school, the fight, Jameel stabbed, the hospital, meeting Mary. They had found chairs and sat in the lobby. As she spoke, she realized this wasn't where she'd wanted the conversation to go. She wanted to hear what he knew, not tell him everything she knew. Still, he nodded and listened thoughtfully. She wrapped things up quickly and decided not to beat around the bush.

"Have you met anybody involved in the accident today?"

"I have. Two, not including you," he said. He had to be careful not to divulge personally identifying information; the hospital chaplain training program had been clear about that.

"Are they okay? I was right there; I mean—right there. I have to know; please."

"You understand the privacy regulations I'm under? I can't give you any personally identifying information."

"Yes, I understand."

"Okay. Based on what you said, I've met both of the families you described." Sean suddenly realized it had been a long day; his conversations with them seemed like ages ago, and he was tired.

"Are they okay?" she repeated.

Sean paused, composing his words. "As far as I know, neither of the two crash victims died. Their injuries are serious, but they are both out of surgery and recovering."

"Thank God. I was so worried. It was horrible—" Her words caught in her mouth, and she looked at him, tears in her eyes. "Why does this happen?" she asked, as she fished in her purse for a tissue. "These people didn't do anything to deserve what happened to them."

He answered her question with another question. "Do you go to church?"

"I used to. I haven't been in a while," she said and blew her nose softly.

"Okay. Your question reminds me of a passage in the book of John." He reached into his folded jacket, now on his lap, and pulled out a small Bible. "I don't know why I feel I have to say this all the time, but I could use my phone," he explained. "I just find the rest of the stuff on there distracting, and I don't want to be distracted when reading Scripture."

He found the passage and continued. "At one point, Jesus and His disciples happened upon a man born blind." Reading, he said, "And His disciples asked Him, saying, "Rabbi, who sinned, this man or his parents, that he was born blind?""

He looked up to face her. "You see, this is not a new question: why do bad things happen to people? The only answer I have is Jesus's answer: 'Neither this man nor his parents sinned, but that the works of God should be revealed in him.'"

"What does that mean?"

"Well, Jesus went on to heal the man, but the healing wasn't the main point; it was the aftermath that mattered. Since the man was a known blind beggar for years and years, and he was undeniably healed, the ruling officials demanded an explanation. They didn't like the explanation they got."

He paused, and Gloria said, "Go on."

"You see, they'd already made up their minds. They'd heard Jesus teaching, and He did not teach the same things they taught, so they viewed him in opposition to the truth. Yet He could perform miracles. This validated Him in the eyes of the people—and, if you read the Old Testament, in Scripture too. They wanted to get rid of Him. They could accept almost any explanation *except* that Jesus healed the man of his blindness. But that was the explanation they got, and rather than modify their beliefs based on the evidence before them or investigate the matter further, they threw the man out of the synagogue. Does any of this sound familiar to you?"

"Yes, I remember the story."

"No, I mean do you detect any parallels in the question you asked? Why do bad things happen to people?"

"No, but that was why I asked you." Gloria smiled, and Sean grinned.

"Okay, fair enough," he said. "After he was thrown out of the synagogue, Jesus found him, revealed Himself to him, and the formerly blind man ultimately accepted that Jesus was the Son of God based on the evidence of his healing. But that isn't even the main point." He turned to the Bible again. "At the end of the story, Jesus says this: 'For judgment I have come into this world, that those who do not see may see, and that those who see may be made blind.' In response to that, some of those nearby who didn't accept Jesus's teaching asked him if they were blind also, and Jesus responded, 'If you were blind, you would have no sin; but now you say, "We see." Therefore your sin remains.'"

He closed the Bible. "The Bible describes a God who is all-knowing, everywhere, and all-powerful, who created the universe and the people in it. Though everything was perfect in the beginning, human beings brought sin and misery upon themselves, and God, out of love, has been revealing Himself to them in many ways down through the ages, through His Word, through His Son, and through His people. What, do you think, has been our response, thinking of humanity as a whole?"

"Not so great?"

"No, not so great. In fact, collectively we've been just like those Jesus was talking to. We think we see, but we're blind. We see bad things happening, and we conclude that there can't be a God in control of it all. Or even worse, we get mad at Him, as though He owed us a good life, when we've spent most of it rejecting Him. But He has a purpose in all of it, as Jesus said at the beginning of that incident: that the works of God may be revealed." Gloria could see the excitement in Sean's animated face as he spoke.

"What does that mean, though? What are the works of God?"

"The works of God are everything that happens. Make no mistake: there are no meaningless events, and history had a beginning and is heading for its end. In the case of the blind man, the works of God were the testimony of His truth to the people involved: those who had seen the blind man healed, the rulers who heard his testimony and rejected it, the man himself who ultimately put his faith in Christ and was saved. His life became part of the continuing testimony of God's truth down through the ages to us, who can read about it now. The point is that God is still working in the things that happen to us every day."

Tingles spread up Gloria's spine. "Yes, but how do I know what His purpose is in a seemingly random car accident that's messed up the lives of so many people?"

Sean shook his head. "You don't. We can look back and see the purpose in what happened to the blind man because it's in the past. We're living this now. Do you think the blind man enjoyed being thrown out of the synagogue? It turned out God had something better for him, something that resulted in his ultimate salvation, but he didn't know it at the time. What happened to him was written down and has comforted thousands, perhaps millions of people about God's purposes for more than 2,000 years. We're not to worry about God's ultimate purpose—it'll be revealed eventually to result in His glory and for Christians, our ultimate good. Our job is to be faithful and, trusting Him, reflect His goodness and love to others, in whatever our situation is, so that, as Jesus said, the works of God may be revealed."

Gloria furrowed her brow in thought. "So you're saying that right now, while we're in it—in whatever we're going through—the works of God are hidden."

"That's right. We don't know what God's purpose is; we just know that He has one. We use an older word—providence—to describe His ultimate plan for His glory and our good. Our job as Christians is to be faithful, and to shine. I didn't read that part, but that passage is also where Jesus said, 'I am the light of the world.' Now that He's in glory preparing a place for us, we are His witnesses in the world, by the power of the Holy Spirit, and we need to be good witnesses. God knows there have been plenty of bad ones."

Gloria looked at the floor. "That's a tall order, Pastor."

"Yes; I won't deny that. But He does promise to sustain us through it. The question is, will we trust His promises, or will we wallow in unbelief and despair? God never promised us easy lives, but He did promise us blessings. And even if we go through something horrible, isn't it better to trust God whom we know has a purpose in it, than to pretend He doesn't exist and descend into anger, fear, and despair? Isn't it better to find grace from our relationship with Him and reflect that grace to other people so they may see the works of God and be encouraged themselves? I mean, that's what it's all about: being a light to the world, so the world can see the works of God and be drawn to Him."

"I suppose so." Gloria smiled. "The way you talk, if I didn't already know, I could tell you were a preacher."

Sean snorted. "Sorry about that. I sometimes have a tendency to lapse into soliloquies."

"No, it's fine. I can appreciate a good, Shakespearean soliloquy, even if my students don't."

"Thank you," Sean said, gazing at the floor. He looked up. "So you're a teacher?"

"Yes, at West Deptford High. But I teach math, actually, not Shakespeare."

"My church is right around the corner from there."

"Really? Maybe I'll come visit."

"I'd love that. You have an automatic after church dinner invitation, if you like," he said and gave her his card. "Would you like to pray for a moment?"

"Not so fast, Pastor, I'm not done with you yet."

Sean's eyes widened. "Oh?"

"I didn't come here alone. I came with a student, you remember. I'd like to visit him; would you come with me?"

33

∞∞∞∞∞

5:00 PM EST/2:00 PM PST

Jenny threw her purse on the bed. "Well, we're not getting anything else done today," she said.

Emma collapsed onto her bed. "I'm exhausted. I don't even want to eat."

"Heh. That didn't stop Tina."

"I'm not Tina." Emma paused, thinking. "She may have been right, though."

"What?"

"That seemed like a big waste of time."

"You never know; there could be some detail in there the police can use."

"Maybe. Maybe we did the right thing."

"I know we did."

They lay back on their beds, staring at the ceiling for a while, the muted sounds of the campus drifting through their window. It almost felt like it could have been any other, normal, day—but it wasn't. Jenny's thoughts turned to her dad, thousands of miles away, in a hospital bed. Mom probably needed her help. There was no way Mom was prepared for something like this, and even though they didn't get along that well, Jenny started to think it might be a good thing to take a semester's break and go home.

"Emma?"

"Hey." Emma turned her head from the ceiling to face Jenny.

"I'm thinking maybe I should go home for the semester. Mom hasn't asked me to, but I honestly don't know if she can handle this." She shook her head. "And I don't know if I can handle being away while all this is happening."

Emma looked thoughtful for a moment, her eyes returning to the ceiling. Then she sat up, facing Jenny, and said, "You know how they tell you never to make major decisions in the middle of a crisis? This might be one of those times."

Jenny sat up. "You think it's a major decision to go home to my parents when my dad almost died in a car accident?"

"I think that today has been a big day. It was a crisis all around. And I think in the middle of that, considering any action that deviates from the normal way your next few months were supposed to go is a major decision. Instead of helping your mom, you might make her mad."

"Well, what am I supposed to do? Stay here? I won't be able to concentrate on my work and I'll flunk out anyway!"

"I'm not telling you what to do," Emma said. "I'm just saying take your time and make any decisions carefully. Talk to your mom about it first. Work out what going home would be like and what staying here would be like. Maybe the university has a policy for this, and you can go home for a partial semester or study remotely or something. Don't just go do something, because in the middle of all this, it may be the wrong thing."

Jenny put her head down and picked at one of her fingernails—a bad habit she thought she'd eradicated years ago. "You're probably right," she said and flopped down on the bed. "I just want to do something."

"Why don't you call your mom again? See how she's doing. I can go somewhere else."

"That sounds like a good idea, though I don't really want to." She thought for a moment and then added, "I don't mind if you stay, Emma. Maybe if we get in a fight again you can help me figure out why."

"Okay."

Jenny grabbed her phone and called her mom.

∞ ∞ ∞

The insistent ringtone from her phone jarred Greta awake; somehow, she'd fallen asleep in the hospital chair. She looked around. Everything remained as it had been before—she supposed the sounds of the monitoring equipment had lulled her to sleep. She sat up and fished the phone out of her purse.

Jenny.

"Hi, Jenny."

"Hey Mom. How is everything?"

Greta yawned. "I'm sorry. I fell asleep here in the hospital chair. Uh, everything is pretty much the same as it was before. I don't think we're going to know anything for a while."

"Okay. How are you?"

"I don't know. I guess I'm managing."

"What are your plans? Have you decided what to do about your classes and your semester?"

Greta sighed. "No, Jenny. I don't know yet." She felt a brief flash of anger. Jenny reminded her of things she really didn't want to think about right now: her semester, her students, her research. Her life, put on hold.

"Mom, I think I should come home and help."

Greta sat bolt upright, her reaction immediate: "No. No way."

"Why? I could sit with Dad while you teach. I could help out at the house, try to make things—"

Greta cut her off. "No. No, your job is to be at school, get your degree. Your father and I both sacrificed too much for this, for you. He would never want you to stop prematurely."

"But it would only be for one semester. I could go back. Under the circumstances, I'm sure it would be all right."

"I really appreciate your offer, Jenny, but 'only for one semester' are dangerous words. Once you stop, it's so much harder to start again; trust me."

"How am I supposed do this, to be away from you and Dad during all of this, and still go to school? I can't, Mom!"

Greta sighed again. She was so very tired, and she could feel a headache coming on. She didn't want to fight with Jenny again. She had no idea what to do or to say. She was the Mom. Wasn't she supposed to be the voice of experience, of reason? Where was it now, when she needed to call on it?

"I don't know what to tell you, Jenny. We all have to do difficult things in life, to push through circumstances that aren't ideal. Studies have shown that kids who learn to delay gratification are more successful as a population than—"

"Mom," Jenny's voice was trembling, but she controlled it. "I'm not a kid anymore, and this is not gratification."

The words danced at the tip of her tongue: *But it is. You want to be home, in the thick of it, with me, in this prison of our circumstances. Instead, you should be off, flying, becoming who you should become. Gratification is what you want to do, not what you need to do, but if my life is on hold, I need yours not to be.* She almost said it, blurted it, knowing it would escalate things. Under normal circumstances, she wouldn't care: Jenny needed to be corrected, and she was her mother, the perfect one to do it. But she stopped herself, her motivations for stopping unclear. Was she just too tired to start another fight? Was she holding on to Jenny, afraid to break an already tenuous relationship? Right now it didn't matter; what she said next mattered, and it made all the difference.

"I understand. You love your dad, and you love me. It's not clear right now how any of us will navigate this, but please do me a favor and wait, okay? Wait till I've had a chance to think and plan and come up with something. I love you, Jenny, and all I want is the best for you." She saw something on the floor and bent down to pick it up: the minister's card. It must've fallen out of her purse when she'd grabbed her phone.

For her part, Jenny was momentarily paralyzed. Mom rarely used the "love" word, especially as a motivator for anything she did. She preferred "science has found," "studies have shown," or some such other phrase. Mom had stopped talking, perhaps waiting for her response.

"Okay, Mom. But maybe we can think and plan and come up with something together. It shouldn't be all up to you."

Greta suddenly realized Jenny really wasn't a kid anymore. Jenny had intuitively understood something that perhaps Greta had been unwilling to face: this was very likely beyond her ability to handle by herself. And since her dream world of a public service that would handle most of it didn't exist, she needed to consider the options she did have, especially so that Jenny wouldn't have to drop everything and come home. She looked down at the card in her hand and realized something.

She'd already been offered help.

As every fiber of her being began to recoil from that idea, she realized she owed Jenny a response, and Jenny had been right.

"You're right, Jenny. It shouldn't be all up to me." She looked down at the card again. "I'm sure there are some options I can pursue; I just don't know what they all are yet. Give me some time to work through this. Give me a call tomorrow, okay? Or I'll call you."

"Okay, Mom. I love you."

"I love you too, Jenny."

She hung up. Almost as soon as the call ended, her phone rang again in her hand.

David.

David, her research partner. David, her pursuer, who'd made a pass at her—a pass she'd returned enthusiastically—before all of this had happened, this morning: a lifetime ago. She looked over at Gerry and thought about her conversation with Jenny. David presented another possible source of help. David could take care of things; he was always so helpful. He—

His help came with a price. David represented help and attention, thoughtfulness and concern, but only for her. His involvement would tear her family apart, because she represented his only interest. And what motivated that interest? Honestly, she didn't know, because she hadn't let the relationship get past a certain point where she'd be able to tell if his attention waned and wandered somewhere else.

But wait a minute. She did know, because David knew she had a daughter, a daughter who would be devastated (as any child would) at the break-up of her parents' marriage, at the prospect of future awkward family gatherings, of home and family never being the same. And David knew she loved her daughter, and had sacrificed much to get her to where she was today. If David *really* loved her, he'd recognize that and stay away. If her marriage failed on its own, fine, but he didn't have to try to make it fail.

David's love was selfish, which meant it wasn't love at all.

She threw the phone into her purse, unanswered.

34

∞∞∞∞

5:00 PM

Sal pulled out of the hospital and headed east, toward Route 130, as the sun began to set. Mary sat quietly next to him. Neither of them seemed anxious to begin a conversation; neither of them could tell whether that represented anxiety or a reserved personality on the part of the other.

"I guess you're feeling better?" Sal finally asked, breaking the ice.

"Yes, I am; thank you for asking." Mary fidgeted with her fingers, rubbing them back and forth. "And thank you for driving me home."

"It's no problem really. It actually helps me," he indicated his phone with a GPS app running, sitting in a dashboard mount. "I'm all set up to do that job I was supposed to do earlier; I just want to find the place, and it's right by here. So you're actually doing me a favor."

"That's what I don't get. Couldn't you just use the GPS tomorrow morning? It's getting dark. How are you going to see anything?"

"Oh," he cleared his throat nervously. "I think we'll make it before dark. I hope so, anyway. There's a key under a rock I'm supposed to be able to find."

"Salvatoré, I don't think you're telling me everything, and quite frankly, I'm getting a little nervous. Is this safe?"

"Yeah; I'm sure it's safe. Why wouldn't it be safe? It's just another job."

"What is this place? Does anybody live there?"

"No, it's abandoned, but the guy who owns it is fixing it up to rent. There's a busted pipe in the kitchen he wants me to fix."

"So you're taking me to an abandoned house?"

He could hear the almost-panic in her voice. "Yeah, but it's a row house, in a big neighborhood of row houses. Lots of people around. Don't worry; nothing bad can happen."

"Sounds like famous last words to me."

"You can stay in the truck while I check it out. Even lock the doors, okay? It'll be all right."

"Okay; I'm trusting you, Salvatoré. It's not easy for me."

He turned north onto Route 130. "So then why'd you call me? I'm sure you could've called somebody else."

She fidgeted again. "I-I wanted to see you again. And—I don't know."

"What?"

"Nothing." *I hoped you might want to see me.*

"Okay. Well, I am glad to see ya. I'm glad you're doing better; I felt real bad about what happened. That's never, ever happened to me before." He paused and added, "Ever."

"It seems to upset you."

"It does. I'm a professional, you know? I take pride in my work, and I don't screw up. And to have it affect you, just minding yer own business going to work—it burns me up."

"It does?"

"Yeah; you didn't do nothing wrong. That's why I have to know." His heart jumped in his chest; he'd said too much.

Her eyes narrowed as he pulled off 130 and into an area Mary didn't recognize. "Know what?"

He knew he was defeated. How could he explain this? The truth would sound as bad as a lie. Sal knew he wasn't a good liar, and lying wouldn't help him engender her trust anyway. He'd already sent this woman to the hospital, and now he'd done a bait and switch, taking her to an abandoned house. He decided to come clean.

"Ah, you'll think I'm going crazy."

She reached out and put her hand on his arm. He almost jumped. "Try me."

He explained his discovery of the cut ties, the police report, and his conversations with the two different Blackfields. While he spoke, the GPS indicated several turns into a neighborhood of row houses. He finished by saying, "I was just going out the door when you called me, and I figured I could still stop by the place after picking you up."

"And you don't think this is dangerous in any way? Obviously, somebody doesn't want you there today, somebody pretty powerful who can tap phone lines and impersonate people and stuff."

He indicated the outside. "Today is fast becoming tonight. I probably missed whatever is going on."

"And what if you didn't? We could both get killed!"

"Why would somebody want to kill a random plumber that they hired in the first place?"

"Because somebody is pretending to be somebody, and he isn't the somebody you think somebody is. He's somebody else."

He turned to face her. "Huh? You're not making any—"

HONK!

Sal whipped his head back to the road and swerved when he saw an oncoming white van. Narrowly missing it, he overshot his swerve and pointed his truck at a parked car. Spinning the wheel as fast as he could the other way, he slammed on the brakes, and the truck ground to a halt. Thankfully, he hadn't hit anything.

"You all right?" he asked.

"I almost peed my pants."

He grinned. "Don't do that; it's a new truck." He rolled down his window and leaned his head out to see the white van at the end of the block just finishing making a turn onto another street, where it disappeared from view. "I guess we didn't hit him; he kept going."

"It would have been the second time today—and in my life—that I was in a car accident." She paused, then added, "And both of them involved you."

"Ha. I'm not normally that dangerous. But I want you to notice something. I didn't lose anything off my truck, and that was just about as bad as what happened this morning."

"So?"

"So it proves my system is good, and somebody messed it up."

They were on a residential street, rows of connected houses on both sides. Darkness had nearly replaced the twilight, but street lights provided artificial light in regular intervals. It didn't look dangerous.

"GPS says the house is right up this street. We're almost there," he said and started the truck moving again. They went halfway up the block, where the GPS triumphantly announced they'd reached their destination. The house was on the left; made of brick, it had an empty driveway in front of a garage and dark windows. Sal pulled into the driveway and killed the engine.

"You can stay here; I'll be right back," he said.

"Be careful."

"I'm always careful." He shut the door, locked it, and gave her a thumbs up.

The front walk connected to the driveway pad and then turned 90 degrees up to two concrete steps leading to the front door. Before the steps sat a tiny flower garden area, overgrown with brown, dead weeds. The rock and the key were in there somewhere. Sal lit his keychain flashlight and bent down to search for the fake plastic rock, which he soon found. Inside was indeed a key. He grabbed the key and opened the front door.

Strange. He'd expected a moldy, musty odor; instead, he smelled fresh paint. He fumbled at his left on the wall for a light switch. Finding two, he switched them both, but nothing happened. This meant probably no ceiling fixtures; he bet one controlled one of the outlets in the room and the other turned on the outside light, which had a dead bulb. He went back to his truck and rummaged in one of his compartments for a real flashlight; the keychain wasn't powerful enough. Mary waved at him as he passed by, and he pointed at his flashlight.

He entered the house again. The entranceway had no coat closet; stairs rose parallel to the room on his right, a narrow hallway opened in front of him, and eerie shadows from the streetlights illuminated the living room to his left. He could definitely smell fresh paint. He touched the door jamb: still tacky. Blackfield had told him clearly that he had to get the plumbing done because his contractor was coming to fix up the place on Wednesday, but it seemed like the contractor had already been here. He shined his flashlight onto the floor: it looked like new carpet.

He decided to check out the job he'd been hired to do. Heading down the hall, he entered a kitchen area and clicked a light switch, and this time the light in the ceiling fan came on. Here, the house's age was more apparent. Green-and-orange, pockmarked, 70s-era vinyl covered the floor. A small table sat in front of him, blocking the way to the back door. Cabinets freshly painted white, an old electric stove, and a sink sat around the perimeter of the room.

Going directly to the sink, he bent down and opened the cabinets. A bare interior stared back at him. Shining his flashlight in revealed a large hole cut in the bottom of the cabinet. Leaning into the cabinet, he pointed the flashlight down the hole, squinting. An old copper pipe sat flush with the sub-floor underneath the cabinet.

This was not a broken pipe; this pipe had been cut, deliberately. Why would someone cut a pipe flush with the sub-floor? He'd probably have to get in the crawlspace to fix it. Still, depending on how clear it was to access, the job wouldn't take that long.

He stood up and a shadow made him nearly jump out of his skin. "Yaahh!" escaped his mouth before he knew he'd made any sound. He raised the flashlight to strike whoever it was and stopped. Mary. She'd left the truck and come into the house.

She jumped back in surprise, and then immediately started laughing, as Sal bent, breathing heavily, his hands on his knees. After he'd recovered for a moment, he chuckled. "Don't do that."

"Seems like you may have been a bit nervous after all, Mr. Who-Would-Kill-A-Plumber," she said.

"Yeah, well, there's nothing here. Just a job. It can wait till tomorrow."

"Then let's get out of here. I want to go home."

"Yeah. Yeah; that's a good idea."

They both walked out. Sal locked the door and replaced the key. As they backed out of the driveway, Mary said, "Thanks for letting me into your world a little. I had no idea being a plumber could be such an adventure."

"Ha. It usually isn't."

Mary directed Sal to her small house in Westville, and this portion of their trip went smoothly. Night had completely fallen. Streetlights lit their way for the entire journey, keeping the shadows at bay. They talked. Sal told Mary about his fresh move and getting his business going. Mary spoke about her love of books and stories and learning, and how she particularly liked helping students researching papers for school. Before they knew it, Sal had pulled his truck in front of her house.

"Thank you again for driving me home, even if you had to go on a little adventure first," she said.

"It's no problem. Least I could do, after all the trouble I caused you."

"Well, to your point, you didn't do it on purpose. Somebody else did it to you."

"Yeah, but I shoulda checked everything before taking off this morning."

"Nobody's perfect."

Suddenly, Mary's stomach growled, which gave her an idea. "Hey, do you have anything planned for tonight?"

"Not really. Dinner, TV, bed."

"Would you like to share a pizza before going home? I've suddenly realized I'm starved. The hospital only gave me some chicken soup."

Sal considered his options. He could go home now—by way of Wawa for dinner, watch some TV he'd never remember later—or he could stay with Mary for a while and enjoy some companionship. Seemed like a no-brainer.

"Sure; I'd like that." He thought for a moment, and just to make sure she didn't think this had any extra meaning to it, added "I'll pay half."

"Sounds good to me."

He shut off the truck, came around to the passenger side, and opened the door for her.

"Thank you," she said, as she stepped out.

They went up the walk and into the house.

35

∞∞∞∞∞

5:30 PM

"So," Gloria finished, "I have no idea how a kid like Jameel could have gotten mixed up with a bad seed like Freddie. I want some answers."

"Uh," said Sean, and cleared his throat. "This might not be the best time for a complete debriefing."

They'd reached the nurses' station in the middle of the floor and checked the signs to see which hallway contained the right room.

"I don't care," Gloria replied. "I need to know. He's got a bright future ahead of him if he stays out of trouble, and Freddie is trouble."

"I'm sure he knows that—particularly now. He's just been dealt a hard lesson. Let's try and see what he's learned from it first and guide him from there, rather than lecture him."

"Okay, Pastor. I'll follow your lead. But don't expect me to stay silent."

Sean smiled. "I wouldn't dream of it."

They entered the room. An empty bed separated by a curtain which hid the other bed beyond greeted them. Sean let Gloria take the lead, as she seemed anxious to see the patient, and she moved quickly past the empty bed to the occupied one. There was only one chair again, opposite the bed, but Gloria went right to the bedside, where Jameel lay motionless. Sean could see immediately that he was tall. If he hadn't bent his legs under the covers, they'd easily have stuck out uncomfortably beyond the foot of the bed. His head faced opposite them. Gloria touched his shoulder gently.

"Jameel?"

His head whipped around, his eyes wide. He'd been crying. Quickly wiping the tears away, he said tiredly, "Ms. Williams."

"Oh, honey, how are you?"

He ignored her question. "Mom just left. She's a mess. Plans to go talk to the Principal about school security. I couldn't tell her the truth." He looked away again.

"The truth?" Gloria asked. "I don't even know the truth, Jameel, and I was there. What were you doing, fighting with Freddie?"

Jameel turned back to face her, then seemed to notice Sean for the first time. His eyes narrowed suspiciously. "Who's that guy?"

Sean came forward and stuck out a hand, which Jameel ignored. "Sean Peterson. I'm a minister on staff at the hospital. I met Ms. Williams earlier today, and she wanted to bring me along, in case I could help."

"Well, you can't, so you might as well go."

"Jameel!" Gloria exclaimed. "That's awfully rude."

"I didn't tell my own mom what really happened today; what makes you think I'm gonna tell some random guy?"

"Because he can bring in a neutral perspective, as an outsider. And you can trust him to keep things confidential, right Pastor?"

"Absolutely. Unless you're confessing to abusing a child, I must report that. Have you abused a child?"

Jameel looked annoyed. "No, I haven't abused a child."

"Well that's something, then." Sean smiled. "If it helps, you can pretend I'm not here while you catch up with your teacher."

Jameel still looked as if he didn't trust him, but he seemed placated. He lay back staring at the ceiling, but didn't speak, forcing Gloria to take the first step.

"Jameel," Gloria sat on the edge of the bed and took his hand. "I can't help you if you won't talk to me."

"Don't you understand? I don't want your help! I don't want anybody's help! I have to handle this myself."

"Why? Jameel, everybody needs help at some point in their life."

"Yeah, well 'help' always seems to get me in trouble."

"That doesn't make any sense. You're not in trouble and as far as I can tell, you're one of those kids everybody likes."

"Shows how much *you* know."

Gloria threw up her hands and looked up at Sean, helplessly.

"Well," Sean said, "*I* don't know anything about you, but it's my job to help anyone who finds themselves here at the hospital in any way I can. Sometimes it helps to begin with a small piece of the problem, if the whole thing is too big to handle. Ms. Williams tells me you were stabbed today, and it gave her something of a shock—"

"—to say the least," Gloria muttered, her hand at her chest.

"—so maybe you can start with why somebody would want to stab you in the first place."

"Because I owed him money," Jameel said, looking out the window.

Gloria's eyes narrowed. "You owed Freddie Dietrich money? Why?"

Jameel's head whipped around to face her. "Why do you think?"

"I don't know."

"Oh, come on. It's not that hard. You just don't want to say it."

"Why do you think that?"

"Because." Jameel paused. "Because I'm your poster boy; your great example. Except I'm not. I'm no better than my father, who died drunk in the gutter." He turned toward the window again. "I suck."

"That's not true—" Gloria began, and Sean cut her off with a wave of his hand.

"Jameel, that's the truest thing you've said. You do suck," said Sean.

Jameel turned to face him, but Sean continued, "You owed him drug money, didn't you?"

"What?!" Gloria looked at Jameel, then back at Sean, then back at Jameel again. Jameel's intelligent eyes studied Sean's, assessing, measuring. They relaxed when he made his decision.

"Yeah. Yeah, I did." He looked away again. Gloria's mouth dropped to an O shape, but she didn't speak, and she closed it when she realized it was hanging open.

"How? How did this happen?" she said.

"Doesn't matter. I let it happen," said Jameel, still not facing her. "I couldn't keep up. Couldn't do it all. Everybody cheered me on, gave me respect as long as I could perform. As long as I was their example black boy, who could do everything. When I couldn't perform, that was it. Nobody helped me, and I didn't want nobody's help."

"*Anybody's* help," said Gloria reflexively. That made Jameel turn, roll his eyes at her, and turn back.

Sean broke in. "But Freddie helped you, didn't he?"

"Yeah. He gave me the stuff for nothing. I knew using was wrong; I knew it was dangerous. But Freddie and I grew up together. At first I thought he had my back. And I had no intention of using the stuff till it was gone; maybe just a couple of times, that's it. But I couldn't keep up."

"You keep saying that. What do you mean?"

Jameel turned to face him. "AP classes. Honor society. The play. Basketball. A job. Taking care of my little brother, 'cause my mom works. I'm tired all the time. On the meth, I could do it all—I didn't need to sleep. But after the first batch, Freddie said I had to pay, and my job doesn't cover my share of our rent plus that. I got behind."

"I get it. Get you hooked, then squeeze you dry," said Sean. Gloria eyed him quizzically and he smirked, saying, "I wasn't always a minister." Jameel looked at him with new respect, then scowled.

"Doesn't change anything. It just means I was fooling myself all along, that I was gonna make it out. But not now. Now I'm stuck where I am, like everybody that came before me, and everybody that'll come after me. No magic scholarships, no college. Just the same dead end."

"And that's why you suck."

"Yeah, pretty much." He stared out the window again.

"Jameel, I'm going to let you in on a little secret," said Sean. "We all suck." Jameel turned to face him and he continued, "You've just learned a lesson that some people never learn: nobody measures up. You've learned it the hard way, but you've learned it early, and probably more thoroughly than most people. Don't waste it."

"I don't get how that helps me."

"There are people who spend their entire lives comparing themselves to other people, trying to 'measure up.' It's a trap. Don't fall for it. We all fail, because there's something wrong with all of us. What made you think you could juggle all that stuff and survive?"

"I didn't think about that. I needed to survive. I'd do any—" he cut himself off and turned away.

"What is it, Jameel?" asked Gloria.

"Nothing."

"Jameel, we can't help you if you don't tell us what happened."

Jameel's head turned back, first to face Gloria, then Sean, then back to Gloria. "The last time I trusted somebody to help me, I got stabbed."

"That's because you trusted the wrong person," said Gloria.

"Yeah, but I had reason to trust him. I've known him since I was five. You're just a teacher, and you—" He indicated Sean, "—I don't know you at all."

"All that proves is that perhaps *you* aren't the best arbiter of who to trust," said Sean. "Instead of trusting yourself, trust that she's a teacher of—how many years?"

"Ten."

"Of ten years' experience, who met all the qualifications of the State to gain that position, and that I'm a minister of 11 years' experience who met all the qualifications of the church to gain my position. Furthermore, trust that both positions—a teacher and a minister—are roles within society that traditionally support, coach, and counsel other people to help them do what is wise and good and just. All that is solid evidence to trust us both, but I realize in the end because of those who haven't fulfilled those roles properly, you ultimately have to exercise faith."

Silence hung in the air as Jameel looked from one to the other. Finally, he snorted in attempted laughter, but grimaced in pain from the sudden contraction of his muscles around his wound. This did not prevent Sean and Gloria from laughing out loud, and Gloria placed a reassuring hand on Jameel's forearm to help him regain control.

After taking a few deep breaths, Jameel said, "You're crazy uptight."

Sean smiled. "I've had a long day," he said, and they laughed some more, causing Jameel to lose control of his breathing again.

When Jameel had recovered, Sean said, "So what do you say, are you ready to talk? If I'm crazy uptight, you're crazy intense. Why are you so intense?"

Jameel took a few deep breaths. "I was five when my father died. I didn't know why or how he died until later. I just knew he wasn't there anymore, and that other kids had dads and I didn't. I'm not even sure if I missed him in particular, or if I just missed the idea of having a dad, because I don't remember him that well.

"I don't know when or how old I was, but at some point I was feeling really low about this. I sat on my front steps and looked at the sidewalk, and I thought my dad amounted to nothing and died. My granddad was killed in the Army, young. Grandmom had to work to make ends meet; Mom had to work to make ends meet. They tried to teach us right from wrong, but with no Dad around and them working all the time, kids for generations were left mostly alone. I realized everybody in my past, my ancestors, they had nobody to guide them, to love them, to bring them up right. That's why we were poor; that's why nobody ever succeeded at anything, because nobody had their back. They did what they wanted, and they never amounted to anything. We're all in apartments or on food stamps, have menial jobs, drink or use drugs, or have been in jail.

"I swore that day that I would be the one to break that pattern. I would start working hard, and do well, and succeed. My kids—when I have them—would have me around to teach them right, and I would have a good job, and they wouldn't be poor. Since that day, my whole life has been focused on that."

Jameel paused, staring at his bed sheets. "The problem was, I just couldn't keep up. I couldn't do it. I worked as hard as I could, and still, stuff would slip. I hadn't thought of that before, that I wasn't up to the task of making it. So many other people do it: they get good grades, they graduate, they go to college, they get good jobs."

"Why do you think you can't make it?" asked Gloria.

"Well, look at me! I cheated with drugs because I couldn't make it on my own, and it landed me in the hospital."

"You think everybody makes it on their own?" asked Sean.

"No. Most people get help and support from their families. But lots don't. They just do it."

"See? That's trying to measure up to an impossible standard. That's the trap: thinking the standard is reachable, but it's not. It's just there to taunt you and make you feel bad when you learn you can't reach it. You may think other people do it, but they don't. It's the same with the standard given us by God."

"God? What does God have to do with it?"

"Did you ever wonder why so many people who say they're Christians or follow God wind up doing things that are wrong, that God hates?" asked Sean.

"No, not really."

"Why?"

"Because. Because all them people—" Gloria's eyes flashed, and Jameel noticed. "Because all *those* people are hypocrites. Some people say everybody who talks about God has an angle. They use God to manipulate people, make them do what they want."

"What do you think?"

"I don't know. My mom, she loves church. Says it always makes her feel better."

"What about you?"

Jameel cleared his throat. "I don't have time for church. I haven't been there in a long time."

Sean frowned and said, "When you did go, did you ever notice somebody—even somebody in leadership like the minister—do something you knew was wrong?"

"Maybe. I don't know, really. I was just a kid."

"What did you see?"

"I came running in from outside to get a drink—we were playing basketball after the service, and I got thirsty. I caught him yelling at somebody."

"Him? Who, your pastor?" Sean asked.

"Yeah. He was screaming at the guy; I don't know who the guy was, though. They stopped when they saw me. I got my drink and left real quick."

"All right, I can work with that. What did you think at the time?"

"At the time? I don't know. I don't think I thought anything. I just wanted to get back to the game. I forgot about the whole thing until now."

"I don't think so. I think your brain filed that little incident away until somebody put it in context later."

"In context? What do you mean?" Jameel asked.

"You said before that some people say anybody who talks about God has an angle and is manipulating people. I think at some point you heard that and your brain connected it to this experience. Your minister once did something that didn't match up with what he preached, and—boom—suddenly you believed it."

"I didn't say I believed it."

"Yeah, but it was, like, one of the first things you said about people who believe in God, so it's right there, in your head. It's something you think about."

"Maybe. I can't say I actively think about it."

"Maybe not, but it's one of those ideas that bounce around in your head."

"Okay, so what?"

"So the minister at your church doesn't measure up. You've got a standard in your head that says what kind of person he should be—"

"No, no, that's not my standard. That's *his* standard."

"Bingo! You've got it." Sean raised both fists in the air.

Jameel looked confused. "Uh, got what?"

"You're measuring your pastor according to the standard that he himself has set, and you found he doesn't measure up."

"Okay, right."

"Well, you're doing the same thing to yourself: measuring yourself to a standard you set for yourself, and finding you don't measure up."

"So what are you saying, I'm a hypocrite, just like Reverend Wilson?"

"I didn't say it; you just said it. But I'm going to give you a different way to think about it, are you ready?"

"I'm not sure."

"Everybody's a hypocrite. Nobody measures up. We all screw up, all the time. What matters is whether you expect it and are introspective enough to recognize it for what it is, because that makes all the difference in what you do in response. Tell me, what was the first thing you thought about today, lying here on this bed? How did you process what happened today?"

Jameel looked away. He said quietly, "I thought about how I am a failure."

Sean leaned forward and asked, "Did you decide to do anything with that information? Be honest."

"Yes."

"What was it, Jameel?"

"I decided it was no use. I've been fooling myself that I'm different. I'm nobody, and I'm no better than my father or anybody else, and I might as well accept it."

"Now Jameel, how is that going to help you achieve your goals?"

"But you don't understand! I *can't* achieve my goals! I'm not good enough. If I've done anything, I've proved that!"

Sean sat back. "No you haven't. All you've proved is that you don't measure up to the standard you set for yourself."

"Isn't that the same thing?"

"No. Let me give you a parallel. God's standard—His law, which is in the ten commandments—is so high that no one can reach it. What you saw your pastor doing was just an example. What you did to yourself was the same thing: you set a standard for yourself so high that you couldn't reach it. The problem is when you realized that, you cheated with drugs instead of seeking help. We should hold people—including ourselves—to a high standard, but we can't expect that they'll be able to meet that standard. Only one person ever has."

"Who?"

"Jesus Christ. That's the whole point of going to church, and probably the reason why your mom loves it so much. Jesus met God's standard, and He took the punishment on Himself that we deserved for not meeting the standard. The Christian trusts in Jesus to meet that standard and God forgives us, fully and completely. He sees Jesus's perfection instead of our imperfection. And in response, we study God's Word to learn about ourselves and where we often go wrong. On a daily basis, we ask God's forgiveness, turn away from those things, and seek to live more like Jesus lived."

Jameel smirked. "I don't see how that makes a difference."

"It makes all the difference. It means that when we fail, we can be forgiven, pick ourselves up, and try again. It can be a privilege—a joy even—to go to God and ask His forgiveness. We can ask forgiveness of other people affected by our failures too. We don't have to hide it when we don't measure up, and we don't have to try to present a false image of our 'perfect' selves to the world."

Jameel seemed lost in thought for a while. Gloria looked expectantly at Sean, who locked his gaze on Jameel's face.

Finally Jameel turned and faced Sean. "That's a whole new way of thinking."

"Yes it is. I daresay it's a better and more productive way of thinking. It changes the trajectory of your life. Embracing forgiveness and redemption means you can never be canceled, no matter what happens."

"You think if God forgives me, if my mom forgives me, and if I forgive myself, that it'll fix everything? I'll get that basketball scholarship, I'll get a degree, and I'll pull my family out of this hole?"

"No, Jameel, I can't make any promises like that. What I can say is that God promises a life that's more abundant and that's eternal. I can promise that your life will never be the same. I don't know what God has in store for you, but I know that God will give you grace to get through whatever life throws at you. And that is far better than wallowing in your failure to meet a standard that's impossible anyway."

Jameel took a deep breath. "Thank you. You've definitely given me something to think about, bro."

Gloria smiled. "So it was okay I brought him here?"

"Yeah. Yeah, it's okay. In fact, maybe we can talk again some time?"

"I'll stop by tomorrow. For now, though, we should let you get some rest." Sean yawned. "I think I need some rest too."

Gloria stood up. "Thanks for letting us visit, Jameel."

"I appreciate you coming."

A man entered the room, wheeling a cart. "Looks like your dinner's here anyway. Actually smells good," said Sean.

"I'll let you know," said Jameel.

"Okay, see you later."

Sean motioned for Gloria to precede him out of the room, and they walked out.

36

∞∞∞∞

7:00 PM

Gloria had insisted she could drive herself home left-footed, so Sean had dropped her off by her car and waited in the parking lot to watch her pull out. Though her exit wasn't the cleanest he'd ever seen, he thought she had a more than 95 percent chance of making it home alive.

He pulled into his driveway, put the car into park, and sat for a bit with the car (and its heater) running, rubbing his bleary eyes. He couldn't remember ever having a day quite like this one, and his burning eyes wanted badly to close. He shut off the car and entered the house.

The smell of fried chicken and the sound of a beater mashing potatoes greeted him warmly. He put his coat in the closet, snuck into the bathroom to wash his hands (a good idea always, but particularly wise when he'd spent all day at the hospital), and entered the kitchen, making Wendy jump.

"Oh! I didn't hear you come in."

"This smells delicious!" He pulled her close, beater and all, and kissed her firmly.

"You look exhausted," she said.

"I am. Very busy at the hospital. There was a big car accident this morning, and I think I met all of the main people involved, along with some others."

"Oh wow. Emotional day?"

"Definitely. I'll tell you all about it over dinner."

It had taken an hour to tell her about his day, and now he was more exhausted than ever. Sean cleared the dishes in silence. The day replayed itself in his brain while his hands rinsed dinnerware automatically.

As he placed a plate in the dishwasher, he said, "I was thinking on the way home about the providence of God...." he trailed off and grabbed a glass.

"What about it?" asked Wendy.

"Well, every person I met today had their day irrevocably changed by one event this morning. Some of them more than others, of course. It makes me think of all the events in a single day, and how one event can affect hundreds, perhaps thousands of people."

"What do you mean?"

"Well, take the accident this morning. I may have met some of the people involved but think about it: that accident caused a traffic jam that changed how all those people's days were going to work out. They got to where they were going later than they would have. That may have caused something else to happen differently, and then something else, cascading way out from the original event."

"And yet God planned it all."

"Yeah, that's what gets me. I mean, we study these things and have kids memorize catechisms saying that God 'hath foreordained whatsoever comes to pass,' but I don't think we ever stop to think about what that means. There are millions of events happening to people all the time, events we know nothing about, but are so important to the people involved in them, and God knows about all of them. God can hear somebody praying in Bangladesh right now, while He also hears the good night prayers of a child a few houses over. Doesn't that fill you with awe?"

"Now that you describe it like that, yes."

"Well, I think when we're done with these dishes, we should sit down and spend some time praising Him. I want to thank God for the small part I have to play in His plan, and ask Him to help me be faithful."

"Okay."

"And I want to pray for all the people I met. I feel like something was put in motion, something bigger than just what happened today. And I want to be prepared for whatever comes next."

Wendy put the pot she was drying down, dried off her hands, and faced Sean. "It's this, you know."

"What?"

"This is why I love you. You love God first, and then that love spills over to other people." She pulled him into an embrace. "And I'm the first one in line."

"Always, my love. Always."

Epilogue
∞∞∞∞

Six months later

The bright, June sun beamed down upon the church's backyard. Several oblong tables festooned with plastic white tablecloths formed two lines with a wide aisle between them. A breeze momentarily puffed up the tablecloths before subsiding, revealing that they'd been somehow fastened to the empty tables to keep them from blowing away.

The back door to the church banged open, and a four-months pregnant Wendy Peterson emerged, carrying a hot casserole pan covered in tin foil between two mittened hands. Close behind her came Sean, close behind him came Gloria, and close behind her came Jameel, each burdened with a pot, a dish, or a pan of some kind laden with food. They all placed their payloads on the first table, making it a buffet.

"I think we're just about all set!" said Wendy.

"Just in time," said Sean, indicating cars arriving in the parking lot. "How do I look?"

Wendy inspected his face and wiped some crumbs off the corner of his mouth. "You've been sampling one of the desserts."

"Maybe not just one," said Gloria.

"I can't believe you threw me under the bus!" he said in mock disbelief. "I'll remember that."

Sean quickly untied his apron, crumpled it up, and handed it to Wendy.

"Pray for me," he said.

"Absolutely."

He headed toward the parking lot. Two cars had arrived and parked side by side. The doors opened on the white Toyota Camry. Dan Livingston emerged from the driver's side, and Colin Donnell exited the passenger's side. Dan immediately trotted over to the other car—a maroon Honda Civic—to meet its driver at its already popped open trunk.

"Welcome!" Sean called as he approached. "Can I give you a hand?"

"I think we're okay over here," said Dan, pulling crutches out of the trunk. "But Colin might need help with the food."

"Hey Colin, let me grab that," Sean said as Colin passed him a covered crock pot. "Hey Nat!" he called over the top of the car as Dan helped Margaret's son, Nathaniel, out of the car while Margaret handed him the crutches.

"Hey, Pastor Sean! Thanks for doing this; I think it'll mean a lot."

Sean smiled as Nat settled himself on his crutches and Margaret pulled his daughter, Terri, out of the car seat in the back. "I've been looking forward to this for a long time," he said.

As Sean placed the crock pot on the table his phone buzzed, and he pulled it out of his pocket.

Had some last minute trouble getting him to agree to come, but we're on our way.

Awesome! he tapped back.

More vehicles arrived: a red Dodge RAM that Sean recognized immediately and a beat up Toyota Corolla. He jogged toward the Corolla, but Jameel came from behind, overtook him, and arrived there first. The back door opened.

"Daryl!" Jameel exclaimed. The young boy—already tall for his age—exited the car, smiled up at Jameel, and leaped into his arms.

"Hi Carynne," Sean said, as Jameel's mother closed the driver's side door, having popped the trunk. "Anything I can help you with?"

"No, I'm good, I'm good," she said as he came over anyway. Rather than hand him something to carry, she gave him a hug and a peck on the cheek. "I got my boys here; they'll be glad to help me, won't you, boys?"

"Yeah, mom," said Jameel, while Daryl squealed "Let me! Let me!"

Sean turned to the truck, whose occupants had already disembarked and were approaching. The man carried a big box, presumably containing food items for the picnic, but his mind did not seem to be on the box. His eyes darted furtively around, taking in the parking lot, the church building, and the people busily moving as they carried things through the yard to the left, beyond which the tables could barely be seen around the corner. As Sean approached, his eyes locked on him, and he smiled with relief.

"I'm so glad you could make it, Sal," said Sean. "You need any help with that?"

"Hey Pasta." Sal used the affectionate nickname he'd developed for Sean. Growing up Catholic, he had not been used to protestant titles for clergy and still found them awkward. "Naw, I got it. Where do I go with it?"

"Back behind the church, we have tables set up for all the food." He turned to Mary, who'd arrived with Sal. "Hi Mary; it's so nice to see you. I think the two of you have an important part to play today."

Sal visibly blushed, and Mary smiled. "To tell you the truth, I'm worried," she said. "This could go well, or it could go poorly. And you know I'm not one to be relied on to say the right thing."

"Well," Sean said, "you won't be alone. We're in this together, and I'll be praying whenever I'm not speaking. May God give us grace to be a blessing this day."

They passed by him carrying their contribution of food for the meal, and Sean took a deep breath. *Won't be long now*, he thought as he exhaled. *Oh Lord, help us to encourage and to edify.*

He followed Sal and Mary back to where a huge spread, much more than was necessary for the amount of people in attendance, had been set up on a conjoined row of fold-up tables hidden by white plastic tablecloths. Sal and Mary placed their item—a gumbo soup of Mary's own design—in the row and found a table at which to sit. Most of the gathered people greeted each other in groups of three or four, not willing yet to sit.

A flash of sun glare off a windshield caught Sean's eye, and he turned to see a blue minivan enter the parking lot. He found Wendy straightening the items on the banquet table and said, "Well, here goes nothing."

She squeezed his arm. "This is what you've been waiting for, what you wanted to do from that first night when everything happened. You've been thinking about this and preparing for it, and designing everything about today to be encouraging, uplifting, and a help."

"Yes, but I can't stop wondering what if it doesn't go well? What if we make things worse?"

"You've done everything in your power to keep that from happening. Now it's time to give it your best and watch God work. You're not in control of what happens; just be faithful. You told me last night you couldn't live with yourself if you'd done nothing."

"That's right."

"Okay, so go do what God has so clearly called you to do, and leave the results up to Him."

He smiled and kissed her. "I love you."

She winked at him. "I know."

He smiled at the familiar reference, took a deep breath, and headed for the parking lot one more time.

Two blond women had already gotten out of the minivan as its rear door rose automatically. They disappeared behind it, and then one of them—the younger one, he saw—emerged, pushing a wheelchair. The side door opened automatically as the back door closed, and the woman lined the wheelchair up with the opening, locking its wheels.

Sean wasn't sure whether he should approach or leave them be. The older woman and the younger woman now flanked each other, clearly seeking to help the third occupant out of the vehicle and into the wheelchair. Hands waved from inside the minivan, and Sean could hear snatches of stressed conversation. The older woman spoke sharply to the occupant—something about "coming out or we're dragging you out," and Sean decided to stay where he was for the moment. He turned away, faced downward, and cradled his chin with thumb and forefinger as though lost in thought, to give them privacy.

After hearing some grunting and the clatter of the chair, he turned to face them again. The third person—a man—now sat in the chair. The older woman locked its left arm into place, while the younger one stood ready to push. Sean approached.

"Hello!" he called and waved. "I'm so glad you could make it today."

The two women—Greta Stratton-Foster and her daughter, Jenny—smiled. The man in the chair, Gerald Foster, scowled and looked at his shoes.

"It's nice to see you too, Sean," said Greta. "It's been a while."

He shook her hand. "Yes; it's been too long since we've had a brain-bending conversation, but today is not the day for such heavy things, right?"

"That's right. This is our daughter Jenny; she's home from school for the summer."

He shook Jenny's hand. "It's very nice to meet you, Jenny. I understand you have a harrowing tale to tell yourself."

She smiled. "Yes I do. Dad hasn't even heard it yet."

"Really?"

"Yeah; it's been a long recovery."

Sean reached out to shake Gerald's hand. "It's good to see you again, Gerry."

Gerry looked up at him, squinting in the sun. He did not return the handshake. "I know what you're trying to do."

Sean retracted his hand and squatted down to face him so he wouldn't have to squint. "What am I trying to do, Gerry?"

"You think you're going to make me *feel* better. You think your stupid picnic and religious platitudes will somehow *comfort* me, and make me feel like it's okay to be disabled."

"It is okay to be disabled, Gerry," said Greta.

"No it's not! I'm less than half the man I was, and nothing's going to change that. That's reality. There is no God, there are no miracle cures, and there's nothing you can say to make me feel better. This is a complete waste of time, and I'm only doing this for them." He pointed his left and right thumbs at the two women.

"I'm sorry that you feel that way, Gerry. But there are a lot of people here, and we've put this thing together not just for you, but to help all of us process what happened that day."

"I don't know any of these people. Are they church people?"

"Some are, yes, but not all."

He looked at him quizzically. "I don't see how a picnic with a bunch of strangers is going to solve anything."

"We're not here to solve anything, Gerry," said Sean. "We're here to have a good time, and to share that good time with you. That's all."

"Why?"

Sean glanced up at Greta, then faced Gerry again. "Because we want to share this day with you. Everyone has brought some food to share, and we want to have a good summer picnic and enjoy each other's company."

"No religious mumbo-jumbo?"

"This is a church, Gerry. There's going to be some religious mumbo-jumbo. I think you can handle it."

"Come on, Dad," Jenny said. "Mom and I think this is a good idea. It's something small, to get you out of the house, get you socializing with people again."

"Why these people? Why not anybody we know? Why *religious* people?"

"Just trust us, Dad. Please."

Gerry faced Sean sternly. "I'm doing this for her. If you've done anything to her, brainwashed her with religious garbage, so help me God, I'll—"

"So help you God?" Sean asked.

"It's a saying. I'll make you pay. I don't know how yet—" he looked down at his useless legs, "—but I will. I love her more than life itself."

Sean clapped Gerry on the shoulder, and Gerry visibly jumped. "It's that love that gives me hope for you, Gerry."

They made their way across the parking lot to the sidewalk, and then into the lawn area that comprised the church's side yard. The wheelchair got bound up in the spongy New Jersey grass, and Sean helped Jenny navigate it around to the back of the church, seating Gerry at the first table facing the banquet.

As Gerry came into view, heads swiveled to look at him. He noticed and scowled, muttering something to himself. Sean placed him at that first table for two reasons: to make it so he wouldn't easily see the people staring at him, and to give him the best view of the proceedings to follow. So far, all his choreography had worked out perfectly, but the day wasn't over yet.

Sean stood in front of the banquet table and faced the assembly. "Now that everyone is here, why don't we all take our seats so we can begin enjoying this delicious meal everyone has brought!" he said, thankful that he'd been blessed with a loud voice.

The milling people took their seats at various tables. Sean could see that his choreography continued to work: there were no extra seats. Everyone had to share a table with someone else. This way, hopefully, they would get to know one another and have good conversations.

Once everyone was settled, Sean said, bowing his head, "Let's pray. Dear Father in heaven, we thank You for this beautiful day You have made and for Your direction to rejoice and be glad in it. We want to do that today, even if in some ways we may be hurting and suffering. Though it's hard to do, we want to rejoice even in that, knowing that we have a part in the sufferings of our Lord Jesus Christ, who died to restore our fellowship with God so that we might be delivered from suffering forever. Though we know we'll never be free of suffering in this life because of sin, Jesus paid the penalty for our sin if we put our faith and trust in Him, and now we can live our lives according to His teachings: loving our friends, our neighbors, even our enemies, that the light of Your gospel may shine throughout this world and point people to You, the source of all that is good and true and beautiful. Bless this food which we are about to eat, and bless our fellowship together. In Jesus' name, Amen."

Sean looked up quickly and saw that Gerry, Greta, and Jenny had not been praying. Gerry had his head down, shaking it, Greta had been calmly watching Sean and now turned away, and Jenny looked thoughtful. He continued, "Okay, we're doing this buffet style. The line starts here—" he indicated the end of the table, "—where you can grab your plates and go down the line. Take as much as you want, and make as many trips as you want!"

Because there were so many "chefs," there was a great variety of food. Fresh watermelon, cantaloupe, and honeydew decorated plates filled with pieces of chicken, potato salad, or barbecued ribs. Bowls filled with salad or Mary's gumbo soup traveled down the line as people grabbed fresh Italian bread or handfuls of chips. Mayonnaise and mustard spread over rolls filled with deli ham, roast beef, and varieties of cheese mixed with the tangy smell of kosher dill pickles. People ate their fill, and the sounds of conversation caught in the warm summer breeze. Sean surveyed the scene and smiled at Wendy. So far, so good.

Sean and Wendy sat with the Foster family, and Sean helped Greta with the mechanics of getting a plate filled with food for Gerry. He seemed to eat well, even if he didn't talk much. Sean had met with Greta several times since the day of the accident, and the church had provided meals for them periodically. She'd taken a leave of absence from the University, with the hope of coming back to work full time for the fall semester.

Jenny had come home to visit her family shortly after the accident, but this was the first time Sean had met her face to face. She seemed still to be getting used to her new reality, which made sense. Greta had made her go back after a week or so and continue with her studies. No wonder she seemed a bit shell shocked. But when Sean had proposed this idea,

Jenny had been instantly enthusiastic about it, which gave Sean hope: if Jenny wanted this done, he'd thought, it would be done. And here they were now, doing it. He prayed, *Dear God, bless our ministry to this man, to this family. Heal them and save them by Your grace.*

He looked around and saw that most people were finishing up. He took a deep breath and exhaled slowly, hoping to exhale some of his nervousness with the air. It was time to start. He stood.

"Hey everybody!" Conversation started to die down. "Your attention, please. Thank you. I think it's time to get started. If you have trash to get rid of, please do it now, and then take your seats."

He ran up the stairs, grabbed a small podium from one of the nearby Sunday school classrooms, and brought it outside as Jameel and Sal moved the banquet table aside. He placed the podium where the table had been. Jameel appeared with the portable, battery-powered PA system Sean had bought for the occasion and plugged a lapel mic receiver into it. As everyone took their seats again, Sean saw Gerry whispering furiously to Greta while she tried unsuccessfully to shush him.

Sean cleared his throat. "The reason I wanted to get everyone here today is simple: we all have something in common. All the people here had their lives forever altered on the same day: the day of the accident."

He surveyed the assembled people; all gazed at him expectantly. A warm breeze fluttered the tablecloths; Sal waved away a bee that had investigated Mary's hair.

Sean continued, "I'm not the main speaker today; in fact, I'm not sure if there is a main speaker. We are here to share how our lives have changed because of a single event on a single day. We Christians believe in something called providence, which is the outworking of God's plan, according to His will, each and every day. Our church's doctrinal statement calls this the 'decrees' of God: His 'eternal purpose, according to the counsel of his will, whereby, for his own glory, he hath foreordained whatsoever comes to pass.'

"A secular concept for this is Fate, that there is somehow an inevitability to life: people must follow the path laid out for them. To me, this is nothing but the same concept with God taken out. When you take God out, you lose the sense of purpose, that there's a reason for the path laid out for us. I believe there is a reason, and I believe our paths have been planned out from before the foundation of the world, for God's glory and our good.

"Many people had paths planned out that day, and all of them were altered, some drastically, some slightly, by the accident. It was one event that cascaded out to hundreds, perhaps thousands of people, changing what would have happened forever. I count myself blessed that some of those path alterations brought all of us together, since none of us knew each other before that day."

Sean cleared his throat and looked over at Wendy, who gave him an encouraging nod. "Sometimes our paths take us through valleys of suffering. What you believe makes all the difference in how you respond to suffering. If you believe there's no reason for it, you then become focused on yourself and the cruel, random, unjust circumstances that brought you the suffering. If you believe there is a reason for suffering, you can focus yourself on that reason instead of on yourself and your own misery, and perhaps even rise to become something greater than you were.

"Few people who experience suffering are offered insight into the reasons why. But today, we are afforded a rare opportunity to see how suffering has affected the lives of everyone here. It is my hope that today we'll learn more about how to respond to suffering by seeing the effect one car accident had on all of our lives.

"Our first speaker is Gloria Williams, a math teacher at West Deptford High."

There was scattered applause as Sean took his seat and Gloria went to the podium. As Sean sat down, Gerald leaned over to him and said, "I know what you're trying to do, and it isn't going to work."

Sean tamped down a flash of anger. "You think this is all about you? You're not the only person who lost something that day. You should keep an open mind and listen."

Gerry sat back in his seat as though he'd been shoved. Sean stared him down, and he gazed down into his lap, picking at his thumbnails.

Gloria had finished clipping on the lapel mic Sean had left on the podium for her. "Can everyone hear me?" People nodded their assent.

"Hi. As Sean said, I'm Gloria Williams. I'm here to talk about how my life—and the lives of some of my students—were changed on the day of the accident."

She shuffled her notes into place after a breeze threatened to blow the pages away. "I was driving the car directly in front of the accident." She glanced quickly at Gerald. "It was horrific. One car landed upside down on another car. I thought everybody was dead. In fact, I thought I'd confirmed one death."

Her eyes met Gerald's. "I was the first person to see you after the accident, before the cops or anybody arrived. I also saw the car you landed on," she indicated Nathaniel. "A car containing someone who will tell his own story, I'm sure.

"But I didn't know what to think after they whisked both of you away. I have responsibilities; my emotions, not my car or body, were the only things damaged, and I continued on to work.

"Because I was late, I had to park in an unusual area, where the students usually park. As a result and to keep a long story short, I witnessed one student stab another over drug money. But because I was there, at exactly the right time, I was able to alert the authorities and get help for the stabbed student.

"I found out later that the other student—the one who did the stabbing—was himself killed as his handler/supplier/whatever-you-call-them used him as a human shield to make his own escape from the police. So you see —and I've thought long and hard about this—because I was delayed by the accident, there was a reversal of fortunes. A student who was stabbed and would've been left for dead survived, and the assailant who would have escaped was killed, likely as a result of his own misdeeds.

"The student who survived—who is here to speak to you today—is a good kid, though he was fighting demons of his own. Is that justice? I don't know, and I've asked the Pastor here, and he claims not to know either, which I actually found comforting." Titters came from the assembly.

"He did say, though," she continued, "that that wasn't the question to ask, even though it seems the most natural. We aren't in control of the big picture. We only have our part to play in it. In fact, most of the time, we can't even see the big picture. The question we have to ask ourselves is what are we going to do about what we can see? The answer to that question determines whether we grow from our experiences or shrink within ourselves. It makes the difference in whether we lift people up or tear them down. In whether we are ultimately remembered for the blessing we were or as that nasty old person always focused on some past, unjust event and never quite aware of the potential of each day's new events.

"After some things I'd been through in my life, I wasn't sure if I believed in God anymore when this all happened. But that perspective—that I am a small player in God's reality with my own responsibilities in that reality—has helped. I hope it helps you too. I think maybe this opportunity of getting to see some of that bigger picture isn't always afforded to people. I can only speak for myself, but knowing just some of it has helped me think better about the part I have to play. Thank you."

Applause rang out as she collected her papers and left the mic on the podium. Sean quickly jumped up, gave her a hug, and grabbed the mic, holding it up so he could be heard.

"Thank you, Gloria! Now, we don't actually have a plan for the rest of this. I asked everyone I met from that day to think about what happened and prepare something to say that only they could share. Gloria actually called me and asked if she could go first. Does anybody else have something they'd like to share?"

Silence greeted him. Birds chirped in the distance, and the sun disappeared briefly behind a cloud. He scanned those assembled; most refused eye contact. Finally, as the sun broke its way through the clouds, Nathaniel raised his hand.

"I'd like to speak, but I can't stand at that podium in my current condition."

Sean smiled. "I'll bring the mic to you, and you can speak from there."

"No, I want to be up front. I want to face everybody."

People shifted uncomfortably in their seats. Gerald briefly put his head in his hands, then turned to Greta, pleading to help him get out of there. She shook her head, face resolute.

Nathaniel stood with the help of his crutches. Sean grabbed his own chair, moved the podium aside, and placed the chair where the podium had been. When Nathaniel arrived at the chair, he sat down heavily, leaning the crutches on the podium beside him, and pulled a folded piece of paper from his back pocket. Sean pinned the mic on his shirt and stood to the side.

"Hi everybody; I'm Nathaniel Fitzpatrick. Most people call me Nat." He turned and faced Gerald directly. "I'm told the man who caused the accident is over there, and his name is Gerald Foster. I'm the one your car landed on."

Murmurings came from the assembled people, and the tension they already felt ratcheted up a few notches. Gerald, who had been pointedly whispering to his wife, swiveled his head around to face Nathaniel.

"I'm not here," Nathaniel continued, looking down at his notes, "to accuse you of anything, to blame you for my injuries, or really to say anything negative to you or about you, so everybody can relax." He faced the audience and grinned from ear to ear. "I just couldn't think of any way to start this without making everybody nervous."

It seemed like a collective sigh went through those assembled. A small giggle escaped from Mary before she put her hands to her mouth.

"I believe everything happens for a reason. That didn't keep me from feeling sorry for myself at first. The accident obviously seriously affected my life. I've had pins and screws and all other manner of hardware inserted into my legs over multiple procedures. I'm recovering from the second-to-last round of it. I have one more procedure next month, and then I'm done.

"All this time recovering from surgeries and not being able to walk has given me a lot of opportunity to think. It forced me to really assess what I believe. A lot of us say we believe one thing, but then we live like we believe the opposite. And after a while, I had to admit to myself that I'd done that. I was living for what is practical, for what is the most safe, for what seemed logically to work best. I was not applying the beliefs that I'd been brought up with to my everyday decisions. And so in the midst of my bitterness and selfishness and pain over my injuries and the interruption to my life, I began to ask myself one question: what could God's purpose be in all of this? Because ultimately, He's in control.

"This led to more questions: is there something in my life that God is calling me to change? And even worse: is there something I need to correct in my own life and behavior?

"Unfortunately, the answer to the last two questions was 'yes.' And then through a lot of soul-searching, I figured out what it was."

He looked up at the small assembly, and a tear coursed down his right cheek. "I have this problem. I go on auto-pilot. I don't recognize when the people around me—the people I love most—need me. I just go on my merry way focused on my own responsibilities until something blows up in my face. And boy, it sure did.

"At the time of the accident, my life was a shambles. I'd just been through a divorce, and it was all my fault. I'm not going to go into all the details, but I'd failed to recognize when my wife needed me, and I drove her away, into—well, something that had previously given her comfort.

Because of my actions, or rather inaction, I showed her that the church—and by extension, God—was unreliable and wasn't there when she needed help the most. Because the church, you see, is God's hands and feet on Earth. And who should be right there in the trenches with her the most, but her husband, who claims to love both her and Jesus? I'd been blaming her all this time, but it was really all my own fault.

"As I drove to work that day, I was angry. Angry my marriage had failed. Angry I'd just had to drop my daughter off at her mother's house. Angry that my ex-wife wouldn't even speak to me, and that I had no idea if she was caring properly for our daughter. And then out of nowhere, a car came flying at me and changed my world. And if that hadn't happened, I would never have understood the depths of my own sin and blindness."

He turned and faced Gerald directly. "You and I have both been through unbelievable physical suffering because of that day. But I want to thank you. I know you didn't mean to throw your car at me that day, but it has changed my life. I have you to thank for the incredible privilege of confessing my sins before God and receiving the beauty of His forgiveness. I have you to thank for the experience of making multiple attempts to confess to my ex-wife. I have you to thank that the drive to do this with such persistence has shown her the change in me. I have you to thank for a renewed relationship with my daughter, whom I love so much. And I have you to thank for more maturity of thought. I am now much more aware of my own imperfections, and that being a Christian does not mean I or anybody else is perfect. I need to work on my relationship with the Lord every day, so that my life reflects more of the fruit of His Spirit than the whims of my own wicked heart.

"I don't know your heart, Mr. Foster. But I hope you'll take the things I've said seriously, and consider your relationship with God. You should seek Him while He may be found. I guarantee it'll change your life, as it has changed mine." He turned to face the small audience generally. "Thank you for listening."

Sean leaped forward to help Nathaniel stand as vigorous applause and some *whoop whoops* came from Pastor Dan in the audience. Nathaniel dropped his papers as he grabbed his crutches, and Sean caught them before they blew away. He followed Nathaniel to his seat and handed them to him there before returning and replacing the chair with the podium. Glancing over at Gerald, he saw him gazing into the distance, a look that he couldn't read.

"Well, that was something," he said into the lapel mic. "Does anyone else wish to speak?"

"I'll go," said Mary, standing. She walked calmly up to the podium carrying a small notebook. Sean handed the mic to her and then sat down.

"Hi," she said after pinning the mic to her blouse. She adjusted her glasses. "I'm Mary Simmons. I'm a Librarian. But maybe you could tell."

People shifted uncomfortably. She plowed ahead. "I was also on my way to work on the day of the accident, though I didn't know anything about it. It seems that your accident caused my accident. I mean to say that I also had an accident." She sighed. "Maybe I better just stick to my notes."

She looked down at her notebook, adjusting her glasses again. "Oh yes, there we are. I didn't know the one accident caused the other one that day, because I was nowhere near it. Your accident, I mean," she pointed at Gerald, whose face had turned pale.

"It turns out," she continued, "that Salvatoré over there—wave Sal!" Sal darted his hand up and down quickly. "Salvatoré diverted himself off the highway onto the back roads when he saw the traffic jam, and wound up in Westville, where I was. Then he lost his pipes."

She looked up from her notes. "He's a plumber, you see. He can explain this part better than me. Salvatoré, would you come up here, please?"

Sal shook his head vigorously. "Oh come on, Sal!" she said, sharply. "Don't be obtuse. They'll understand it better if you say it!"

Sal appeared to be wrestling with himself. His legs shifted, and he clasped his hands first in one direction and then the other, five or six times. Then, with resignation on his face, he stood and shuffled slowly to the podium. Mary detached the mic from her blouse and handed it to Sal but left the transmitter clipped to her own belt, effectively handcuffing them together while Sal spoke.

"Hey, uh. I'm Sal. Sal Fuchetti. My truck's out in the parking lot; you can call me if any of yous ever need plumbing work done."

Mary slapped him on the shoulder and said something the mic did not pick up.

Sal continued, "I'm, uh, supposed to get to the point. I have a pipe rack. I built it myself; it's in my truck bed. You put your pipes in the rack—copper, PVC, PEX, it don't matter—and then all you have to do is secure them with cheap plastic ties. Worked for me for years, no problem. Cheap, easy way to carry enough even for big jobs."

Sal seemed to be gaining momentum, and Mary smiled at him. "That day, I hit a pothole, and everything I was carrying—lots of white PVC—just fell off! I couldn't believe it! It went bouncing all over the street and cars were swerving to get out of the way. Except one—hers." He pointed his left thumb at Mary. "She skidded right into a telephone pole."

A loud *whumphf* sounded as Mary snatched the mic from him. "Yes, well, I already said I had an accident, didn't I?" She glared at him, holding the mic now instead of reattaching it.

"Anyway," she continued, "Salvatoré was very apologetic and nice to me that day. I had a concussion. He gave me his card and offered to drive me home from the hospital. I wasn't sure I should trust him, but Gloria over there—oh, I guess I should say something about that."

Her notes had been completely forgotten. "I was in my little ER compartment recovering when Gloria over there barged into my room."

Sal leaned down into the mic. "She couldn't barge, she was on crutches."

"Oh yes, she'd broken her leg or something fighting with that mad stabber guy." Mary frowned. "That might not be right. I had a concussion; I'm not altogether clear on the facts." Gloria had her head in her hands.

Mary pressed on. "Well, however she got there, she wanted to talk to me, because she heard me from the next compartment talking about my car accident, and she thought it was *the* car accident, which it wasn't, but how else could she know it wasn't unless she asked me if it was, so that's what she did, and I told her it wasn't."

Looks of confusion passed over the various people in the audience. "But I guess that doesn't matter," she said. "What matters is that she convinced me to call Sal, and she gave me her number in case Sal was a pervert, which he wasn't."

"I'm not," Sal said helpfully, leaning into the mic again. Now people started to chuckle.

"Sal! Would you stop doing that?" Mary said.

Sal leaned into the mic again. "She's the reverse of my mother. When she yells at me I'm 'Sal,' at all other times, I'm 'Salvatoré.'"

The audience laughed again, and Sal grinned. He had clearly begun to enjoy himself.

"I'm regretting bringing him up here," said Mary.

"That's the idea," Sal said, leaning into the mic again.

Now the tables roared with laughter. Mary glared at Sal.

"I'm trying to tell a beautiful story, and you're messing it all up!" she said.

Sal took her non-miked hand in his, kissed it, and said "I'm sorry" into the miked one. "I'll behave."

"Well," Mary said, "I don't have that much more to go. I called Salvatoré, though—" she glared at him again, "—now I wonder at the wisdom of that, and he picked me up from the hospital and drove me home, after a strange detour into a not-so-nice place he was working on."

"That's another story," Sal added into the mic.

"Yes, quite right, quite right," she said. "Well, we've been seeing each other ever since, and now—" She held her left hand up proudly, with its back toward the audience. A ring glinted from the third finger. "—we're engaged! And we never would've met if he hadn't gotten off the highway because of the accident, and if Gloria hadn't been there for me! Isn't that a great story?" She pointed alternately at Sal and Gloria.

Apparently she was done, because she detached the microphone and slammed it down on the podium, creating a loud *poof!* from the speaker. Sal took her in his arms and kissed her, and the audience cheered as they sat back down. Sean took up the microphone again.

"Well, I think we can all agree that that was a great story," he said. "And we'll be starting a new and even more interesting story next week when the three of us get together for your first pre-marital counseling session." He faced the audience gravely. "Pray for me," he said, and the audience chuckled.

"Okay," he said, "does anyone else want to speak?"

After a pause, Jameel stood. "I do," he said. He shuffled slowly up to the podium, a yellow sheet from a legal pad in his hand. Sean attached the mic to his shirt and handed him the transmitter.

"You can clip that on yourself," he said and smiled.

"Thanks," Jameel said, obviously nervous. Sean sat and Jameel faced the people. "I'm Jameel. Jameel Jones. I'm also, uh, the kid who got stabbed."

Another round of applause ensued. Gerald looked down at his shoes.

"Yeah, well," Jameel continued as the applause died down, "I didn't go out that day to be stabbed. It was a bad day for me, yeah, a bad day. I was the highest scorer on the basketball team, about to beat the school record. I worked most nights busing tables. I was in the honor society. In the play. Trying to make straight As. It was too much. I couldn't keep up. I was tired all the time.

"Freddie—that's the other guy, the stabber—Freddie and I grew up on the same street. He saw how bad off I was. He offered to help me and I took it. I was so tired. Maybe you understand, maybe you don't; I don't know. I don't even know if he really wanted to help me or if he was just in it for himself. I sorta think now maybe he was in it for himself." He glanced quickly at Sean. "Though the Pastor here tells me we can never know now, so I shouldn't judge."

The audience chuckled, causing Jameel to look up from his notes unexpectedly and smile.

"Anyway, after what Ms. Williams said—and I knew some of what she was gonna say, because we talked—I got to wondering." He turned to face Gerald. "Do I in some weird way owe my life to you? Did you, without volunteering it, somehow give up your legs to save my life? I mean, it's strange, this bigger picture Ms. Williams was talking about. Usually you only see your own experience, like if you pushed me out of the way of a moving car and lost your legs or something, we'd have both been there and seen it. You'd have done it on purpose. You'd be a hero. But you didn't mean to save my life. You were doing your thing, and I was doing mine.

"Yeah, well. I, uh, I don't know how to process that. I talked with my mom, Ms. Williams, and Pastor Sean. I think this is the first time in my life I've had to *decide* how to feel, how to react. After thinking about it a lot, I decided to feel the same way I'd feel if you had pushed me away from a moving car: grateful. I'm sorry you can't walk any more."

Jameel started to choke up. He put a hooked index finger to his nose and looked down, struggling to keep control. "But thank you, Mr. Foster. Thank you for my life. Thank you for giving me a future. I will use it to the best of my ability to be a force for good in this world." He paused, getting himself under more control. "I will work hard. You know I will, because I always worked hard."

A look of surprise crossed his face, as though he realized something, and Jameel quickly corrected himself. "Not so hard that I'll ever cheat with drugs again," he said, and the audience responded with grunts of assent and scattered applause. Jameel grinned. "But hard. I have to, actually.

"See, because I was stupid, I lost the basketball scholarship I was going after, the one that was gonna give me a free ride. I got others, but I've had to change my plans. I'm gonna stay home. Work. Go to a local school, Rowan. Do things smarter. No free ride for me. And I'm gonna be the first college graduate from my family, ever. He's gonna be the second." He pointed out at his brother, Daryl, watching from his table. "And then I'm gonna keep going. And I'll be the best doctor you ever saw. And I'm gonna have a wife and a family, and I'm gonna build a legacy where none of my kids or my grandkids will ever remember having nothing. We'll be helping others, and not taking nothing from nobody." He grinned and glanced quickly at Gloria, feeling her glare. "Sorry, Ms. Williams," he said and smiled. "It just comes out. I don't write that way, honest."

"Okay. Pastor Sean helped me with this part. I've felt this way all my life, that I wanted to be the way my family escapes from scraping by just to survive. When I first talked to Pastor Sean, he said it was like a big, hairy beast was riding on my back, whipping me and driving me. The beast had gotten so big I couldn't see anything else, and I would do anything to feed it. It was the meaning of my life. Scary picture.

"He told me that the meaning of life is to 'glorify God and enjoy Him forever.' I never heard that before, and I wasn't sure I wanted to hear any of this God stuff. To be honest, sometimes I'm afraid to talk about it. I'm new at it, so I'm no good at describing it. If you want to talk about God and Jesus, go talk to Pastor Sean. He'll tell you about the 'enjoy Him' part, which I'm still learning myself. I'm gonna focus on the 'glorify God' part.

"What does that even mean? I think it means to do the things God would do, if He were living your life instead of you. So what are some of the things God would do? Well, I think you can get that from the things He told us to do. Help people—all people, like the good Samaritan, who didn't let racism or the idea of being paid back stop him when he saw somebody in need. Love everybody, even your enemies. Do good even to people who wrong you. You could summarize these things by saying *be redemptive*, because Jesus was redemptive. Take things that are broken and fix them, like He did with us. Make that the pattern of your life.

"That made me see the beast. I wanted to be the One, the savior who rescued my family, and that was good, but I was obsessed and unbalanced. I could've hurt my family and I almost got myself killed, because all I wanted was to prove something: that I'm better—that my family is better—than everybody else thinks we are because we have nothing. I wanted everybody to know that. I was gonna prove it.

Everything I ever did was trying to prove it.

Jameel put his head down and gripped the podium as though his life depended on it. The gathered people silently hung on his words as he looked back up at them, leaning on the podium with his elbows. "The first thing I had to realize was that I was—and still am—really, really broken. We all are. Don't trust the ideas that just pop into your head. They might be coming from that beast that's driving you. Compare those ideas with better ones, the ones from God that I was talking about earlier. If what you're thinking doesn't agree with God's ideas, go with His. Be redemptive. Do good even if you think you've been wronged. You can take the hit. It's not gonna be as hard a hit as the one Jesus took for you, to save you, and He asks nothing in return except for faith in Him.

"I did that, and now that beast is dead. I know now that it's okay to admit when you need help. It's important to surround yourself with people—redemptive people—who have your back.

"I still have the same goals, but for different reasons. I want to help my family and other people. I want to be redemptive, like Jesus was. I want to glorify God and enjoy Him forever. So I want to thank you for that also, Mr. Foster. Because even if I'd somehow survived being stabbed, I woulda never learned that lesson, not in a million years. I woulda never killed that beast. It woulda driven me to my death. So without knowing it, you kept my life from being cut short, and you also preserved my life so it would be worth living for the long term.

"That's why I'm grateful. Thank you, Mr. Foster. And thank you to God."

He paused, looking down at the podium, then raised his head. "I guess I'm done now. I'm gonna steal some of this for my Valedictorian speech next week, so thanks for listening."

Forceful applause—way more than expected from the small audience—shook Jameel. Everyone who could stand, stood. Sal whistled loudly. Daryl whooped. Tears streamed from his mother's eyes, and, he noticed, from the eyes of Mr. Foster's family. Mr. Foster's head was down, whether because he was moved or because of something else, he couldn't tell. Jameel grinned and removed the mic from his shirt. Sean clapped him on the back, shook his hand, decided that wasn't enough, and embraced him tightly. Jameel returned the hug and then returned to his table, where his mother nearly crushed him in her embrace.

Once the sound died down, Sean asked, "Does anyone else wish to speak?"

He scanned the audience of hopeful, bright faces until he reached the table he shared with the Fosters. Greta looked contemplative. Gerald's blank face revealed nothing. Jenny was crying. He scanned the audience again and didn't see anyone volunteering. As he was about to thank everyone for coming, Jenny Foster stood.

"I would like to speak," she said.

Greta grabbed her hand. "Are you sure?" she said.

"Yeah," Jenny replied. "I'm sure."

She came to the front, no notes in hand, wiping the tears from her eyes. Sean handed her the microphone.

"They're all yours," he said and sat down. He looked over at Gerald, but Jenny had all of Gerald's attention.

"Hi," she said and sniffed, wiping her nose. "Actually, does anybody have a tissue?"

Greta and Sean immediately leaped up, but Sean was closer. He grabbed the box from the table and pitched it to Jenny, who caught it easily. She turned her back and blew her nose—loudly, the attached mic amplifying the sound. After tossing the tissue into the trash can by the first table, she returned to the podium.

"Thank you. I don't know anybody here, but you all seem like nice people. Did you all know each other before the accident?"

Murmurs of no and shakes of the head came from every table.

"Wow, that's—that's amazing. Well, I guess you all know that my family has been through a lot, but you probably don't know anything about us. After that speech—" She pointed at Jameel. "—that was a great speech. I want to go to your graduation and hear it again."

The crowd chuckled, and Jameel looked down at his shoes.

"After that speech," she continued, "I felt I had to say something, because you see, Dad has saved my life too, countless times. And, I'm realizing, he saved it again, unwittingly, just like he saved yours, by having that accident that day.

"That day was also the day of the shooting at Berkeley, where I go to school." Nods and murmurs of recognition passed through the audience. "I had a class at the same time and in the same building where the shooting happened, and not far from it. I could've been killed that day. But I wasn't in class. I'd skipped class so I could be ready in case Mom called with an update on Dad. Plus I was upset. I wanted to know anything and everything about what had happened to Dad. So in that way, Dad also saved my life that day."

She looked over at Gerald, who had his arms crossed on the table and his head down on them. His ribs shook.

"I've been trying to tell Dad this since I got home; actually even before that. But he wouldn't listen. He kept saying his life was over, and that nothing I could say would comfort him, so I may as well not try. I don't know why he says this; it's not like him at all. But now he's a captive audience, so I had to take the opportunity.

"I'm intrigued by the things said here today. Yes, this is an amazing opportunity to see past your own experiences, to the bigger picture of the effects of a single event. Is this how you convinced Mom to come here?" she asked, looking at Sean, who nodded.

"I have to admit, I wasn't sure about this. I've never been to a church—well, except for weddings. And all that Jesus stuff is stuff my family has sort of made fun of for years. I came because of the hope of breaking Dad out of this, this—depression he's been in. When you're up against a wall and you've tried everything you know, then you start being willing to try anything. And I want my dad back." Her face turned red as she began to struggle with tears. "By some miracle, he didn't die in that accident, but I still don't have him back."

Now she began to cry freely. She grabbed a tissue from the box and wiped her face with it. Some people began to stand, as though they'd approach the podium, but she raised a hand. "I'm not done yet. You all have to understand what kind of person Dad is.

"Dad used to dress himself up like Santa Claus on Christmas morning and pretend to escape out the door—because we have a gas fireplace—just as I was coming down the stairs to look at my presents. Sometimes he'd throw a half-eaten cookie behind him as he 'escaped.' Dad took me on countless trips to give me different experiences: up to the mountains to ski or hike, to lakes to fish, down the shore for rides, for the beach, for crabbing or jet skiing.

"Dad's not very handy, but he always tried his best. He built me a swing set that was great for a while, but it eventually fell apart. He got me a goat because he heard me call one cute, and we had to get rid of it because it got away and ate our neighbor's Fourth of July flags she had out on her lawn, not to mention all her little flowers.

"Our garage is filled with failed projects he attempted: pieces of a bike he could never put together, so he bought me a new, preassembled one; a fort kit still in its box; pieces of a zip line that fell down. All of these things were things I wanted and that he did for me, even though he knew working with mechanical things wasn't one of his strengths.

"We tried sleeping in a tent in the backyard once. I don't think he put it up right, because it fell down on us in the middle of the night. He'd been talking about going camping, but we never tried it after that. There were so many things; so many things.

"Dad was what you were talking about: a redemptive person, at least, and always, with me. Maybe not with everybody; I don't know. But always with me. Always positive, always encouraging, always cheering me on and helping me explore anything I wanted to explore. So deep down inside, I know that in some fashion, he agrees—or he did once agree—with what you said. Be redemptive. I like it. That may become my motto. I really have no experience with religion, but if that's what Jesus taught, then I agree with it, and I want to hear more, and I want to be around more people who are redemptive, who are like my Dad."

She turned to face Gerald and began to cry again. "Dad, please come back to me. I don't care if you can't walk. I don't mind pushing you, or getting things down from a shelf for you, or anything else. I want *you*. I *need* you. I was so afraid you were gone, that I'd never hear your crazy ideas, experience your thoughtfulness, or have you help me through some problem again. I was really, really scared. And now that you're here and can listen to me, I don't recognize the person you've become, and that makes me even more scared. Please, Dad. Let go of whatever it is that's keeping you from being my Dad. I need you so bad. I need all the things you've always been. I need the Dad who always loved me no matter what. I love you! I love you! I love you!"

She said these words to a man who looked directly at her, tears in his eyes. As she spoke, he reached both arms out to her, and she left the podium, dissolving now completely but not caring, simply rushing into the arms of her father. He embraced her with a surprising strength, and both sobbed and sobbed until their shirts were soaked with tears. Gerald grabbed Greta's blouse and pulled her into the embrace, and the family wept together in a catharsis of tears and proclamations of love and devotion and dedication and sacrifice.

The rest of the group could not escape the display, and they looked at each other, each in their own groups, some of them with tears in their eyes, until Jameel's mom stood and approached Margaret and hugged her. She in turn brought Nathaniel into the embrace, who brought Theresa and Colin and Dan.

Dan grabbed Sal, who held on to Mary for dear life. Sean stood and with Wendy, leaned down and embraced the Foster family, crying with them, as he felt the embraces of the other group begin to form around them as they pushed tables out of the way to make room.

Sean thanked God for this day, and for the providence that had brought him—all of them—here. As Jameel's words echoed in his mind, he remembered where in God's plan, His providence ultimately leads.

Redemption.

Afterword
∞∞∞∞

A novel—especially your first—starts as a solitary task and ends with the help of many people. I'd decided after I finished the book that I'd want to gather maybe around 10 "beta readers" to read my novel and tell me about any plot holes, inaccuracies, bumpy sentences, crappy dialogue, or anything else representing me getting in the way of the story.

My "alpha reader," of course, is my wife Deborah, who read the book multiple times in its various stages, and her comments were always insightful and helpful. I then ran it past my mother-in-law Ruth Kostas—a nurse—to make sure I hadn't messed up any medical stuff, and my father-in-law George Kostas—a pastor—to make sure I got the pastor right. After that, I had maybe only four other people in mind: one teacher, my pastor, and a couple others whom I knew were readers. If you're keeping count, that does not add up to 10. I really wanted (needed) at least one other teacher and most especially a police officer, as I thought it highly likely I'd messed up some police procedure. Well, the book is called Providence, so I decided to place my beta reader problem into the hands of Providence.

I sent a plea out on Facebook.

Beta reading isn't a joke: you don't just read the book for pleasure and then put it aside. I had a questionnaire and a reading log, and I let potential readers know this wouldn't just be passive reading. Yet I was overwhelmed by the interest, from people at all stages of my life—some I hadn't seen since high school. And who happened to be in that group? You guessed it: multiple teachers, a retired police officer, and a book editor, among a distinguished group of people. I decided to expand my beta reader group with those volunteers and a few others who approached me. My initial beta reader group had more than doubled in size. God is good.

I am beyond grateful to my beta readers; their comments were insightful and helpful, and the product you hold in your hands wouldn't be nearly as good without them. Thank you to Marlene Abraham, Laura Bailey, Russell Bohl, Joshua DeLaurentis, Fred and Jenny Dohner, Dick Ellis, Bonny Beth Elwell, Gina Endres, Stephanie Farrell, Nicola Hairgrove, Matt Hartel, Michele Hughes, George Kuhn, Nathan Rao, Barbara Richards, Sandee Rodriguez, Jon Steever, Marian Stevenson, and Paul Williams. Any mistakes or inaccuracies remaining in the novel are my fault, not theirs.

Thank you to my mom, Constance Hunter, who never wavered in her support of me from the day I told her as a teenager that I wanted to be a writer. Thank you to my stepfather, Paul Sutton, for also being a beta reader. And thank you to my daughter Julia, who was the first to grab my rough draft and read it all the way through. What an encouragement!

I am not very visually astute, and so I only had vague ideas about what the cover of this book should look like. But I knew Louis Ciavolella would create something astounding, and he proved me right. Thank you, Lou, for an awesome cover.

Thank you to James R. Hannibal for your kind comments and wisdom.

Most especially, I thank God for the inspiration and the downright temerity to make this strange little story my first novel. Soli Deo Gloria!

And finally, thank you to you, the reader of this book. If you enjoyed it, please feel free to let people know, to pass it along, to review it. The biggest struggle a first time author has is with obscurity. I could use any and all help to get the word out.

I first got the idea for this story from sitting in morning traffic on my way to work. Most mornings, I would bemoan my circumstances when I'd run into delays that would make me late for work. On one particular morning, however, I started thinking about all the people in the cars surrounding me. If I was frustrated at having my day altered by this delay, what were these other people going through? How would their day change because they were now delayed? What if something happened that drastically altered the day of many unrelated people, and it brought them together somehow?

A story was born.

I thought this would be a short story initially. Once I hit 20,000 words, however, I began to suspect I had a much larger beast by its tail. Writing proceeded pretty quickly until my son was born, and then it slowed considerably. What I initially thought would take 6-12 months to write in my spare time wound up taking 6 years, plus one more to get it through the beta reader and editing process.

The experts say to write what you know, so I did. The novel is set in South Jersey, where I grew up and currently live. My alma mater is Rowan University; I needed a professor, so I put her there. The campus has changed quite a bit since I went there, so hopefully none of my details are out of date. I have, however, never been to Berkeley; every bit of detail came from research I found online: course descriptions, campus maps, and even a Wikipedia description of Wheeler Hall. My apologies to Berkeley alums and students if I got anything wrong. If it helps, I wanted events on the east coast to affect events on the west coast, so I chose an institution that would be widely recognized.

Jameel's school is real (I've never been there, except to scout out the parking lot near the woods), but Sean and Dan's churches are figments of my imagination.

This is the first of what I hope to be many novels. You may have noticed that I left the Brick Johnson/Brent Jensen storyline hanging. Though this is a standalone novel, the description here of Brick and his organization is like a string hanging off the corner of a tapestry to be unraveled in a future series.

I have a website; on that website is a blog. I'm also on social media. Feel free to stop by or follow me. And thank you again, for reading my book.

https://www.richardsezov.com

Twitter: @sez11a

Facebook: @richardsezov

Gab: richsezov

Colophon
∞∞∞∞

My background is in computers and specifically open source software. This book was composed, edited, and typeset entirely on open source software, with the exception of the cover. Open source developers do what they do because they love doing it, and their projects make the barrier to entry for *our* projects only as challenging as learning how to use the software. That is an incredible gift. It's important for users of that software, when they can, to give back.

The book was composed in NeoVim, specifically in my distribution which I call VimStar, using Commonmark syntax. For beta readers, I used Pandoc to convert my Markdown manuscript to an OpenDocument I could use with LibreOffice. I then formatted the manuscript (added page numbers, etc.), printed it, and sent it out for comments.

The print layout was done in Scribus. I designed my RS monogram on the title page in Inkscape. For the ebook, I used Pandoc again to convert the manuscript to an ePub, which I then edited using Calibre and exported to both ePub and Amazon formats.

The book is typeset in Alegreya and the titles are in Alegreya Sans, both open source fonts.